Defen ____g

the Forest

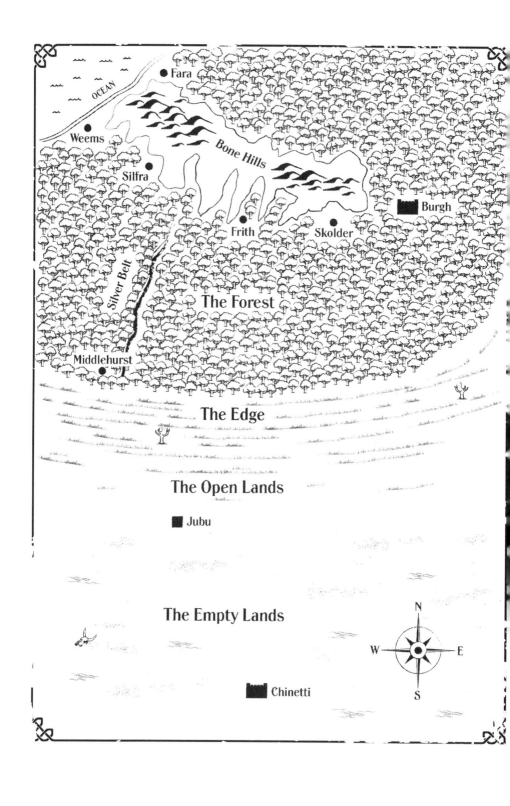

Defending

^the Forest

Graham Scott

The Message Medium

2018

Published by
Phillimore Book Publishing
The Message Medium

© Graham Scott, 2018

ISBN 978-1-9999381-1-6

E: Author@treelogy.world

Contents

Read This

I really hope you read this book. If you do or don't, then read another book. And enjoy it, because reading is meant to be one of life's pleasures! As far as we know, and compared to most other pleasures, it won't make you ill, within reason it won't cost too much, and it's only mildly addictive!

I've written millions of words as a writer for magazines and websites and everything else over the decades, but writing the Treelogy series is proving to be the most enjoyable, fulfilling, intense writing I've ever done. I hope that comes out in the books, and I hope you catch some of that joy in reading them.

If you'd like to contact me then please do email me at the link below. I'd love to hear from you and I'll reply personally. If you were a parent or teacher wanting a school talk, or a reader wanting to know something about the books, whatever it is, please just email at the address below, it comes straight to me.

Author@treelogy.world

Or you can keep up to date and join in the conversation through the Facebook page at:

https://www.facebook.com/Treelogy.world

My thanks to the exceptional Nick Plackett for the cover and all the other artwork.

Nick Plackett / http://frontsidedesign.co.uk

My huge thanks too to Andrew Illes for his thankless task of trying to keep me right in terms of production and technical competence.

My equally huge thanks to Christian Skelton for his very effective work at starting to market the Treelogy series so the word gets out there louder.

Yet more huge thanks to Alison Bowen for constant encouragement and support and for making me think like a publisher. I wish everyone had a sister like her.

Finally, my biggest thanks to my son, Sam, to whom this book is dedicated. If it wasn't for him the series would never have been written.

Chapter 1

Tom stumbled forward, deathly white. He knew he was covered in the remains of tiny dead animals. He'd been told that the Bone Hills were named because long ago countless numbers of little things with shells on had died, and the hills were the mounds of their crushed and powdered bodies. He hoped all their spirits were not still there.

He pressed on, limping when his bare feet encountered one of the many patches of splintered flint amid the great boulders and islands of grass. He licked his pale lips and looked around again for some sign of water.

Nothing. Just a landscape of glaring white, with a few bits of green under a pale blue sky. He snorted the dust out of his nose and looked at the piece of bark in his hand. Right now he didn't really understand.

He remembered the elders in Frith had given him the map and a pair of woollen breeches and that was it. His memory wasn't working too well. Two days and nights of fasting in a tiny hut. Two days and nights of listening to stories, secrets, Instruction from the elder men.

Then dawn on the third day and being sent out of Frith and into the Bone Hills. Sent out as a boy, to be welcomed back as a man. That was yesterday, he thought.

No weapon, no food, no drink, just this map. He looked again.

The tree, there it was, drawn by a hot poker on the beech bark. He had to get to the tree. He remembered now. In the tree was something he had to bring back. He stopped, his head down, his flaxen hair falling over his face, savouring the moment when he would return to the village in triumph. A man. No longer a boy.

He touched the rough piece of oak on the cord round his neck. His spirit tree was back near the village. He would return to it. He pushed on, a new strength in his stride.

In Burgh, the old stone city from where he had been banished, there was no manhood ceremony. There was just a sort of gradual change, but he found he welcomed the ways of the forest, and he knew when he returned to Frith it would be clear cut. He would be a man, he would be treated like a man from that day on. And, he pondered, he'd also have to act like a man too.

He tucked the map in the top of his breeches, tightened the drawstrings, and walked on into the bleached land. He was wobbly through lack of food and sleep, and he was parched by thirst, but he had no thought of turning back.

High above, a large black shape drifted on the thermals. She looked down and saw clearly the mortal moving across the land. Her gaze took in the other two mortals, much further back, as they trudged westward. Letting the thermal coming off the ridge carry her higher, she saw, with a tilt of her head, how all three were heading roughly in the right direction.

She turned, her ragged wings tilting her. The three were deep in the Bone Hills but she was quickly over the long crest that flowed along the side of the hills. She flew over the wooded valleys and green hillsides that flanked the boys' progress. She turned for home. She felt some sense of happiness as she knew the three boys and she knew where they were going. She had good news to deliver.

It wouldn't take her long to get back to Frith, then she could rest. But she knew she would then have to go out again and that second journey, south, would be much more hazardous. She felt the tension rising at the thought.

Below she saw a buzzard circling a rookery, its inhabitants piling up into the air to defend their young.

She dropped down, mobbed the buzzard, made it steer suddenly away as it screeched in annoyance. Feeling better, she regained height, away from the clamouring rooks. It wouldn't do for the queen of the crows to fly with the rooks.

Tom walked for hours and then stood, his eyes down. The ground on the hills was cracked and fissured, great areas pushed up and tumbled down by the massive earthdins that rumbled through the land.

He remembered the last one, the night before the final battle for Frith, and he remembered that he hadn't been sure if it was an omen or not. He hoped there wasn't another one while they were in the hills. There was so little to anchor the ground together when it shook up here.

He looked around, considering. Somewhere out there were Rick and Grant, unless they'd turned back. He didn't think they'd give up. He wished they were together but knew that wasn't allowed, and that crows and Watchers would see if they banded together. They had to do this the way the elders demanded or they'd stay boys for ever.

He looked down again. Rabbit droppings. His eyes took in the faint signs of its passing. There were too many places in this broken landscape for it to make a burrow, but he could see a faint path that it and others took. He could make a snare. What with? He considered. The cord that held his spirit wood round his neck? The drawstring of his trousers? Perhaps the cord – even out here he didn't fancy hanging about completely naked with his breeches round his ankles.

He grinned and then winced as his dry lips went tight and felt close to cracking. He'd need some wood or something to make a dead-weight snare. A loop of the cord on the track, tied to an upright piece of wood. One end of the wood on the ground with the cord, the other supporting a big rock balanced against the wood. He nodded. That would work.

But there was no wood, nothing to use, just rock and tufts of grass. He looked at the light. And no time either. It would be half a day before the rabbit came this way again, and he couldn't spare the time.

He sighed. He'd quite like some meat, even if he had to eat it raw. And he could badly do with drinking the blood. He snorted again as he moved forward, trying to keep his lips compressed. What had he become?

He, Tom Haywood, a boy who went to school in Burgh, the greatest of stone cities, who lived with his parents in a nice lane in a stone house. He, Tom Haywood, who always had the latest haircut, who had good friends, like Abi; he whose greatest outdoor adventure had been spending the night under a cover in the garden with his friend Rick.

Tom put his head up and sniffed. Something there. A smell he had never smelt before. What was it? Salt? Something that smelt fresh in the warmth of the dusty air up here. He drew out the map again. Could it be the ocean that was marked vaguely on his map? He'd never seen it, but they'd told him about it, and he knew that the tree he had to find was within a long walk to this ocean.

Heartened, he pressed on, his thirst forgotten. This was the new Tom. The Tom who had got caught up in the murder of that old man one evening back in the city. He didn't even feel angry about that any more, it wasn't just, it wasn't right, he and Rick had done nothing wrong. But he at least vaguely understood why the Burghmen had taken all five of them into the cells.

Being banished for a year and a day had seemed like the end of his life to him at the time. Yet here we was, much of the way through his sentence, happy to live in the village of Frith, deep in the forest, and now well on his way to becoming a man.

As he breathed in the freshening air, he amused himself by thinking that even his parents would probably struggle to recognise him right then. He was leaner and so much more muscular than that slightly flabby boy with the silly haircut and the buckles in his shoes who had been ejected from the city, bewildered and scared. And of course right now he was bone white all over.

His blonde hair had grown long, hiding the dark scar on his temple from when he'd fallen into that enormous hollowed oak, his spirit tree. And all the training with axe and scaramax blade and shield had toughened his young body. He still had nightmares about standing in the shield wall in that hideous battle to save the village, but he kept those nightmares to himself.

And now, ahead, he saw something. He looked at it carefully. Something in the distance. It was the top of a tree, an oak, in full leaf. Either that or a big bush nearby. He walked forward and leapt up on a big boulder of the soft, white rock. It was a tree. He'd found it. Now, all he had to do was get to it, find whatever it was that was hidden in the tree, and get back. He hoped some food and water were there too.

Eagerly he jumped down and strode on. He was close to finishing the manhood ceremony. But he was tired, so tired and weak. He felt his legs wobbling a bit, but he couldn't rest now. Another few paces and he seemed to be having trouble walking at all. Puzzled he swayed to a stop. He seemed to hear buzzing in his head. He frowned.

Then he realised it wasn't just him. An earthdin. Already the ground was starting to tremble, with smaller rocks beginning to slide. He looked around and saw how huge and dangerously balanced some of the rocks were.

As the white dust swirled up and the great menacing roar of the earthdin started to rise in rage, Tom knew he had one chance. He had to reach the tree, reach those stabilising roots and high branches. He ran forward and was swallowed by the wall of white dust.

Chapter 2

Where were they? Pine Leaf had been flying south for hours, riding thermals where she could, or else having to keep going by using her great wing muscles. She was tiring, no longer as strong as when she was young, some of her feathers no longer black but dull and grey. Where were they?

She had already flown over the outer reaches of the forest and out into the Open Lands. She'd seen the winds blowing the patterns in the long grasses, like the patterns she'd seen over the ocean.

Pine Leaf found Jubu again, flew over the edge of the brown and grimy town, but veered away. She was used to how shrill, high-pitched sounds reached her so clearly when she was in the air, but deeper sounds didn't seem to be so loud. It was almost the opposite when she was perched in a tree or on the ground. And the sounds coming up to her from Jubu were foul.

She could hear the shrieks and wails of women, the high voices of children in fear and the great clanging of metal on metal in the forges.

Gaining height on a thermal near the town, Pine Leaf saw the forest as a smudge far in the distance. She started to fly back there, but taking a route that would take her more westerly, covering new ground. Gazing down as the grasslands passed, she found what she was looking for.

They were closer to Jubu than she'd expected. She felt this was good. Smart enough not to circle over what she saw, the great crow started to beat her way back towards Frith. Blakelock would be pleased with the news. It was going well.

Felix finally dropped his gaze.

'Was that one of ours, a crow?' One of his men stopped shielding his eyes as the bird flew into the distance. He twisted where he lay on the ground and looked questioningly at Felix.

Felix nodded. 'I think so. It might have been Pine Leaf herself. Blakelock will know where we are soon. That's good.'

The other man grunted and shifted his grip on his spear. 'And she'll be back in Frith long before we are, that's for certain.'

Felix smiled ruefully. 'That is certain. As a crow flies, she'll be back in one hour or so. It'll take us a lot longer than that to get back. Particularly if we succeed here.'

They both looked forward, raising their heads slightly so they could just see through the tops of the grasses in which they lay. The outer walls of Jubu were about as near as they could get with a whole warband without being spotted. Even so, Felix was worried about enemy patrols.

Having brought his warband from Frith, and having got them near the walls of Jubu, he was now uncertain what to do next. He ran a hand through his flaxen hair and tried to think.

It had seemed so easy to make the plan. After fighting off Lord Gutta's warriors on the very outskirts of Frith, they'd needed time to recover, tend the wounded and bury the dead under their spirit trees. He'd been one of the men most praised by the villagers for his role in holding the great shied wall together even at moments of utmost peril. So they'd listened to him.

They'd listened when he spoke under the moot tree. How in his anger and pride he'd told them that they must send a rescue party to Jubu, how they had to rescue the women and children taken by Lord Gutta's army from the forest village of Middlehurst. Everyone in Frith knew, thanks to the bravery of boys like Tom and Grant, how their own kin were being worked like slaves, probably worked to death.

There was no argument that a rescue mission had to be launched. But Felix, looking carefully now at the mud-brown walls, had to admit that he'd dismissed the concerns of the elders he respected, like Donald and even Lord Gregory himself. Felix's sharp eyes counted the sentries on the wall while another part of his mind wished he'd spent more time thinking of how they'd actually rescue their women and children, and less time getting his own way.

He smiled and rolled on his side to look at his men. What was it Donald had said to him? Oh yes. 'Sometimes you find the only thing worse than not getting what you want is to get what you want.'

He studied his men. They lay in the grasses trying to stay concealed, using the shade of the few stunted trees that grew here. He saw the grey hair and beards beneath leather helmets. Saw the axes and spears and heavy scaramax blades, all tools they used every day, not made especially for war. Only the wooden shields, the great circular willow-board shields, marked them out as anything other than a bunch of villagers.

He noted how the two groups he'd managed to get together, his Frith warriors and the fewer men he'd found from Middlehurst, tended to stay separate, even in the same warband. He hoped they'd be able to fight as one.

Felix looked away. Yet with these men he had to take that walled town then get all the women and children across the endless grassy plains to the forest. Right now he wished he hadn't had his youthful way, he wished he was back in Frith. He suppressed a smile as he remembered something the wise old Donald had also said: 'Absence of body is better than presence of mind'.

Well, their bodies were here, and they were going to rescue their kinfolk. Or they'd die trying.

Within the hour they were in position. Felix had spotted the work party outside the walls, where they had to chop up the vast trunks and branches of the trees that had been dragged to Jubu from the forest. Tom and Grant had told them about how this worked, so Felix knew that towards the end of the day the villagers they could see trying to chop logs with bad axes would be rounded up and taken back to the town.

There were only a few guards as the villagers were worn-out women and boys. The wooden gates would open to let them in. That's when Felix and his warband would strike. They'd advanced cautiously, using all their stealth, but there wasn't a man there who didn't wish he had the cover of the forest canopy over him. Out here in the Open Lands they all felt exposed, vulnerable, beneath a sky that was fading blue as the day wore down.

The men slithered forward like the dreadful death worms, using animal trails in the long grasses so the tops hardly fluttered as they crawled closer and closer. There weren't many guards and they were all bored, looking forward to the end of the day, but the forest men took no chances.

Felix, at the head of the crawling columns, halted and sent word back. The villagers by the dead trees were being rounded up. Everyone was to look to their weapons, no weapon glint. They knew what to do. Through the gate, kill the guards there, so they at least held the gate. Men to form a shield wall in the gateway, the rest to head like an arrow for anything that looked like guarded slave quarters.

After that, who knew how it would go.

The men checked their weapons, while those with spears crawled closer to the front. They'd be needed first. These weren't warriors, they were villagers, but they'd been in battle enough to know what to do, and what was to come.

They felt the tension rising as they waited for Felix's command. They gripped the hafts of axe and spear, or wiped the sweat from their hand so they could hold the bone handles of their heavy scaramax blades tight.

They heard the shouts in the distance as the returning party demanded the gates were opened. Breathing was shallow, mouths were dry, muscles were tensed.

And then the land fell apart.

It started with a noise, a deep booming that swelled and swelled. Felix looked round wildly. The ground thundered and shook and the men of Frith heard the grasses around them swaying and hissing as if every death worm in the land were coming for them. The fear kept them flat on the ground, paralysed. The hissing turned to a grinding, groaning roar that hurt their lungs as land and air were turned upside down.

They vaguely heard screams and crashes but every man tried to bury himself in an earth that threatened to crack and swallow him at any moment. The great earthdin went on and on, the men choking on dust and dirt and terror. It was the worst they had ever endured.

Slowly, it faded, receded into the distance, taking its destruction with it. There was a sort of choking silence, thickened by dust and debris. Felix raised his head and looked forward. He was half covered in bits of earth, dead grasses and dust and he felt completely disorientated. He spat out some dust and staggered to his feet.

He raised his shield in his left hand, his big war axe in his right and shook his arms, debris spraying out into the dust-dimmed air. The land seemed silent. He looked around, at the dusty shapes lying on the ground like so many dead and half-buried men. He drew a huge, wavering breath.

'Now! Now! Men of the forest, up. Forward, forward, spearmen to the front. Axes and blades, we go to war, we go to rescue our people. For Frith's sake, forward!'

Without waiting to see who followed, he ran into the chaos of Jubu.

Chapter 3

As Tom ran he saw the tree, not far ahead. But the ground was quaking so much he seemed only able to stagger towards it. He leapt to one side as a boulder rolled across. He ran again, getting nearer. The tree was shaking, its crown of green leaves fading as the white dust swirled upwards. Was the tree too going to fall?

He kept going forward, his breathing wild, choking in the white air. His feet, which felt like they were bleeding raw on the rough flints and white rocks being thrown up, finally felt the reassurance of the tree's root system. He looked up. The big oak's branches were nearly over him.

Even though the tree was shaking and swaying, Tom felt safer. He ran across the roots writhing into the soil. He saw a lower branch, kept running, leapt, hit the trunk with one foot and thrust himself up until his hands just caught the lateral branch.

Back in Burgh he'd now have been stuck, unable to pull himself up. But the axe and shield training and the long days hunting and working in Frith now paid off. He pulled himself up easily and rolled onto the branch, scratching his chest on the rough bark.

He kept on climbing, up into the crown. He didn't know what else to do.

As the clouds of white dust roiled into the air, they completely hid Rick and Grant. They'd been desperate to stick to the rules, and had been keeping an eye out to make sure they didn't start walking together towards where they thought the tree was.

Fortunately they'd both had a good grasp of the right direction and their different routes were slowly converging. The earthdin terrified and confused them. The ground shook and rolled like there was a giant old man under the earth, turning over in his blankets. Perhaps it was true, perhaps that was what was happening.

Grant saw what looked like a stable area of ground through the clouds of dust and ran for it as hard as he could. He scrambled over a boulder and leapt down as it rolled away. He heard a grunting noise.

Grant spun to a halt as the juddering ground started to slightly settle. What he'd thought was a big white rock unfolded and stared at him with wild red eyes. Grant screamed.

Rick looked up to see a terrifying apparition leap down near him. It was completely white except for big, red-rimmed eyes, which were now staring at him. The apparition made a dry, hideous screaming sound. Rick screamed, a bellow of a scream.

They stared at each other as the ground started to settle into a mutter. A big solid block of flint rolled towards Grant who jumped nimbly out of the way, but Rick stopped it with a foot.

'Rick?'

'Grant?'

They stared some more, the white dust billowing between them, making them wheeze and cough.

'Oh, right, I thought it was you.'

'Yes, I recognised you at once.'

There was a pause, punctuated by coughing.

'Any idea where we are?'

Rick looked around. They couldn't see any distance, it was all like a white cloud with the sun just a pale diffused glow.

'Not entirely. A bit disorientated. Have you seen Tom?'

'No. No idea. Perhaps he's that rock over there.'

As the thundering faded into the distance, Tom sat up in one of the highest branches, from where he could see out into the new world of white. His arm stretched a little way round the upper trunk, and he felt safe. But he had a lot to think about, mostly to do with the three bags tied to the branch beside him.

When he'd first seen them he'd thought 'three bags, weapons, food, water'. But they all contained the same thing, an axe. Tom leant his back against the trunk as the tree settled, dangled his legs astride the branch and drew out one of the axes again. It was a good one. He could see where the cutting edge was made of a different grade of metal to the rest, which curled round the smooth wooden haft.

This was a Mister Weyland axe, he thought. Only his Weapons Master could make an axe this beautiful. He idly went to chop the blade into the branch but stopped himself. A living tree. You didn't hurt a living tree, not in the wildwood.

He put the axe back in the bag, careful not to drop it as the ground was a long way down, and tied the bag back to the branch, beside the other two. What should he do? He had his axe. He knew all he had to do now was get back to Frith, by whatever route he chose. That meant he could go sideways, westerly, get to the edge of this hideous white world and then be back in the relative safety of the forest.

The land was still covered in white but he knew where he was from the starting point of the tree. He knew which way to go. He looked right. That way. He'd survived. And when he got back he'd be a man.

He'd survived two days of sleepless initiation, then two days out here, all without food and hardly any water. He'd survived the worst earthdin ever and now he'd found his man axe and all he had to do was return safely to Frith. Back to a hero's welcome. He smiled and leant against the trunk.

But the other two axes bothered him. At one level of course he was thrilled. It meant he was the first one to the tree. As they'd kept telling the boys, it wasn't a race. So it wasn't a race and nobody had won. But it was still Tom who was first to the axes. He smiled a small smile, but it faded.

Where were Grant and Rick? Were they still alive after that horror of a ground quake? Should he go and try to find them? If so, should he take their axes for them? He knew that wasn't allowed. But would there be any Watchers or crows up here after what had just happened? Confused and unsure, but feeling temporarily safe, Tom settled against the trunk and at once fell into an exhausted doze.

You found us. That is good. We keep you safe, as safe as anything can be in the forest.

Tom's head lolled back against the trunk, his eyes closed, his mouth slackly open. A small frown passed over his face.

'You're not my spirit tree are you?'

We are oak, we are all one tree, we are the forest. You know this.

One part of Tom's mind remembered Blakelock talking about the forest being all connected under the ground as well as somehow above ground. Tom himself had felt the messages coursing between the root system, down at the Silver Belt, hadn't he? His head nodded slightly. He remembered the wood-wide web.

'You called me didn't you? I remember you telling me you'd called me from the city.' There was a hint of smugness in Tom's thought. 'But we're safe now aren't we? The enemy is defeated, they've left the forest. I just want to pass this, become a man. I don't want to be in any more fights. No more shield walls. You're safe now, aren't you.'

The roots below your feet are damaged by the earthdin, the leaves around you are choking, filled with dust, unable to breathe. There were mice living under our roots, but their home has collapsed, killing all of

them. The forest is damaged. This is not for you to repair. But it is for
you to protect.

Tom shifted on the high branch, the dim light through the leaves
appearing to make the scar on his temple even darker.

'I know the earthdin did some damage, but I'm sure the forest will
recover, it must have endured worse ones than that. I just want to go
back to Frith.'

Right now Tom didn't care about going back as a man, he felt like
a tired boy who just wanted to be home. And home now felt like his
wooden home in Frith, not the solid stone home in Burgh. He longed
to be in his bed up in the sleeping chamber amid the trees. He thought
longingly of it, his mind and body exhausted.

You can see Frith. You can see your friends. Now.

It was as if Tom was slowly leaving his own body, floating up into
the canopy around him. His viewpoint gradually lifted, as if he was no
more than the warmth that was rising through and above the tree. Clear
of even the topmost leaves, Tom's vision showed him the devastation
before him. His attention locked on two shapes moving through the
desolation.

Rick! Grant! Tom wanted to call but he had no voice. They were
walking in the wrong direction now, away from the tree, away from the
edge of the escarpment, going deeper into the wilderness where there
was no water or food.

On the branch, Tom's legs kicked and his head lolled sideways. It
was like a horrible dream. His point of view kept rising. In the distance
now he could make out Frith, clearer than he'd have thought possible
given the distance. The village looked damaged but still standing. Then
he looked further and saw Burgh.

He saw what had been his home, the great brooding grey bulk of
Burgh. He looked, his mouth now a circle of horror. It was as if his sight
darkened, and everything was seen through blackened smoke. He wanted
to leave but his vision was turned, to the right, as if he couldn't control it.

Up, up he went, his sight extending over the forest, out into the Open
Lands and finally coming to rest on Jubu. He saw what was there, and
he felt too the hot anger and hatred. He knew who was there. Lord
Gutta. And he knew now what Lord Gutta wanted.

He somehow tore his gaze away. The boy in him wanted to turn
more so he could see the ocean behind him, but the fear of what he'd
seen seemed to make him weak and useless. It all started to fade, and
Tom focused once again on his friends while his mind whirled, like fallen
leaves in a wind.

He opened his eyes. He didn't move for a moment while he gazed
unseeing ahead of him. He nodded. He untied all three bags, slung them

over his neck and under his arm and started to climb down the tree as quickly as he could. At the bottom he stopped. He put one hand on the rough bark of the trunk. His feet rested on a root that was thicker than any death worm.

'I haven't passed my manhood ceremony yet', he explained to the tree. 'I'm just Tom Haywood. I'm going to find my friends and get us all home. I can't do any more than that. I'm not like Felix.' He turned his head and looked out in the direction of Jubu. 'I'm not that brave or skilful. I know what I am, I'm just me.'

He let go of the bark, stepped off the root and trudged away on sore feet.

Chapter 4

Felix drove himself forward, dust and broken dry grasses swirling in his wake. The earthdin had scared him terribly but it had broken the tension and indecision he felt. Now all the fear was replaced by an awareness of time. He'd been given a moment, a moment of confusion when nobody knew what was happening. It wouldn't last long.

He ran over solid wood and realised it was the gates of the archway, and the gates were on the ground. He glanced up as he ran under where the arch should be. It wasn't there. He leapt over fallen blocks of mud bricks and masonry. He was inside Jubu.

People were running around, confused, all going in different directions. Others were still on the ground, stunned or dead. Felix gripped the handle of his axe tighter and pulled his shield close to his left side.

He saw boys running from behind him. He recognised them as the boys who'd been on the work party. He didn't know them, but they were from the forest.

'Boys! Boys of the forest! Boys of the wildwood! To me, to me!'

The boys ran to him. They were terrified and confused but this big warrior seemed like home. Other woodland warriors ran up, looking around, weapons raised.

'Ives, the gate is gone, get a shield wall in the gateway. Hold it. We'll be coming out this way.'

Ives nodded and grabbed warriors who formed a line in the gap where the gates would have been, their shields interlocking, facing into what was left of Jubu.

Felix looked down at the boys. His face was that of a warrior, all doubt gone, his mind focused on his mission.

'Where are the women from Middlehurst? Where are your mothers? And the other boys? We're going home.'

One boy went to speak but then he made a noise somewhere between a scream and a shout. Felix saw the man coming, with another close behind. His men saw them too and moved. But Felix moved faster.

As a woodland warrior he had been drilled to always protect above all else, and he had perhaps a dozen boys around him. He leapt forward, clear of the boys.

He had already dismissed the first attacker in his mind. The young man looked terrified and unsure. Felix ran at him, hitting him hard with the metal boss of his limewood shield. The man spun sideways, his flailing sword missing Felix. The axe in the hand of the man behind Felix didn't miss and the enemy fell without a sound.

The second man had more time to prepare, but he was still unsure who these people were, or where they'd come from. Felix knew that everyone else was the enemy, and it gave him the edge.

He threw his axe as they charged at each other. He threw it a little wide, to the man's left side, where his shield was. The man flung his arm out to catch the axe on his shield. He was focusing on the whirring blade coming in and didn't see Felix whip the scaramax from his belt. The heavy, one-sided blade with the pointed tip thrust forward.

The man was swinging his sword but Felix's shield was rising to meet it. The man's own shield was still wide of his body and Felix thrust hard with the tip of the blade as the enemy's shield swung back in to protect his body. The shield moved across too slowly.

The man's sword hit Felix's shield as Felix's scaramax plunged into his body. The man screamed but Felix was still moving forward, the momentum driving the blade right through the man. He fell as Felix barged him away and withdrew his scaramax. He put the blade away, grabbed his axe from the fallen shield and stood ready for the next attack. The boys hadn't moved.

'Where are they? Where are our people? Tell me, tell me now.' Felix was breathing hard and harsh and the violence so close to them had stunned the boys. One finally spoke.

'My lord, they are over there.' He pointed to where some sheds stood, or half-stood. 'Or,' the boy faltered, 'that's where I think they were.'

'Ives, hold the gateway. Everyone else on me. Arrowhead. We take those huts, we get the people out and back to the gate. Quickly, quickly, before they realise what's happening and regroup.'

The forest men ran across the dusty ground. Around them was chaos, and they brought more. Groups of men were running around, trying to get people out of fallen huts, or just running aimlessly. It was like an ant's nest and Felix intended to keep on kicking it.

Off to their right there were flames leaping up and Felix, glancing that way, saw that there were furnaces breached, molten metal pouring, fires spreading amid the smoke and chaos.

He kept running but shouted over his shoulder. 'Three men, go right, get some of that burning stuff, spread it around, go.'

As three men peeled away his run had brought Felix to within shouting distance of the huts the boy had indicated. Some seemed half fallen down, but he realised they were in pretty poor condition anyway. A few men with spears were trying to stop people getting out of the long huts. That was sign enough for Felix.

The men with spears died. They didn't have a chance, they didn't even know the city was under attack, and just thought more men were coming to help them control the slaves.

The forest men plunged into the huts and soon a slow-moving stream of women and boys were struggling out of the huts, looking around in confusion. Felix saw how slowly they were thinking and moving.

'Get them to the gate, to the gate, now. The rest of you keep looking.'

He saw what he'd feared off to his right. A bunch of enemy regrouping, looking at them and realising they'd been invaded. Speed was on Felix's side, even if time wasn't. He knew that the enemy needed time to work out that the city was under attack, something that wasn't even in their minds before the earthdin.

'Men, wheel right. A few of you keep looking for more of our people, the rest wheel right, shield wall, move forward, trot.'

He didn't need to say who should search and who should fight, the men just worked it out for themselves, they'd done this before. They wheeled right, and started moving forward at a trot towards the gaggle of warriors ahead. Their big shields met, overlapped, locked. They picked up pace.

The Jubu men had so little time to think or organise. They were from different groups and tribes from out in the Empty Lands, and they had never seen a shield wall before. They just charged.

And died. The shield wall was a moving barricade that they simply smashed against. From the gaps in the wall blades stabbed through. Over the top the axe heads crushed down on the light shields the enemy tried to use to protect themselves. The axes thundered through, bludgeoning, maiming, killing.

The Frith men simply ran over the enemy, and left behind them a ground soaked in blood and bodies. The few survivors fled in different directions, but Felix, wiping his blade and axe on an enemy piece of clothing, knew that word would spread fast.

'Men, back, back to the huts.' There must be more Frith or Middlehurst people here, but where were they? He knew that he'd split his men, some at the gate, some looking for survivors, and he was dangerously extended. If the enemy got organised none of them would ever get out.

He thought of what would happen if they did get out. It was probably two days to the forest with this bunch of women and boys, and he didn't know how they'd survive out in the Open if they were pursued. He shook off the thought. That wasn't the problem right now. Right now they had to find their people and get to the shield wall in the gateway. If they couldn't do that, nothing else was worth worrying about. But, all the same, he worried. This was taking too long.

In a building that was almost untouched by damage, a man knelt in front of Lord Gutta. Dizdah Azmih was a senior and experienced commander of the city, a man worthy of respect, but he knelt. He kept his eyes fixed firmly on the floor of coloured rugs.

'This can not be,' the surprisingly mild, slightly high-pitched voice said. 'You say we are being invaded at the same time as we suffer a severe earthdin? That is not likely. I wonder if you are perhaps too scared to think clearly. Perhaps you should be replaced as Dizdah by a steadier man.'

The warrior heard the threat and shifted his knees. 'I can only tell what is, my lord. A group of enemy vermin has broken in as the earthdin struck. Like rats that come out after such an event, they are here. But they seem only interested in releasing the slaves, not winning the city. If we move quickly we can crush them.'

Lord Gutta slumped in his ornate chair. Gazing up through his eyebrows, the warrior could see the chainmail covering the vast body, see the huge dark beard covering his chest and feel the gaze upon him which was both hot and cold.

A pale shape to one side swayed forward. Azmih looked down at the floor. Lord Gutta scared him but the pale ghost made him want to crawl away every time he was in his company. From the white cowl that covered the face, the voice slithered out.

'Your man is a fool. Your men are scattered all over the city, and these squirrels will be gone before your men can act like warriors. You should let them go. As you know, I have pursued our enemy to the forest. It will take them two days if they have weeping women and whining children with them. Let them go and we will pursue them, catch them, destroy them, in the open, where our horsemen can simply ride them down.'

Gutta growled. That sounded like an enjoyable end to this problem. But the black rage was still on him. It had never left, not since his men got back from the raid on the forest to tell him Enver, his beloved warlord brother, was dead. Killed by a boy. And Heller, Gutta thought, that useless scheming brother, he'd not come back either. There were rumours he'd been killed. By a woman.

And now some of those forest rats were here, in his city. Perhaps the two who had killed his brothers. He wanted them dead. Eventually. The forest scum had killed his brothers and they must pay. He was going to burn the whole forest down. And take the stone city of Burgh and make anyone left his slaves, begging for death. But he would settle with these fools first.

'No, Zala, we finish this here.' He turned to the man at his feet. 'You, Dizdah, get the men organised. We outnumber them. They don't leave the city. Seal the gates, kill all the slaves and then kill these peasants from the forest. Go now, make it happen quickly. On your head be it.'

Azmih got up from his knees, and retreated bowing. He turned and ran from the building, shouting for his men. He knew what had to be done. And it had to be done, or it was his head. The thought drove him forward.

Behind him Lord Gutta smiled. 'They have over-extended themselves Zala. If we somehow fail to crush them in the city then we can pursue and destroy them at our leisure. They cannot get to the forest with our mounted men to ride them down. They should have stayed in that dank forest of theirs. They have doomed themselves and all the slaves.'

Deep in his cowl, Zala allowed himself a small smile. He rather hoped at least some of them, particularly the women and children, would escape and make a run for it.

Chapter 5

Just waiting in the ruined gateway was putting Ives on edge. As a
seasoned warrior as well as a forester, he'd been given and accepted
the task of protecting the gate without hesitation. But now he and his
men just waited. People occasionally glanced their way but then ran
on, warriors and city folk alike. He'd lost sight of all the rest of the forest
warriors, although he could hear some shouting and fighting in the
distance.

He stepped out of his place in the centre of the shield wall where the
gates used to stand. He gazed at the men he was now responsible for.
They looked nervous under their leather helmets, shields tight, weapons
gripped hard.

He looked at the disposition of his men again. If they were attacked
from inside the city they were well placed, both flanks anchored by the
pillars that had held the gates. There were walkways for sentries higher
up the inside of the walls but they'd fallen down in places and nobody
was up there. That was all good.

But if the enemy got out of the city and attacked them from the
outside then they were in trouble as he didn't have enough men to form
a wall facing both directions. And if they came at him in force from the
inside then he was in trouble because as soon as they were driven back
from the gate posts they could be flanked, surrounded and cut down in
no time. And then all the rest of the forest folk would be unable to get
out. They'd be trapped. He looked at his men again.

One of them was looking past Ives's shoulder. 'Ives, you'd better turn
round.'

Azmih was using his head, while it was still on his shoulders. There
was no point running around the ruined city trying to find the enemy.
He'd take the northern gateway and then they'd be trapped. He wasn't
sure, but he thought the rest of the walls were still standing, and he'd
heard no reports from the southern gate. He'd have them then, like rats
in a hole. And Lord Gutta could chase them down, killing them at his
leisure.

He brought his men out from the shelter of what was left of one group
of huts and looked across the grimy yellow space between him and
the gates. Yes, the gates were gone, and so was the arch above them,

and he saw a thin line of men in the gateway. He pondered trying to get round behind them, but there wasn't time.

He would go straight through. He smiled a snarl as he organised his men. What was that old joke? What's the best way to a man's heart? Straight through his chest.

'Forward. Archers, out front. The rest, get on the archers' flanks.'

He was in a hurry but he waited as the men jostled into position. They were close now. He glanced around. Milling people, no sign of any more of the rats.

'Halt. Archers, three volleys. Men, as soon as the last arrow flies, we charge. There are hardly any of them and the arrows will thin them more. We go straight through. Turn, kill every one of them. Then we have the rest trapped and we can deal with them as slowly and as painfully as we like.'

The men cheered. An easy victory and then the chance of inflicting pain and terror.

Things were not going Felix's way. People were straggling back towards the gateway, but they were being harried now by little groups of warriors. Half a dozen men would dart out at them from some alley between buildings still standing. They'd cut and hack and then run when the foresters caught up with them.

Felix was losing one man here, a woman there, a child right in front of him. The enemy's long sword chopped the boy down like he was a stalk of grass. Felix, pulling his axe from the enemy's sprawling body, looked down at the boy's face. He wished he hadn't. He couldn't understand how a man could kill a child like that, or an unarmed woman. But these creatures seemed to enjoy it.

'Keep together, keep together, warriors at front and rear. Keep going, we're nearly at the gate.'

Another rush of the enemy, another desperate little action, another of his men wounded. The mob of women and children had warriors trying to protect them and to keep everyone moving, but they were so slow. Felix noticed the enemy was falling away at the front as they came towards the open area that, he thought, would give them a clear run to the gate. Unless they were lost in the tangle of the ruined city.

Bringing up the rear, Felix noticed the enemy massing on his flank.

'Men of the forest, to me. Rearguard.' He hoped the front of the wandering column could now just about make a run for the gate while he brought up the rear. There was a shout from the front.

'Felix. They're attacking the gate, they're attacking the gate.'

'When I say, double shields. Be ready, move fast you hear? Move fast.'

Ives' face was taut. The long grooves that ran from his nose down beside his mouth were even deeper. There were a lot of the enemy. And no sign of Felix. He had a feeling this was going to be a last stand.

'Loose!'

Ives heard the enemy command.

'Now! Double shields, double shields.'

His men snapped into action. Those in the front rank knelt, their shields virtually resting on the ground, most of their body hidden behind the wooden barrier. The second row, what there was of it, put their shields on top, while they cowered behind this makeshift wall. The round shields left gaps between them.

The arrows thudded into the wood, making some of the shields wobble, but nothing worse. The second volley hit, and somewhere in his line a man screamed as an arrow found a gap. How many more volleys? Ives knew if they just kept it up eventually he'd lose too many men to keep even one line.

Azmih had worked out the same thing. He went to shout an order to keep firing, but he had only a partial command on this rag-tag of warriors he had amassed.

The third arrows were launched and the men leapt forward with a howl, drowning out his command. He ran after them, cursing. They'd have to do this the hard way. He'd lose more men but the outcome would be the same.

It was instantly chaos. The enemy's ragged run hit the shield wall, which had had time to regroup as the enemy ran at them. The enemy expected the line to buckle but it didn't. It bent, but it didn't break.

And, just as they had discovered when they attacked the shield wall outside Frith, the enemy found out that their long swords were hard to swing when they were crushed up against the shields, pressed forward by their own men behind.

Ives knew how this would go, at least at first. As the enemy tried to hack and swing with their unwieldy long blades, his men stabbed through the gaps between the shields, the scaramax blades heavy and with a fierce point.

At the same time the few men in the second rank swung over the top with the battle axes, chopping down into heads and shoulders and arms, just as the scaramax blades stabbed into torsos and thighs. The enemy tried to recoil, but they were pressed forward in their eagerness and it killed them.

But there were more and more of them coming, joining the fight. It looked like an easy fight to most of them and they ran up to join the rear ranks, taking the place of men who fell.

Slowly, Ives' second rank became fewer and fewer as they had to step forward to take the place of a fallen comrade. The line of shields bowed, close to being pulled away from the anchors of the gate posts. Behind the shield wall of foresters a few bodies lay still or writhed in pain. They couldn't hold the line for much longer, and then they'd all be dead in moments.

Felix was desperate. His men had fought off another savage rush, this time one that had struck home hard. There were more dead forest women and children. And two more of his men were limping or staggering with wounds.

Felix shouted in frustration. The enemy still lurked at the rear of the column, but he had to get to the front with his men and try to clear the gate. But if he did that the enemy would fall on the women and children and slaughter them all. Felix couldn't understand how men could do that, but he knew the enemy would kill defenceless women and children without mercy.

He was trapped.

'Go, you go, find a way out of here.'

Felix turned, his face a snarl of anger and frustration.

A woman stood near him. She stood straight, her eyes steady on Felix. She looked thin and ragged and exhausted. She looked like a slave, but she stood like a free woman. Her wide mouth was just a line in her face, devoid of emotion.

'I am Rohana. From Middlehurst. You came to save us but it was too late. My husband is dead. My son is dead. And it is time we stopped dying without fighting.'

She looked around, and called some names out.

'Pick up weapons. We have to defend ourselves. It is time we fought back. Come. Remember what they have done to us. Remember all our loved ones lost. We fight, we revenge our lost ones, the humiliation, the deaths. And we defend our loved ones so they might escape. For Middlehurst, for the forest!'

There was a ragged cheer and, to Felix's astonishment, a line of women somehow appeared, all with scavenged weapons. Among them were a few brave boys, while the younger ones and the older women cowered behind.

'Go! Get going! Find a way out. And remember us if you do.'

Felix shook his head.

'Men, with me, to the front, quickly. We have to clear the gate. Move.'

As he started forward down the line of women he paused and looked at Rohana. The young warrior guessed she must be about ten years older than him, but she stood like a younger woman. He sensed the resolve and he admired it.

'Keep everyone moving to the gate. We will not abandon you. And use their swords with both hands on the grip, you'll have some control then. Here.' He drew his own scaramax and gave it to the woman handle first.

'Hold it tight, stab straight with all your force. You don't have the strength or bulk, so use your speed instead. May the forest be with you Rohana. We will meet again.'

And then he was gone, running forward, shouting commands to his men. Rohana hefted the surprisingly heavy blade in her hands. She took a deep breath. She knew the enemy would attack at any moment.

Chapter 6

Tom staggered. He put a hand up and touched the scar on the very top of his head. It was still fairly fresh. The memory flashed of the warlord Enver smashing his great sword down at Tom again and again, splintering his shield, making Tom's arm numb. Then that final, crushing blow that sundered shield and crunched down onto Tom's metal helm.

He shook his head and winced. He had walked far further than the other two, and had carried the axes for a long way before finding his friends, and he was nearly done. Days without rest or food or water were grinding him to a husk.

Rick watched his friend. 'What's wrong? Are you hurt?'

Tom pulled his hand away from his flaxen hair and saw there was blood on it.

'I think my old wound has opened up Rick. With all the strain I suppose. Will you take a look?'

'Here, let me.' Grant put down his axe bag and came over. The light was fading, the long day ending. In the near distance they could see trees. That meant they'd nearly made it to the edge of the Bone Hills.

Grant had a look. 'Huh, it's so dusty and dirty it's hard to see. But it looks like the old wound has opened up. I'm surprised, I thought Miss Goode really fixed it.'

Tom smiled gently. 'Yes, she fixed it even though she didn't want to.' He smiled at Rick. 'And Rick fixed that warlord Enver, didn't you Rick?'

Rick actually managed to look embarrassed at the memory but it was Grant's turn to grin.

'Oh yes, our berserker. Don't make him angry Tom.'

Tom was swaying now.

'We're nearly there, nearly to the edge. If we get there we can find water at least, although I'm really famished too. Let's keep going.'

He set off but couldn't hold a straight line. He put his hand up to his head and looked at the blood on his fingers. Rick and Grant were shattered but they exchanged glances. Each one shifted their axe bag to the other shoulder and got an arm round Tom. Nobody said anything, but they trudged on together.

Tom awoke. He tried to work out what was going on. He was lying on some young bracken, with other bracken and greenery over him. He was gazing up at a sky that was turning from medium blue to dark blue. He was looking at the sky through some dark branches above him. He seemed to be alone. He moistened his lips. They were wet with cool water. He had no idea how or why. It went from dark blue to black.

Mortals and trees, we are not so dissimilar.

Like always, it was a voice that he seemed to hear inside his head, not through his ears. It was so deep and slow that sometimes it was hard to make out, but he'd learned to just let the gaps grow because eventually they would be filled. It always surprised him that he could hear the voice of the forest when he wasn't actually inside the hollowed trunk of his great oak, his spirit tree.

We survive best when we look after one another. A single oak is not as strong as a forest. A forest has the shade and the dampness that we need. A single tree on its own has a harsher time. We prop up one another when we fall. And we will feed not just our young but our neighbours too, if they fall on hard times.

We do this because it is the right thing to do. And because it benefits every tree. It makes the forest stronger and so it makes every tree stronger. You mortals are the same. Help others, and accept help in your turn. Now it is your turn. You must be strong. What is approaching will need all our strength.

'Why? What? What is approaching?'

Tom opened his eyes, confused. Above him he saw the branches of the oak tree spread out above him, nodding gently in a warm breeze. The thousands of leaves he could see kept the morning sun off his face so he just felt a steady warmth. He felt no need to move.

'What's approaching? Breakfast is.'

Rick was crouched down, pulling things from his axe bag. An axe didn't seem to be one of the things. There were green plants of several sorts, which Tom suspected he should have learnt about by now, and some pale roots.

Rick looked up, past Tom. 'Oh and Grant's coming in too.'

Tom gently turned his head and saw Grant walking in. He seemed to have a stick in his hand, which he was paying close attention to.

He knelt down by Tom, his face focused. Tom saw that the stick was actually two bent sticks, put together to form a rough circle. And in the circle was a dense mass of cobwebs, with some dew drops still sticking to it in places.

'Uh, Grant is that meant to be breakfast?'

Tom could feel his sense of drowsy contentment fading quickly.

'This is for your head. Although if you keep talking it will be for your mouth. Lie still.'

Tom looked at his friend in surprise. He still remembered Grant as one of the scary boys from the Shambles area in Burgh. But, somehow, he seemed to have changed. And he was learning, learning everything fast. Tom knew that Grant just adored the Word Mistress, Mistress Hazeling, and he'd been reading everything he could get his hands on. It looked like reading about physicians was one of the things.

'But what are you going to do?'

Grant sighed. 'I've already cleaned the top of your filthy and stupid head. The cobwebs have something in them, something that keeps sickness and bad things from getting into wounds. I thought everyone knew that. Now lie still because this is difficult. I don't want to get this in your hair.'

Tom lay still.

'And you're sure the spiders aren't in the webs aren't you Grant?'

'I've kept a really big fat hairy one to shove in your mouth if you open it again.'

Tom was reasonably sure that physicians didn't talk like that. He kept his mouth firmly shut as Grant laid the mess onto his scalp with surprising delicacy. He looked up into the dark face, aware that only months ago if he'd seen that face this close then he would have been in serious trouble.

Grant knelt back on his heels. Tom felt the need to say something.

'Looks like Miss Goode didn't do such a good job huh?'

Grant didn't smile. 'I saw her. You were in a bad way. I don't think you realise how badly hurt you were. You could have died, there was blood everywhere and this big gash in your head. And she was concentrating so hard on you. She worked on you for a long time. She knows stuff we'll never know. You probably owe her your life.'

He paused. 'Strange though. She doesn't seem to like you, yet she put all her skills and energy into you to try to make you live. What's that about then?'

Tom stirred uncomfortably and looked sideways.

'You got a fire going! How did you do that?'

Rick looked up and talked as if to a child. 'We have an axe, it's steel, and Mister Weyland made sure some of the steel near the haft can take a flint strike. And there were lots of flints up on the crest weren't there? See?'

He turned back to sort the plants he'd foraged. Tom realised something else.

'And you've both got rid of all that white dust. How did you do that?'

Rick sighed but didn't look up from what he was doing. 'There is water Tom, just beyond those bushes, a small stream. We cleaned ourselves. We've even cleaned some of you. Although,' here he did look up briefly, 'there are some bits of you you're going to have to clean yourself, let me tell you.'

Tom smiled and sat up. Grant looked thoughtful. 'Don't touch your hair Tom, just leave it be for a day or so, let the wound fix. If I see you scratching the top of your head I swear I'm going to go get those spiders I made homeless.'

'Thank you Grant, I feel better already. And thank you Rick, you've both done all the work while I was sleeping.'

Rick grunted. 'No change there then. I seem to spend my whole time having to rescue you from one mess or another.'

Tom stood up slowly and threw a small stick at his friend, but he threw it gently. He wandered off, thinking how Rick was right, he couldn't do everything himself. But he felt the strain, knowing things the others didn't know.

He kept walking and realised he was in a beautiful spot. It was a small crest that curved out from the surrounding slopes, a lovely flat area with steep sides falling away, and huge views in several directions. He looked south. He caught his breath and turned quickly, losing his balance slightly as he did. He went back to the others.

'This is a lovely place, but we have to go. We have to go now. Come on, follow me.'

But for once Rick just shook his head. 'No, we're staying here today. You're all in. So are we. Grant and I discussed it. We need to find more food, some meat, and we need to keep drinking water. And we have food here to eat, so sit down and shut up.'

While Tom just gaped at his friend Grant nodded in agreement. 'We rest. And then we'll be quicker on the way back. It's still a couple of days I'm guessing to Frith.'

Tom opened his mouth again. 'But...they...the forest...Felix and the villagers are struggling. I'm sure. We need to get back to Frith. We need to go.'

Tom's head hurt. He went to put a hand up to it, but then put it down again. He sat down in a heap. He decided just to rest for a moment while he got his strength back to argue with Rick, who never went against him. He lay down with his head on a tuffet of grass. He was asleep in moments.

Chapter 7

Felix led his men towards the ruined gateway. He ran down beside the straggling column of women and children, which seemed to have halted just as it broke clear of some ramshackle huts. Felix and his men kept going. The gateway was just there, across a clearing, but in front of the fallen arch was a struggling mass of warriors.

Felix swore. They had to clear that gateway fast and get out of here. On an impulse he sheathed his axe and scooped up an enemy sword lying on the ground. With no scaramax, he wanted to have a blade.

'On me, shields, we clear the gate. We go in at an angle. We clear the gate, we're out of here. Shields, lock.' Still at a trot, the men aligned themselves on Felix, locked shields and ran into the back of the enemy who were attacking what was left of Ives's thin line in the gateway.

The stabbing, clashing, screaming horror began again. Felix struggled with the long sword, which felt cumbersome to him, but the enemy were dismayed. They liked short, sharp raids, where they rushed in and outnumbered the enemy. This grinding fighting with the grim enemy behind those heavy shields was not to their liking at all. They began to give way as they came under attack from two sides.

Felix smashed his way through. He could see the line of men in the gateway, still somehow holding. They were the anvil. And he and his men were the hammer. He had time to wish he had Mister Weyland with him, along with some of the other warriors from Frith, but then he saw a man in a fancy helmet. He seemed to be struggling to get away, screaming at his men.

With a great lunge, Felix pushed his section of shields forward and smashed his sword onto the expensive-looking helmet. The man went down. Felix was sure he hadn't killed him, but it didn't matter, the enemy was running, and the two lines of foresters met in the gateway.

Felix and Ives met in the centre of their depleted lines. Ives looked terrible, Felix thought. Like he'd died. He was pale, breathing hard, and he had a strange look in his eye. Felix grinned at him, noting the tattered ear, and remembering how Ives got it, in that terrible little fight back on the edge of Middlehurst.

'Well done for holding the gateway Ives, men, well done. We're going to get out of here. We're going home.'

The men cheered, but it wasn't much of a cheer and Ives' expression didn't change. He felt his death was moments away. The woodsmen were exhausted after their fighting and needed a break. But they couldn't have one.

Felix saw that the light was fading faster now. Night would help them, but only if they could get out. He looked at the scattered enemy. They had no stomach for a fight right now, and they had a lot of wounded and a lot of dead men scattered on the dusty yellow-brown soil. He looked around for their leader, but he wasn't on the ground, he must have been dragged away.

'Ives, you stay here, most of my men will stay here too, you're safe now. The rest of us are going to get the women and children.'

As he picked out the men to go back with him, they could see the first of the Middlehurst survivors streaming towards the ruined gateway. He and his men trotted back past them, heading for the rear of the column. Felix wondered if any of the women back there would be alive.

Rohana watched the men coming towards the women and children almost as soon as Felix and his men had run for the gate. She didn't know if the warrior would come back. She saw one of the forester's shields lying on the ground in a tangle of kit. She picked it up but grunted in surprise at the weight. She dropped it. She didn't feel so brave now.

An old lady sidled up beside her, with a dagger in each hand.

'Well, Rohana, what do we do now?'

Rohana's quick glance took in the daggers.

'What are you doing with those daggers, mother? Don't be silly.'

'Well. I've looked after you since you born and I've been with you since we were brought to this rotten place. I'm here beside you.'

Rohana just didn't have time for this. She heard a shout. A warrior was close now, swinging his sword. He was smiling. That infuriated Rohana, and she heard a growl from down beside her.

All the time they were edging sideways, heading towards the gateway and what might be safety. The man lunged at one of the girls near Rohana. The girl screamed and tried to parry the blade with a sword she'd picked up. She managed it, but was off balance. The man almost casually back-swung his blade and caught the girl. She fell backwards, blood spraying. It was too easy.

But another woman had picked up a spear and she lunged as the man swung. The man's laugh stopped abruptly as he folded over the spear in his middle. Now the other men came.

It wasn't an equal fight. The enemy warriors killed women and children, killed them as if they didn't matter. They could always get more slaves. They were careless. In the sprawling fight at the rear of the column, a warrior charged at the tall, straight form of Rohana. He swung a huge overhead blow at her that would have split her in two.

She stood motionless as the blade whistled down to her head. At the last moment she simply stepped to one side. The blade swung past her and into the ground. The man ran onto the scaramax that Rohana held with both hands.

He screamed, his head right by her ear. She staggered under the weight and went to pull the blade out. As she struggled to disentangle herself, she saw another warrior attack her mother, another great downswing that would crush the old woman.

Her mother raised both the daggers, crossed and locked above her head. The sword clanged into them and stopped. The man was puzzled by how she'd had the strength, but his frown changed to a wince of pain as her foot lashed out. He bent over as he drew back his sword, his mouth twisted in agony. The old lady stabbed one of the daggers into his throat and he collapsed.

'Treat your elders with respect, boy. Now you've got eternity on the naughty step.' The old lady cackled and checked on Rohana, who was standing free again, her front spattered with blood.

Rohana didn't speak, she leapt forward. This warrior was running fast, angry at the deaths of his comrades at the hands of women. Being killed by a woman was the worst possible death and his anger put a lot of force into the great swinging blow he aimed at the girl with blood on her front. He swung sideways as he ran, aiming to cut her across the middle.

Rohana froze as the screaming warrior swung at her. Time slowed and she remembered the warrior with golden hair telling her to use her speed. She was quick now, and the man seemed to have slowed down, his scream turned to silence. She ducked. She seemed to have so much time.

She heard the blade whirr over her head. She crouched, swung her blade up, her legs braced. His momentum carried him straight into her, his blade safely off to one side. The impact jolted her out of where she'd been.

She kept rising, her arms thrusting upwards as hard as she could. The man just stopped. She could smell him, feel the cloth of his uniform on her cheek, feel his warm blood running down her hand. He made a kind of whimpering noise and started a backswing with his blade. Unable to see as she was so close, Rohana felt another impact. The man just collapsed where he was.

Rohana stood up. Her mother stood the other side of the body, looking hideously pleased with herself. The enemy seemed to have backed away. She couldn't believe they'd scared the warriors off.

Then she saw the blonde warrior running back with his men. She felt nothing.

'Rohana! Good work.' Felix looked around and winced. There were a lot of dead and injured. Men, women and children. He couldn't change that, he had to focus on the living.

'Keep moving, keep moving to the gateway. It's clear, we're getting out, move, move.' Felix and his men shepherded the survivors back to the gateway. Felix turned to Rohana, who was beside him. He put out his hand to take back his scaramax. He looked at it, covered in blood, blood that covered the grip, and her hand and her arm. She held it tightly. He looked at her face and dropped his hand quickly.

'So, blonde boy, they're going to send their horse soldiers as soon as we're clear of the city aren't they?'

Felix looked down, distracted. A small old lady looked up at him. A small old lady with two daggers, both of them covered in blood.

'Uh, well, maybe not at once. We can get some distance in tonight, mistress.'

'That's not much of a plan, blonde boy. I don't want to die out in the Open Lands.'

'My name is Felix. Mistress. Did you have a better idea?'

She nodded beyond where the furnaces had been, and where fires still flared. There weren't many of the enemy in that direction.

'The horses are kept just past the furnaces. Why don't I go and let them loose, they can run out of the city?'

Without waiting for an answer she started to walk in that direction.

'In fact, I'll go and do that now, you young ones keep going.'

Felix was wrong-footed. He called out after the old lady.

'Do you know how to control the horses?'

The thin voice floated back.

'Horses, goats, men, what's the difference?'

Felix sighed, exasperated, as some of the men laughed.

'Who is that dreadful old woman?' he muttered.

'She's my mother.' Rohana stared at him with that same slightly scary expression she'd worn since he'd run back to her. 'I'm going with her.'

Rohana simply followed her mother, her scaramax still held tight in her hand.

Felix thought fast.

'Erik, take three men, go with them, get the horses to follow us. Don't take any chances. And make sure you get those two back as well.' He paused. 'Or at least one of them.'

Shaking his head, he started pushing people out through the gateway. Soon they were clear, with a good rearguard operating, and the darkness falling. Behind he heard a thundering noise and screams, and a mass of frightened horses surged through the gateway and disappeared into the gloom.

Soon Erik and the others joined them.

'How did you do that?' Felix was genuinely impressed.

'Horses don't like fire,' said the old lady smugly. 'But we're still going to be followed and cut down aren't we? They'll round those horses up by morning. Then they'll chase us down and slaughter us all out in the Open. We'll be ripped to pieces, chopped to bits.'

Felix didn't know what to say. The miserable old bag was like some doom-sayer but she was right. He was just taking this one step at a time and he could feel the fatigue fogging his mind.

Erik, one of the older foresters, spoke up.

'Well now Felix. I've been thinking about that. While helping Mistress Yardley here. And I've got an idea.'

In the chamber lit by candles and lamps, Lord Gutta shifted his bulk in his carved wooden seat. The chainmail covering his huge body glinted as it moved in the lights. His rage, never far away, was right there. Everyone could feel it like a force in front of them. Nobody felt safe.

'The forest scum have escaped. We have killed some but the rest, and those worthless slaves, have escaped. Tell me how this could have happened.'

There was silence. The longer it went on, the less anyone felt like breaking it.

'I have a Dizdah, in charge of the forces of this miserable dump. Yet he has not stopped them escaping. Zala,' he turned to the pale robes and cowl nearby, 'did I not say this was on Dizdah Azmih's head?'

'You did my lord.'

Lord Gutta nodded and spoke almost pleasantly. 'Then please bring it to me.'

Zala bowed and went to move away, but he hesitated.

'And who will replace Azmih as Dizdah my Lord Gutta?'

'I will. I can trust nobody. I am surrounded by incompetents. You,' here he turned and stabbed a large finger at a senior warrior, 'get the horses ready, we will ride at first light and ride them down. They cannot escape. The fools will be caught in the open.'

The warrior drew a deep breath.

'I, errr, the horses have run off my lord. They have somehow got out of the city and are spread around the area.'

Everyone looked at their feet. There was a deep silence. They could hear the chainmail clink as Lord Gutta shifted again in his seat.

'Really? They have run off, just like that? That is unfortunate is it not? Then I suggest you go and find them. All of them. Round them up tonight so we are ready to ride at dawn. If, at dawn, we have no horses then I will look forward to adding to my collection of heads.'

The man bowed so low his hair fell forward over his head. Lord Gutta looked at the man's dirty neck. His eyes narrowed.

'What's happening? Where are they?'

Gutta's head snapped round to glare at the newcomer.

'And where have you been? Hiding in your burrow while your fellow tree rats scurry around?'

Gutta stared in open dislike at the pale youth in front of him. He looked so pasty pale compared to the swarthier warriors around him. So thin and so sneaky.

Reese tried to look affronted. But it was hard with Lord Gutta staring at him with such rage in his face.

'No. My Lord Gutta. I was out trying to get the men rounded up. By the time I got some men together the Middlehurst and Frith people had gone. Not my fault.'

Gutta sneered openly at the boy. It was only the boy's knowledge of the layouts of places like Frith and Burgh that kept him alive, but Gutta hated turncoats as much as anyone. Reese would cease to be useful soon. Gutta looked forward to what would happen to him then.

'So what will your fellow forest dwellers do now? Prove your use, tell me something useful. Otherwise what good are you to me?'

Reese looked like he wished he'd not entered the chamber or spoken up.

'They will make a run for the forest my lord. But they'll be slow. There are wounded men, and women and children. And their dead. They never leave their dead men. They take them back to the forest to bury under their spirit trees.'

'So you can catch them easily. Kill them all.' Reese smiled ingratiatingly.

Lord Gutta half closed his heavy-lidded eyes. It sounded so easy. But he'd heard how the battle at Frith had gone. He knew this enemy were no fools, whatever he said. Could they really be so reckless as to charge in here and then leave themselves so exposed on the journey back?

'What if this is a trap? Designed to draw us out of Jubu, even damaged as it is. What if there is a larger force waiting for us to rush out after the bait?' Gutta spoke out loud but nobody answered.

Zala drifted closer. 'My lord, we need to move fast. Slow as they are, we can't give them too much of a head start. We need those horses ready at dawn. We need to get them rounded up overnight. Don't you want to catch them in the open? All those women and children, and some outnumbered and exhausted warriors?'

Gutta licked his lips and gazed up into the recesses of the pale cowl beside him.

'Perhaps you are right Zala. We can avenge ourselves at our leisure then.'

He nodded and drew a breath to speak again, but another man entered the chamber and kneeled before his lord.

'My lord, my lord, there has been another assault on the city. At the southern gateway. It was a major attack but we have repelled the invaders my lord. We fought hard and beat them back. Out of the city.'

Gutta frowned. 'How many? How many of them?'

The man kept his eyes down but paused a moment before answering. 'About, about a hundred my lord. But we fought them back. We won.'

Zala snorted. 'The man exaggerates to keep his tongue in his head. There could not be that many of them.'

But Gutta wasn't sure, wasn't certain. A force had successfully attacked his northern gate and got away. Now there was an attack on his southern gate. He doubted it could be the same people as it was the wrong way to the forest. And a hundred – even if the man exaggerated, it sounded like a serious attack.

He thought of his men running around in the dark outside the city walls looking for the horses. He didn't care about losing men, but he didn't want to give the enemy an easy victory either.

'We will wait. Man the walls, what's left of them, get the northern gateway repaired. We will search for the horses in the morning when it is light. And we will send out reconnaissance squads to find out who's out there. That is all.'

Zala sighed deep inside his cowl. 'But my lord, we will be letting them get away. We must pursue them.'

Gutta growled. 'We will pursue them tomorrow. We will catch them long before the forest and then you can play with the survivors all you like. But tonight we make sure we are not going to be running out into an ambush.'

Zala watched his lord haul his bulk from his throne chair and retire. Tomorrow then. There would still be time. Zala was good at patience. But he knew that every moment they spent behind the walls of Jubu, that little band of desperate tree rats was creeping further and further away.

He shrugged and went off to find Dizdah Azmih and his forfeited head.

Chapter 8

'We're making better progress than I thought.'

The others nodded. They were tired still but were recovering.

Tom gazed southward, always southward.

Rick saw Tom's gaze. 'I'm sure Felix will make it back alright. I'm sure he will, with all the others. That's if he isn't already in Frith, ready for our return.'

Grant looked at Tom, and saw the concern on his face. He stayed silent.

'Well,' said Tom, 'we'll find out soon. If we could just find more food, maybe we could be back tomorrow. If not then we're going to slow down.'

They resumed their walk, moving along animal trails that ran along the hillside. They'd passed lots of fallen trees, brought down by the earthdin. Going round trees fallen across the trails had slowed them down, as had finding routes over or round the great rents in the earth wrought by the shaking and twisting of the ground.

To their right the views stretched over the forest, and out to where the forest ended, the Open Lands. Ahead lay Frith somewhere, perhaps less than a day's walk.

Tom was looking forward to getting back. His feet were sore. The soles of his feet were hardening up, but getting some boots back on would be great. He was famished too. Rick had done marvels, finding and feeding them dandelion and burdock roots and leaves, the tiny peas from vetch and other greens, but the three of them were still low on energy.

He sighed and kept walking, shifting the bag with his axe in from one shoulder to another. The simple drawstrings on their trousers wouldn't hold the axe like his normal belt. That was another thing he was looking forward to putting on. But at least he had his axe, his manhood axe.

'Hey, Rick,' he called. He looked ahead, past Grant, to where Rick was leading along the path. 'When we get back, people are going to see the three of us with three axes. What are you going to say?'

Grant just ahead of him turned his head as he walked. 'You think that hasn't occurred to us Tom? We talked about it while you were sleeping. We had to raise our voices as you were snoring so loud. Maybe there are Watchers out there, we'd never know. Maybe the crows saw. We don't know. But we didn't find the axes, you did. Nothing can change that, whether we were seen or not. We failed. You succeeded.'

He turned his head back and tramped on, the bag cord cutting into his lean shoulder.

'Grant's right.' Rick stopped and turned. 'Imagine the villagers congratulating us, telling us we're men now. But we'd know. I can't do that, I can't live a lie like that. What sort of man would I be?

'Anyway,' he grinned, 'Pad is going to be mad at you so this means he might not be so mad at us.'

Tom nodded and grimaced. He remembered his friend's face when he found out he wasn't to be allowed in the manhood initiation. Tom understood why. Donald, Pad's father, loved him too much to risk him not succeeding. Donald would only let Pad do it when he was sure he could pass.

But Tom remembered how coldly furious Pad had been. How his normally smiling face had been a dark mask of furious rage for days while the boys were prepared for the initiation. Normally Tom and Pad shared the same sleeping chamber, but Tom had been glad he'd had to sleep in a tiny shelter away from the village in preparation.

Tom nodded. 'That's true. He's going to be really angry with me.' He glanced up at Rick. 'But he…'

His voice trailed off. He spoke in a loud whisper. 'Rick. Behind you. What's that?'

Rick turned and looked ahead. They were stopped in a tiny clearing, with a line of trees just ahead. His eyes looked into the dark of the treeline, heavy with shade, while they stood in the sun. Nothing. Nothing moved.

And then it did.

A smallish shape, moving about. What was it – a baby deer, a young warbrock or something? Rick stood still as the other two started to walk up to him. He looked again then turned to the other two. His eyes were wide. He made a motion for them to stop and to be silent. Then he put a hand up to either side of his face and made a gesture - tusks. A boar.

All three boys thought the same. Meat, really tasty meat. But a young boar wouldn't be wandering around on its own. They scanned the treeline again. Because if there were adult boars around then the boys were in danger, real danger.

Tom had never seen a boar but he remembered Felix telling him how their sharp tusks were used to sort of headbutt you in the inner thighs, where all the tubes were that held your blood. If the tusk cut the tube you would bleed to death in moments. Another smaller shape moved. Then a huge shape, more than waist-height to the boys.

The three stood still. The warm breeze, such as it was, blew gently on their faces, and it brought the faint scent of the animals. The breeze wouldn't give the boys away. But any sound would. The boar couldn't see well, but they had uncanny hearing.

The boys were in the open but they stood still as the animals rootled around, just darker shapes in the dark shade of the trees.

Slowly, the group moved away, the faint sound of rooting and grunting receding. Tom relaxed. Rick made a face. He was always hungry. He opened his bag and took out his axe. The other two did the same. Then they all trudged on, senses alert. They disappeared out of the bright sun into the gloom of a big stand of fir trees.

Tom saw Rick rear back. His axe flashed forward in a shaft of sunlight and there was a wet thud. By the time Tom was beside Rick, Rick was retrieving his axe. From the body of a young boar. Tom looked at the prettiness of the brown and cream stripes running down its bristly body. Its skull was a mess, but the rest of the body looked so beautiful. Tom stood, captivated.

'Sorry, it was just there, I reacted.' Rick looked down. 'Meat. We have meat.' He sounded pleased and scared at the same time, like he'd done something dangerous and wrong.

Tom nodded slowly while Grant knelt down and ran a hand over the body. They all heard the sound. They saw the two adults coming back fast through the trees, kicking up last year's leaves and clods of earth.

Tom had time to see the size of the shoulders, the size of the tusks and the wild look in the small eyes.

'Run.' He didn't shout, he didn't need to. He just said it with finality. Because death and revenge were nearly upon them.

The boys scattered. Tom ran as fast as he could, but he knew his mind had to work even faster. The boar could run him down in moments and he knew if it did even his new axe wouldn't save him. There was a screaming bellow behind him. It was closing. By now he'd run clear of the firs and into a patch of beech trees. None had low branches. He snatched a glance back.

It was huge, its eyes glaring, its jaws opening on a red mouth. The shoulders looked enormous. The tusks didn't look quite as big as Tom feared but he still knew he had moments to get out of its way or he was finished.

Gasping, he ran, but there were only big trunks. Ahead he saw a lateral branch but knew he couldn't reach it, it was too high. The grunting, squealing and drumming of hooves was very close now.

He felt the axe in his hand, felt the wooden haft. The thought came. He drew back his arm as he ran and threw the axe at the trunk ahead of him at waist height, all the while running at full tilt.

The axe thunked into the trunk and Tom leapt. He got a foot up onto the axe head, his body thudding into the tree. His leg uncoiled, throwing him up until his arms caught the outlying branch. He hung there for an instant, aware of his legs dangling beneath him.

There was a thud and a squeal and Tom pulled himself up on the branch and lay there, panting.

The boar had hit the trunk. It had been so close it hadn't had time to change course as Tom disappeared upwards and the trunk was revealed. It staggered in a circle, dazed and hurt. Tom watched it, his eyes wide.

It raged. It bellowed and roared and squealed. The din was terrible, but Tom knew he was safe. He looked around but could see no sign of the other boys or the other boar. He really hoped his friends had found a tree.

The noise changed. Tom knew instinctively it was a lament, a sound full of sorrow. He remembered it was the mothers with the smaller tusks. He put his head down on the branch and tried to block out the sound.

The boar, its anger gone, trotted away, squealing, beaten, bereft. It was a while before Tom came down. He retrieved his axe. He apologised to the tree for damaging its trunk, making a wound in the protective bark that it would now have to spend a year repairing.

Cautiously, he slipped through the trees, back to where they'd split up. To his relief he saw both Grant and Rick returning, looking shaken.

'Are you hurt?' Tom looked anxiously at the others.

'Fine.' Rick looked rattled but Grant was grinning.

'That old boar, he seemed to take to Rick. Chased him all over. I just climbed a tree and waited it out.'

'Huh.' Rick gave his friend a shove. 'Thanks. Glad you weren't "bored"'.

The three walked back to the body on the ground. Rick went to lift it and whistled before putting it down again.

'It must weigh 30 pounds. It may only be a young'un but there's lots of meat on here.'

Grant looked around, anxious at the hesitation. 'Come on, come on, let's get out of here before they come back.'

But Tom knelt by the body and put a hand on the itchy bristles. Rick remembered then what some of the hunters had told them. He knelt down too, and put a hand out. The pair looked at the young body, oblivious of what was out in the trees around them.

Rick spoke. 'I am sorry boar, for killing you. My need, and the need of my friends, was stronger even than your will for life. Without you, we might not have made it back home. May your spirit run free in the forest.'

Grant spun round to watch the trees, listening to the background rustling. As his eyes strained at the shadows, he spoke over his shoulder.

'Listen to you two. You've never even been in the Shambles have you? Too rough a part of Burgh for the likes of you. We lived there, in the slaughterhouse district. Trust me, the men didn't pray to the animals' spirits when they slaughtered them. Now let's get out of here, those boar may come back.'

But Tom and Rick felt better. It made sense to honour the dead, particularly if you'd killed it. Tom thought of his spirit tree, that vast, hollowed-out oak, and knew that one day he'd be buried beneath it. In a forest full of such spirit trees, it wasn't sensible not to honour the spirits.

Rick lifted the boar up, grunting with the effort. He managed to get it round his shoulders. A drop of blood dripped onto his bare chest and the rough hairs already chafed on the back of his neck.

'I'll carry him for a bit. When we're clear and somewhere safe I'll butcher it and you two can get a fire going. Let's go.'

The three set off again, through the trees, heading for Frith. They carried food to fill their empty bellies.

Chapter 9

'That's the last of the food.'

Felix nodded. He didn't need telling.

'And we're almost out of water.'

Felix nodded again but didn't look at the forester. He was looking back the way they'd come. He was surprised they'd travelled so far and hadn't even seen the enemy. But, given it was the second day, Felix wasn't surprised they were out of supplies.

Even so, their slow pace had been driving him to distraction. Whatever he did, he simply couldn't get the exhausted women and children to move fast. He'd tried to get Rohana and even her scary mother to force them to speed up, but they stumbled on like a flock of ancient goats.

He realised Erik's plan had worked, and a diversionary attack on the southern gate had delayed the enemy. He'd been glad to see Erik and the others make it back intact, looking like they'd just played a prank on someone. Felix looked ahead. The forest was there, but it was still many hours' walking at this pace. How long could the enemy have been delayed?

He kept walking, moving up and down the column of plodding women and children, trying to chivvy them into more speed. They just looked at him dully, all their spark gone for now. Felix found himself at the head of the column and found something else to worry about.

They'd already passed what looked like big trenches in the ground, with clods of earth and clumps of tall grasses hanging off the edges. He knew it was something to do with the earthdin. They seemed like deep rents in the ground, with stinking smoke or steam seeping from one of them. Right now the column was making its way between two of these deep channels in the ground. Felix looked. If the channels came together they'd be trapped as there was no way they could cross such a big crevasse.

He looked ahead, trying to fathom where the great trenches ended. He was still looking when he heard the cry he'd been dreading.

'Horsemen, horsemen!'

Felix ran back towards the rear of the column, taking with him every man he could find. He waved away Rohana, who tried to join him. He didn't have time to explain how she'd hinder not help in the sort of battle he thought was coming.

'Run! Get them to run, get them running, now!' He waved her towards the column and ran on.

It was as he feared. As he arrived at the rearguard he saw groups of horsemen, who had been cantering across the open, grassy land. The riders slowed to a halt and were obviously waiting for orders.

They'd found the forest filth. Now they just needed to be released into that milling mob with their swords and knives, cutting the men down, keeping some prisoners to enjoy more slowly later.

'Men of the forest, to me.' Felix had seen where he needed to make his stand. The two great tears in the ground were only about twenty men apart at this point. They could protect his flanks, at least for a while. Or would the horsemen jump them? He didn't know. He had no other choices open to him.

'Shield wall, to left and right of me. Spearmen front rank. Axemen second rank. We hold the line, we hold the line. We do not break. We stand, and our forest folk can escape.'

The men ran to get into position, but they were tired. And they were scared. They'd never faced men charging on horses before. Ahead they saw a milling, jostling crowd of warriors on horseback. The horses threw their heads to and fro, great hooves pawing and thumping on the earth.

The forest men licked their dry lips, locked their shields on their neighbours' and gripped their weapons. They knew if they broke then the women and children were at these cruel men's mercy, and they had no mercy. But how could they hold against horses charging at them? And how long could they hold, out here, in the open, far from the safety of the great forest?

Felix fought down his own fear, and studied the men ahead. There, he saw the pale robes again. He knew that man, had seen him at the battle for Frith. And there, there he was. And there was that pasty, gangly body, which had to be Reese. He was riding a horse but looked like he was about to fall off at any moment. Felix scanned the warriors but saw no sign of the great warlord Gutta himself.

'A spear, give me a spear.' Someone gave up their own spear and passed it to Felix. He watched Reese. If he could get a throw at that traitor, then he'd give his own life for it. As yet, Reese might not have told the enemy everything about the defences of Frith and Burgh. It would be worth taking a chance to get him.

But he lost sight of him and the pale rider as someone ahead shouted orders and the huge phalanx of enemy horsemen began to trot forward. Soon they were cantering, heading straight for the shield wall. The noise of the hooves on the ground thundered into the head of every man standing his ground. The earth began to tremble, and the enemy started to shout as they broke into a charge.

And Felix felt the fear sweep across his men like a cold wind, making the hairs on their necks stand. It was a terrifying sight, and his men had never faced such a spectacle. He sensed rather than saw some of the men start edging backwards as the horses covered the ground, getting closer with appalling speed. Some of his men were going to break. To run. To where? If the wall broke then they were all dead.

Felix swallowed hard, his mouth and throat dry. 'Men of Frith! Men of the forest! Stand, stand! Horses will not hit a wall. They will not hit our shield wall. We stand behind the wall, behind the wall of wood, the wall of the forest. Shields, shields, up! Hold fast. When the horses falter, then spear and axe. They will not hit us.'

Felix stopped shouting as the noise of the advancing horde was now too loud. He had no idea if the horses would stop or not, but he had to say something. He had a moment to regret setting out on this whole venture. To regret bringing such trusting and faithful men to their doom.

Then the enemy arrived at full charge.

The men quaking behind their shields expected the horses to just run them over. But it was as Felix had hoped. Horses don't charge walls, even if it's a wall of wooden shields. They were deterred from trying to jump over the wall by the waving spears and axes above the shields. At the last moment they balked. They slid sideways, tried to stop, reared and did everything they could to avoid hitting what looked like a solid object.

The riders were caught off guard and focused on simply not falling off as the momentum of the charge collapsed into chaos.

'Now!' Felix yelled. 'Now, spear and axe and blade.'

The forest men turned their terror into violence. They jammed spears into the sides of the riders as they fought their horses. The second rank reached far over to bring their axes down on legs and arms, while others stabbed between the shields with the scaramax blades, hitting legs, horses' hindquarters and anything they could reach.

Riders fell, yelling and screaming. Those who were injured tried to get up but were felled as soon as they stood. Others were crushed by the mass of animals as the horses struggled to get away from this scary wall of noise and pain.

Felix, stabbing his spear into a rearing rider, shoved him sideways off his horse. The man writhed but was then trampled by his own horse and lay still. Felix looked about, searching for Reese. But the boy had stayed clear, at the back, out of reach. Frustrated, Felix hurled his spear at a rider's back, and drew his axe from his belt as the man threw up his arms and fell sideways.

Then they were gone. The horses had turned and fled, taking the remaining riders with them. A few horses were screaming in pain from their wounds, mixing with the yells of the retreating enemy and the groaning of the wounded lying in front of the shield wall. Felix looked along the wall. They'd taken hardly a single casualty.

He cheered, to put heart in to his men. His brave, strong, courageous men. He saw the relief on their faces. And he'd just shown them they could stand up to a horse charge.

Felix glanced backwards, past the men in the ranks behind him. The women and children were getting away, but they were still in sight. The mass of women and children was slowly disappearing into the long grasses of the open plain. How was he ever going to keep this huge force at bay for long enough?

He looked ahead again. He saw the man in the pale robes shouting instructions, clearly angry at the rout. Half a dozen men left the main group, riding their horses hard down the outside of the great trench to Felix's left. His stomach churned over.

If they could cross that big ditch behind his men then not only were the women and children doomed, but so were he and his men. Everyone watched as the riders curved in fast to the great smoking scar in the land behind the foresters' left shoulders, curving in between them and the retreating villagers.

They jumped. Three made it, three didn't, falling with screams into the chasm, which steamed as they fell. The three who had jumped clear decided to attack the women and children rather than turning to attack the men. Their cowardice proved a mistake.

Felix saw Rohana and others, including a smaller shape that he suspected was the dreadful old mother, forming a line of spears against the men. Felix had begrudged leaving them the spears but now he saw it had been worth it. A noise to the front swung him round, his flaxen hair flying.

Behind him he heard the men dying but the enemy had clearly decided that losing half the men as casualties was worth it. The horsemen separated out. A big central mass was going to attack head-on again. But two large groups went out to either flank, ready to charge round and cross the obstacles, even if they lost a lot of men in the process.

Felix knew he, his men and the women and children were dead at that moment. All he could do was get his wall to face front and rear, but they'd be surrounded with nowhere to go. He determined to sell his life dearly and take as many as he could with him. He glanced back to where Rohana and the others were disappearing again, leaving three horses behind them.

Could he get back and jump on a horse? He snorted. No, he'd never ridden one of the things, and he wasn't going to leave his men now to make a fool of himself on a horse. He'd die here. And they'd all die with him. They knew it.

He could tell from the silence. Each man watched the three masses of the enemy horsemen. Most touched the bits of wood round their necks, wood from their spirit trees. It looked like they'd never get to be buried under them now.

Felix took a deep breath. 'Men of Frith. Men of Middlehurst. We did everything we could. Form two walls, facing front and back. We will die with honour, and perhaps if we die with enough honour our spirits will make it back to our spirit trees. Our axes will spill blood before we fall. Touch wood, touch your spirit tree, touch wood.'

Felix looked back but he couldn't see Rohana. He looked forward. The enemy started moving.

Chapter 10

'Where is everybody?'

Tom walked slowly through the outskirts of Frith. They were home, all three of them home again. But the village seemed silent. They noticed the damage the earthdin had caused. Some of the trees were down, bringing some of the treehouses and sleeping chambers down with them. Other wooden homes looked as if they were leaning strangely.

But most of the village looked unhurt. Tom knew this was because everything was built to move and sway, like the trees in a wind, and it meant the homes could withstand even what had obviously been a fearsome ground tremor.

And he remembered what he thought he'd seen about Burgh. Maybe something that could bend was better than something built strong but rigid.

But that was a thought for another time. Right now Tom was wondering where the villagers were. Had they abandoned the place because of the earthdin? Had they somehow been attacked and driven off or killed? His feet took him almost automatically to the front of his house, with the others trailing behind. Where was Donald, and Mistress Anne? And where was Pad?

'Congratulations.'

All three boys spun round.

'Pad!' Tom smiled, even though he was as unnerved as the others. You just never heard him approaching.

Pad wasn't smiling. He was looking at the axe bags the boys held. His expression was stony.

'So you found the tree, passed the initiation. Well done.'

His tone was at odds with the words. Rick and Grant shuffled their feet.

'Well,' said Rick, 'it wasn't quite like that. We didn't find the tree. Tom did.'

'Is that so?' The new voice made the boys turn, to find Anne standing in the doorway of her house. Tom ran forward and gave her a quick hug. He realised she felt like a second mother to him these days. To his surprise a beaming Grant moved forward and gave her a hug too. Rick just looked embarrassed and waved a hand.

Anne looked like such a sweet older lady.

'You three look a complete mess,' she said severely. 'And you smell. Tom, your hair looks like you've been breeding birds in it. Rick, why is there a rash all over your shoulders? And Grant, you clearly haven't been looking after your feet.'

The three looked down. This wasn't quite the hero's welcome that Tom had been looking forward to.

'And you say Tom found the tree with the three axes?' Anne's
expression under her grey hair hadn't softened one bit. Grant and Rick
just nodded.

'And who saw this?' Anne folded her arms. The boys just shrugged.

'Well,' said Tom, 'I did have the three axes. So I obviously found
the tree. That's what I had to do. For the manhood ceremony.' Even he
could hear the pleading in his voice.

'It may surprise you Tom, to hear that we haven't had the Watchers or
crows to spare to keep an eye on you three. There's been a lot going on
here. Not much of it good. We'll have to talk about this another time.'

Anne sniffed. Tom saw Pad smirking out of the corner of his eye.

'But right now,' continued Anne, 'you three look hungry and dirty. You
go off and fix the last of those and I'll fix the first. In the stream, all of
you, then find some clothes and boots, and I'll have food and drink ready
for you. You probably deserve it.'

Her severe expression softened as she watched the three shamble
off in the direction of the stream.

As word of the boys' return spread, people started wandering in.
Sitting on the eating bench, the boys were working through some of
Anne's fabulous food. They were drinking big draughts of a drink made
months before from birch sap, and generally trying to refill their hungry
frames before Rick finished everything in sight.

People were asking them what had happened, how it had gone, how
come they had the three axes. But the boys noticed how some villagers
were missing, and it took a while to get answers as to where everyone
was.

Beth eventually wandered in and leant against the doorway. She
didn't say anything, but she looked with a smile at the three. Rick gave
her a huge grin but didn't seem capable of saying anything. And not just
because his mouth was full. Tom gave up on the unequal food fight and
smiled back at Beth.

'Beth! How are you?' It was good to see her. Tom wasn't entirely sure
how things were between them, or between her and Rick, but the sight
of her in the doorway made him briefly forget his food.

She nodded. 'I am well. It's good to see you back. I hear you found
your axe tree.' It came out more of a question than Tom expected.

'Yes, yes I did, just as that earthdin hit. It was really bad. And it was
bad here too I see.'

Tom paused. 'Is that why everyone is missing? Where are they?'

Beth tossed her head in the direction to her right, her brown curls whirling.

'Burgh. It's damaged. Lord Mofty has been calling for everyone to go to the city to protect it, get it repaired.'

Tom nodded. He knew most of that, but he didn't let on.

'But you're still here Beth, Pad?'

Pad frowned and went to kick a wooden wall. 'I'm still here. Can't go on the manhood initiation because I'm too young, can't go and help the others at Burgh because I'm too young. I have to stay here and wet-nurse the women.'

Rick halted the wooden fork of food half way to his mouth. Anne, clearing an empty pot from the table, looked up with amusement. Beth lashed out.

Her round-house kick took Pad behind the knees, sending him crashing to the floor. By the time he'd struggled up she had drawn an axe and was swinging it idly.

Beth smiled in her best girly manner. 'Thank you so much for looking after me Pad.'

Tom, watching with his mouth open, was taken aback when Pad stormed off. The friend he knew would have laughed and apologised to Beth. Rick's fork continued its journey to his mouth. No sense in wasting good food.

Beth sighed deeply and stared out the door. 'My brother's still out there. We haven't heard from the crows for ages. He's been gone for days. Maybe I should go and look for him.'

'No.' Anne shook her head. 'Felix is big enough and ugly enough to look after himself. Having you to worry about wouldn't help at all. He'll be back, you'll see, and he'll have all those Middlehurst forest folk with him. Then we can discuss what we do next.'

Tom nodded. 'We can't just sit here if everyone else is in Burgh. But do we know what's happening exactly? Is Blakelock still here? Can his crows or the Watchers tell us what's going on?'

'We wait,' said Anne. 'We wait until at least Felix and his men are back.'

'How long do we wait?' Rick didn't like asking the question and he liked it even less when Beth looked at him imploringly.

Tom rubbed the sooty scar on his temple. He stared at the wooden table as the others discussed possibilities.

'They're near.'

He said it quietly, but everyone heard him and fell silent.

'Who's near?' Beth looked at him, hoping against hope.

'Felix and the others. They're within the forest, they'll be here very soon.'

'How do you know?' Pad had come back in and looked suspiciously at Tom.

Beth looked at Pad in annoyance and then looked past him, out the door. 'Because they're here,' she said quietly. 'I think they're here.'

The village was overwhelmed. There were so many people, many of them wounded or beyond exhaustion, that everyone in Frith was busy. The incoming women and children were in a bad way. They'd been kept as slaves, seen their loved ones killed; they'd been starved, beaten and terrorised. And they'd spent days fleeing a terrible enemy whom they knew would ride them down.

Yet somehow here they were, and kindness, food and drink were working their charms.

Felix looked to the men. They too were shattered by the last days, but they received far less of the immediate attention. They had all faced the fear of fighting, and not one had run away from that fear. And many of them had volunteered for the terror of the front rank in the shield wall. They had stood and fought, even against horses. Many were wounded, all were weary from the aftermath of the rush of combat.

The men seemed resigned to being more ignored than the women and children. They had to keep their fears and terrors among themselves, the only ones who would truly understand, their shield brothers. They talked quietly, or loudly, but they shared the terrors with each other. That way the terrors might eventually go away.

Ives sat on his own. He looked half dead, like he'd been through something that he hadn't fully survived. His food was uneaten beside him. He watched a Middlehurst woman being given a hug of welcome and support by one of his village elders. He rubbed his arm and drew his stinking cloak around him. His head dropped and he saw his hand on the ground was shaking gently. He couldn't seem to stop it.

Felix knew that the Middlehurst men had taken greater casualties. All the bodies had been brought back, wrapped in their capes, and were now held a little way from the village. No man was left behind. The Middlehurst men had been fighting for their own women and children, and they'd fought with a wildness that had cost them dear.

He saw his sister coming back again to him, this time bringing more water and yet more food. He smiled his thanks, and thought how what he really wanted was to sleep safe for a week.

He appeared uninjured, but you didn't fight in armed combat without at least taking cuts and deep bruises. He held up his right hand for the wooden bowl of food. His shield arm was mottled blue and red and too stiff to move easily.

'Thanks Beth, you're doing wonders here.'

She put her hand on his shoulder. It spoke volumes. She looked down where her brother was slumped on the ground. His blonde hair was sticking to his head, dirty and streaked with sweat after days under the leather helmet. His clothing was torn, splashed with blood that now looked almost black.

'You're welcome. It's so good to see you back. And you're looking great.' She took a step away, to go and help some of the other warriors. 'Mind you,' she said over her shoulder, 'you stink like a warbrock.'

She grinned and turned away and saw Ives sitting on his own. She recognised him by the mangled mess of his ear. She hesitated, and then went and sat beside him, drawing his cloak closer around him. She picked up his food bowl and encouraged him to eat.

Felix, smiling, watched her go, glad she'd spotted Ives before he'd had to say something. He glanced up as someone else approached.

'Good morrow Mistress Anne. You're doing wonders too. Thank you.' He smiled his appreciation quickly, before shovelling yet more stew into his mouth.

Anne grunted. 'Yes, well, don't tell anyone, that's all. Now, Felix, you need to come to the moot tree and tell us what happened. We're hearing all sorts of strange things and we need to make a plan.'

Felix sighed and slowly stood up, aching all over. He so wished the village elders were there. He nodded. 'We will have a moot.'

Felix stood on the mound by the river, with the moot oak behind him. He told everyone what had happened. Those who'd been there nodded. He told it straight.

When he'd finished, Tom stepped forward. 'But, sorry Felix, that doesn't make sense. Gutta's men had you trapped. I still don't understand how you escaped.'

Others nodded and muttered agreement. Felix sighed. 'I don't understand it either. They were getting ready for their final assault, that much is clear. They started, but then another group of riders arrived. We thought they had yet more reinforcements.'

A few men listening nodded at the memory. It wasn't a good one. Ives put a hand to his face.

'They called a halt. They seemed to have a big shouting match. There must have been disagreement between the two groups.' Felix shrugged, then winced.

'Then they just turned around. They rode away. We thought it was a trap and we waited for hours. But they were gone. That's all we know. And, well, here we are.'

People frowned. The story didn't make sense. Felix silenced the muttering that had broken out amid the crowd. 'But now we need to hear what has happened here. Where is everyone? Who will speak?'

Anne stepped up to the mound. She seemed an unlikely spokesperson for the village, a homely looking woman with grey hair. But everyone in Frith knew her, trusted her and respected her. And the Middlehurst people didn't care who she was – they just wanted to find out the facts and then get back to their own village.

'There was a bit of a din,' she started. A few laughed at her understatement. 'We had a few trees down. I think my house lost a shingle roof tile. A few others had a bit of damage.'

Again, people laughed as, looking around, they could see houses leaning or with sleeping chambers collapsed.

Anne's friendly face grew sterner. 'But actually it is true. Our village survived almost intact the worst earthdin I have every experienced. We should be proud of that. And just a day later we heard from Burgh. That great city of stone, built on pride and arrogance in its own strength. The outer walls of Burgh have been breached, thrown down.'

There were gasps from the warriors who'd been with Felix. Burgh! Most had at least seen from a distance the vast grey blocks of stone that made up the city's walls. Nothing could damage such a solid structure.

Anne spoke again. 'If you make things too strong they can't bend. If they can't bend then they will break. If you men spent more time reading than waving your axes around you would know this.'

Her gaze searched the crowd till she found Grant, standing near the front. She grinned briefly at him before continuing.

'Our dear Lord Mofty, guardian of Burgh, sent out word demanding our presence at the city. To provide protection while they try to rebuild the walls. Not that there is any enemy near.

'Lord Gregory,' here she glanced at the Middlehurst people, 'our lord, our lord of the forest, has heeded that call. All the remaining warriors and elders have gone to Burgh. So what we need to do is to decide, now, what to do. Do we stay here or do we too go to Burgh? Whatever we do, we have to tend our animals and our crops here in Frith.'

Felix, standing to one side of her nodded and stepped forward. 'And we also need to try and work out why Lord Gutta's men have run away, back into the Open. Not that I mind them running away.'

Men laughed but Tom stepped up on the mound. Some of the Middlehurst people raised eyebrows. A boy, the same one who'd spoken – and been listened to – before.

Tom didn't feel comfortable back on the moot mound. He remembered standing there before, as he looked out at the sea of faces, many of them not known to him. He took a deep breath.

'I think I can answer Felix's question now. It took a day for news of Burgh's walls to reach Frith. Lord Gutta must have spies. Maybe he even used some of Reese's old mates.' He saw people looking blank. 'Reese is from Burgh. Like us.' He indicated Grant and Rick who were standing below him.

'He seems to be on Lord Gutta's side now. So they'd know, a few days later, that Burgh's walls had fallen down. Lord Gutta's drawing all his army together, not wasting it chasing slaves. He's going to attack Burgh. And Reese can lead him straight to it by the quickest route.'

There was muttering and a few shouts now. Tom continued talking as if to himself, his gaze somewhere else, and the noise died down.

'And if Burgh falls, then the forest falls. We will not be saved here in Frith. Lord Gutta will destroy us, destroy the whole forest, destroy us all. He will burn every one of us to the ground. Then there will only be Empty Lands. For ever.'

There was total silence. His quiet voice chilled everyone who heard. Then the shouting rose to a roar.

Chapter 11

Rick threw his kit down beside Tom's. 'Why is everyone in such a bad mood?' he asked. 'Every time I try to talk to anyone they snap and snarl like a warbrock with toothache.'

Tom smiled sympathetically. 'I know. I've given up.' He started sorting through his gear, untying the roll from his shoulders that doubled as either a shelter or a cape. Right now it would be a shelter, once he'd found a few sticks.

'Come on Rick, let's get our telts up, this is a good spot. Let's find some supporting sticks and some bedding.'

They set off into the surrounding trees, anxious to get their bedding sorted for the night before everyone else found all the good greenery. All around them men were starting to forage for ferns and mosses to put between them and the ground for the coming night. Everyone looked tired and it wasn't surprising.

As he searched, Tom noticed how quiet the men were. It was only two days since they'd all got back to Frith, yet here they were again, already a day out from their home, halfway or more to Burgh. The warriors hadn't had enough rest but here they were. Some still had bandages, and many were moving stiffly. A day's march hadn't really helped them much.

Rick was still grumbling as he snapped some sticks that would prop up his shelter. 'We should all be back in Frith. My feet still ache. Although it's nice to get them back into decent boots.' He looked down at the long brown boots he was wearing. 'And nice to get back into some clothes again too. Although it feels too hot today anyway.'

'Rick. Stop grumbling will you. We're all in the same cart aren't we? I'm not surprised the others had a go at you.' Tom picked up an armful of soft greenery and headed back to his gear. Rick followed, looking unhappy.

'But it was meant to be so great. We get back, hero's welcome, new men of the village and all that stuff. Instead nobody's even talking about our manhood ceremony. And anyone who is talking is just shouting at each other.' He started putting up his shelter with more force than was strictly necessary.

Tom nodded. 'I know, it's like we've just been forgotten. I *did* pass the initiation, I *did* find the tree and the axe. Yet here we are still being treated like boys. It's not fair.' He looked around as he pegged down his telt at all the men putting up their own shelters amid the trees and the open glades around them. He shrugged. Fair or not, everyone had other things on their minds.

'So who is having a go at you then?' Tom stuffed in the bedding and crawled into the small space to make sure it was comfortable.

Rick was still pegging his shelter down. 'Well, Felix for one. I know he's exhausted and he feels responsible for the men we lost, but I've never seen him in such a mood. Given I've been living with him and Beth you'd think he'd be a bit more friendly.'

Tom wriggled his hands behind his head and lay on his back looking at the fading blue of the day, and the grey clouds drifting over. 'I reckon he's not angry at you. I reckon he's angry at Beth somehow.'

Rick shoved the bracken and moss into his sleeping space and started to push himself under the shelter. 'Beth! Don't get me started on Beth. You'd think she would be pleased to see her brother. But oh no. As soon as he brings in that Rohana woman and her mother, Beth just went berserk. I've never seen her so angry. Quite scary.'

Rick turned so he could see out of his shelter to Tom. 'And did you see her face when Felix told her she had to stay and guard the village, with Rohana and the rest?' Rick grinned. 'I thought she was going to throw her axes at him!'

Tom nodded thoughtfully. There was something there, something about Beth and the Rohana woman staying that was clearly causing an upset. He couldn't see what it was so he shrugged it off. 'And how about Pad then?'

Rick reared round again and grunted as he hit his shelter and pulled some of the pegs out. 'Seriously, I thought he was going to kill someone. He's changed since we left. He scares me a bit now. I wouldn't have minded being told to stay back and guard the village. Me, Beth and the others. That would have been great.'

Tom gave him a look. 'I'm sure. You and Beth practicing your axe throwing together. Nice. But do you know where Pad is?'

Rick gave a roar of irritation and thrashed about some more. He'd pulled more of the pegs out of the ground and his shelter was folding gently in. 'Fabulous. I've just found I've put my shelter over a big rock or a root or something. It's really uncomfortable.'

He pulled himself out and kicked his feet clear. His shelter collapsed. Tom tried not to laugh.

'Pad?' Rick spoke over his shoulder as he tore it all apart to start again. 'I don't know where he went. He's not in the village and he's not with us is he? Probably sulking somewhere. He'll be there when we get back I'm sure.'

Tom extracted himself from his shelter and nodded. 'Perhaps. Perhaps not.' He started sorting through his gear and weapons, making sure his axe and blade were dry and clean and sharp. He felt sure he was going to need them.

Rick gave up on his shelter and kicked it into a heap. 'I'm going to sleep out tonight. It won't rain. Stupid shelter.' He looked at the sky through the branches. 'Anyway, tomorrow we'll all be tucked up nice and dry in Burgh. And we can see our parents and get some proper food. You looking forward to seeing your parents?'

Tom nodded slowly and kept sharpening his scaramax. He had a feeling. He looked at the trees.

Where was he going? He didn't know. But he crept cautiously out of the camp, moving stealthily so he didn't wake the sleeping men. Some had made shelters like his, others had made little covers out of twigs while others were just rolled in their capes on the ground. It was warm and still in the darkness, but Tom thought he could smell rain.

Once clear and among the trees, the blackness closed in. It seemed even darker after the light from the small fires in the camp. Tom waited to adjust his eyes then moved on, getting into clearer forest where larger trees stood tall. Their branches formed a canopy above him, a bit like a roof.

He felt no fear now, this recent city boy. The Burgh boy would have been terrified by being alone in a forest at night, the noises, the smells, the unseen terrors, the way bracken and questing stems twisted round his legs. But he moved as if he was looking for something. He found it. A vast oak with other smaller oaks around it amid a scattering of beech trees. He could make out the rough trunk in the darkness. It wasn't his tree, his spirit oak, but he felt it was the right tree.

He climbed, he sat, he leant his back against the thick trunk. He waited.

He waited and his mind whirled with all the worries and thoughts. What should he do? He could just go to Burgh with the others. See Abi, see his parents, feel safe. But he wasn't sure he'd be safe in the city now, with Gutta's vengeful army tramping ever closer.

And would he and his friends even be let in? Technically they were still outcasts, cast out by the city. And what would he do to defend the city? He was still classed as a boy, not a man, and he'd be given some safe boyish task which now he thought would be beneath him.

He waited. Slowly, in the absence of anything happening, his mind stopped rushing round and he rested, exhausted from his day. He breathed in the clean night air of the forest.

He smelt it. The burning. Trees burning like candles, even with their summer greenery. Great clouds of smoke and ash drifting over the forest. He felt the fear of fire. Just for a moment his mind seemed to slow enormously and he saw how trees can move, how they colonise one area but retreat from another. But it took generations to achieve, far slower than mortals could notice.

And they couldn't move fast enough to get out of the way of fire. They knew it was coming. The messages through the roots and leaves would have arrived by then. They had to stand there as it got closer and closer, the heat scorching their leaves, the flames burning the roots before the orange fire burned their bark, boiling the sap, flaming the branches and then the mighty trunk.

Tom had his eyes shut but he was breathing fast, sweating.

Now you know. You know what is coming, what is the present and a future. And you know we summoned you to help. We summoned you through the one you call Miss Goode, even though she is a dangerous instrument for us to use.

The big burning is here. If they get to your stone city they will have already burned thousands of us. And if they conquer the city they will burn all of us. All the trees, all the millions of beetles and bugs in every tree, all the animals that live in our shelter. It will all be empty lands.

There was a pause and the oak seemed to change subject.

We told you before how trees survive better if they stand together. How one tree alone will rarely live a long life. So it is with you. And you have others near, approaching. You can rely on them.

Tom guessed the tree meant the men slumbering in the camp. He nodded gently, his mind floating.

You call a group of trees that forms its own community, like a big group of oaks, a stand. Now it is your turn to make a stand. You must form a group in the forest. You can best help the forest by staying in the forest, not being a single mortal out in the open, or behind the big stones. And if you help the forest, that will help the stone city. It will help your ancestors who live in the city.

Make a stand. Make a stand.

A faint background noise brought Tom slowly back to the surface. A big raindrop landed on his nose, making him jump. He nearly lost his balance. The sound was heavy raindrops starting to fall. Feeling confused, Tom slid down the tree and headed back to camp.

Lying in his shelter, Tom tried to sleep. He failed miserably. The rain was strangely comforting, a gentle noise, and it released a sweet, fragrant smell into the night air. Admittedly, Rick didn't feel the same about it. Tom could hear him muttering and thrashing about as he tried to make some sort of instant shelter with his cape. Tom grinned and turned over in his dry, soft bedding.

Now it came to it, he realised how much he wanted to go with the others. Go to Burgh. They'd be there the next day. He could see Abi, see her lovely smile, talk to her again. See his parents, sleep in his old bed, see some of his old friends. Even with the walls damaged, he felt sure he'd feel safe there.

And he'd be surrounded by Lord Mofty's city army and some of them even had horses. And he'd be with his Lord Gregory's men. The finest fighting men Tom could imagine – Mister Weyland the Weapons Master, Donald the best Watcher ever, the terrifying Miss Goode with her quiver of dark, poisoned arrows, and Mister Blakelock, the hub of all the activities of Watchers and crows, the man with overwatch over Frith. Tom remembered seeing him swinging his two-handed sword and felt that thrill that is part pleasure, part fear.

All that was just a day's march away. He realised how scared he was of Lord Gutta and his army. And scared too of the big forest when all the Watchers and crows had been withdrawn. Out there now he'd be on his own. And what could he do? One boy, a boy who'd sort of failed his manhood test. A boy who, up until a few months ago, had been a city boy with buckles on his shoes and a fashionable haircut and not much else to worry about.

He knew the forest had said he could trust people around him. Although it had said people were approaching, which was wrong, as they were already here. Anyway, the men around him were going to Burgh, they weren't going to listen to him, and Felix was in no mood to really listen to Tom.

But the forest had spoken to him. His fingers crept up to his neck, to the wudu, the rough wood on the cord round his neck. He felt the timber of his spirit tree and remembered what he'd heard. He sighed and tried to sleep for a while.

He stood in the dark before dawn. He couldn't take his shelter because it would make too much noise taking it down. He knew he needed to travel light anyway. He left the shield and most of his things.

He felt with his fingers in the near blackness. Axe in his belt on the right side, scaramax on the left, water bottle round his neck. None of them would make a noise against each other.

He hesitated then stepped forward. The gentle rain continued and would mask any sound he made. He knew he had to be clear before dawn, he had to get going. A hand grabbed his ankle.

He stumbled and it took all his effort not to cry out.

'I'm wet. I've had a rotten night's sleep. And where do you think you're going?'

By Rick's standards it was a whisper. A deer on the edge of the clearing leapt away and a few men turned and muttered in their sleep.

'I have to go Rick. I just have to go.' Tom knelt, and put his head near his friend's, keeping his voice a proper whisper. 'I have to go and you can't come with me. Sorry.'

'Why not?' A startled owl took off from a branch nearby but fortunately it made no sound at all.

'Will you stop shouting? Do you remember those two boar that charged us through the woods?'

'Course I do.'

'Well, you make about as much noise as they do. And that's when you're trying to be quiet.' Tom paused and looked at the vague outline of his friend. 'Explain it to Felix will you. Tell him I needed to stay in the forest, to help. And say goodbye to Grant. Tell Abi I was thinking of her. And look after my parents.'

He wanted to say more but couldn't. He reached down and patted Rick's shoulder. Only now did Rick's hand release his ankle. That was it. Tom stood and walked away. He'd never felt so alone.

Chapter 12

Tom tried to get his mind working as he walked. If he thought about what Lord Gutta might do, then perhaps he wouldn't think about how lonely he felt, and how scared he was at the prospect of what lay ahead.

He forced his feet to keep walking. Otherwise he would simply have turned around and gone back to his snug bedding and then on to Burgh, to see his friends, his family, Abi.

He didn't feel he'd gone far when he saw that the dawn was upon him. He was in fairly open wooded land, heading south east, and the sky ahead was brightening. The rain had eased away and the clouds looked like they'd thin and disperse. It might be a good day.

His spirits started to lift a little. He looked ahead and breathed deeply. He heard a noise behind him, someone coming quickly. He looked around for somewhere to hide. Felix must have sent a search party, and they were closing fast.

A couple of small bushes nearby would have to do. He crawled behind them and lay still. There were some small, spindly trees nearby and anyone looking would search those rather than a couple of bushes half in the open.

The thudding steps, more than one person, drew closer. Donald had taught Tom that people often had an ability to know when they were being watched, so he put his head down into the grass. The figures rushed by without pausing. Tom put his head up. He sighed.

Behind Tom a tree's branches seemed to nod as if in a breeze, but it was a still morning.

'What are you doing? Just – what are you doing?'

Tom was exasperated. He had just been getting his head straight and now this.

Rick looked sulky. 'I just couldn't let you go off on your own. I couldn't do it.'

'And why are you here?' Tom glared at Grant.

Grant shrugged. 'Rick woke me up. I haven't got much to go back to in Burgh. Thought I'd tag along.'

Tom didn't know what to say but Grant looked back down the track.

'The thing is, Rick didn't just wake me up. He woke quite a few up – you know what he's like when he's being "quiet". Felix probably sent a search party after us.'

As he said it, they caught a hint of movement through the trees in the distance.

'Run,' said Tom. They ran.

The trees nearby rustled and moved as if a squirrel was leaping from tree to tree. It must have been a large squirrel.

After a while the boys slowed. Tom called a halt and he turned to study the track. The ground was fairly dry despite last night's rain, and they weren't leaving many prints. They moved on, over some grass, and then Tom shifted sideways into the trees. It was an area where there were several fallen trees covered in moss amid the standing survivors, and the boys hid behind one of the fallen trunks. They waited.

Silence. Tom let out a breath, confident nobody was following them.

'Rick, how did you know where I had gone?'

Rick looked defiant. 'I watched the direction you went. I followed that path. Look, don't get all grumpy with me. You always need me to save your sorry bum at some point.'

Grant grinned. 'He has a point. And three can do more than one.'

Tom laughed a bit loudly the other two thought. He leaned in and they leant in to hear. He was smiling broadly but talked in a whisper.

'Don't look up. Rick, don't look up. But there's something in the tree above us. There's something there. On the count of three we get back to the path, and we draw our axes.'

The others nodded and Rick managed to keep his eyes on the ground while he heard the whispered 'One, two …'

There was a thud behind them.

'Good morrow boys.'

'Beth! What are you doing here?'

Beth ignored Tom's question. 'Or should I say "Good morrow men"?'

The three looked at each other and she laughed.

'I thought you were all going to Burgh?'

Tom didn't seem to be able to answer any of her questions. He felt he was being played with like the time he'd seen a fox playing with a mouse. Yes, he thought, looking at her green eyes and brown hair and tanned skin. Just like that.

Beth perched herself on one of the fallen tree trunks, the moss making a comfortable seat.

'Well, if you're not going to answer my questions, I'll answer yours.'

And she told them briefly about how she couldn't be cooped up in the house with her brother gone again. The village didn't feel the same. All the Middlehurst people had left, gone back to their ruined village to rebuild and restart their lives. Since it was in the opposite direction to Burgh, they'd felt no need to accompany Felix, and anyway they had a lot of dead and injured to attend to.

'So all the Middlehurst people left did they?' Tom felt he was missing something.

Beth flicked her hair. 'Well, nearly all of them. That old woman Rohana and her batty old mother stayed.' She gave Tom a fierce stare. 'In our house.'

Rick looked up. 'What, in our house?' Since arriving in Frith with the others, Rick had been taken in by Felix and he viewed it as his home too. 'Why?'

Beth shrugged. 'How do I know? Something about her husband and child being dead. And the really old crone smells of the goats that she's obviously spent her life feeding and killing and skinning. And Rohana is just angry all the time and didn't want Felix to go.'

'A bit like you then?' Tom couldn't help himself.

Beth glared at him but then her glare darted past Tom and her eyes widened.

Pad was there, standing like he'd been there for hours. It was uncanny how he did that, even though everyone knew his father Donald had been the best Watcher ever.

The others were so startled that nobody moved or said a word. Pad broke the silence.

'The search party has given up. They've left, for Burgh. Without you. Which is lucky as you lot are just sitting around chatting loudly with no guards out. Lucky for you it's just me.'

'Have you been following me?' challenged Beth.

'No Beth. Although our paths have crossed once or twice. I prefer moving on the ground. But I'm curious. How did you know Tom and the others were here and not with the main group?'

Beth looked at Rick and grinned. 'I'll admit I was asleep, but Rick caused such a commotion this morning I had time to follow them.'

Rick pulled a face.

'Where were you sleeping?' Tom thought it was creepy that she'd been out there the previous night.

'Oh in a tree,' she said airily. 'And you Pad. What are you doing here, you're meant to be in Frith, "wet-nursing the women" aren't you? How will they survive without you?'

Pad glared at her, and then the others.

'I'm sick of being treated like a child. I could have passed that manhood test long before you lot. I'm not staying in Frith, nothing's going to happen there. And I don't want to go to Burgh either, so I can stand behind a stone wall and get told what to do.' He looked around. 'So I'm here.'

'Well that's just great,' said Grant. He stopped swinging his axe and brought it down on the dead trunk in front of him.

'So what do we do now?'
Everyone looked at everyone else. Then everyone looked at Tom.

Chapter 13

'What do you mean, you don't know where they are?'

Donald strode out of the stone house and stood staring south.

Felix looked tired and guilty. 'I'm sorry Donald. They took off before dawn. I had no idea they'd do that. I don't know why they left. We sent a search party but we found nothing.'

Donald nodded without turning round. His gaze took in the city before him, but he couldn't see far because of the walls. The crumbling walls. He finally turned.

'And Pad? You told him he had to stay and guard the people in Frith, yes?'

Felix could hear the tension in the question. 'I did Donald. Yes. I told him.'

Felix took a deep breath. Right now he'd rather be charging the enemy. But he wouldn't lie to Donald. He knew how he felt about his son.

'I did. He didn't take it well Donald. He stormed off. And I have to say I didn't get a chance to see him again before we left. I had a lot to do.'

Felix ran a hand through his long flaxen hair and stared back at Donald. He'd done all he could. He'd had so much to do, and he needed rest himself. He'd got everyone here that he could. Much as he liked the boys, there were bigger games afoot now.

Donald stared back at him for a moment then scratched his grey beard.

'I know Felix, I know. You've done a lot and we're grateful to you. Hopefully Pad, Beth and the others – plus any Middlehurst stragglers – will be enough to hold the village. I really can't see any threat to them right now. Lord Gutta is already coming up from the south, that much we know. He won't be bothering with Frith, he's got his eye on a bigger prize.

'And, anyway, we have to look after the crops and the animals. We need to have something to go back to.'

Felix joined him outside the doorway as they looked south, their gaze ending at the southern wall some distance away. There were huge gaps in the part they could see, the massive blocks having tumbled down in the disastrous earth tremor.

'Was it wise to recall all the Watchers?' Felix felt he had to ask.

Donald barked a laugh. 'No. It wasn't. I can't imagine Lord Gregory liked doing that one bit. But you know Lord Mofty, he can only see the city. Wants every man here to rebuild and defend the place.'

He sniffed the air and looked around at the streets crowded with people still going about their business. His watchful gaze took in who was going where and who they were. He scanned the buildings, analysing, pondering.

'This place is a dump, isn't it Felix?' Felix laughed as Donald carried on. 'It stinks. Trust Lord Mofty to make us stay down here in the south of the city. No wonder it's called the Shambles, it's a stinking mess. While he lords it up in the fragrant north of the city.'

He turned abruptly and walked back into the house. 'And that's another thing,' he carried on. 'All this stone, it's so cold. It's so dead. Gives me the creeps. Like being in a stone vault in the ground. Give me my sleeping chamber in the trees any day.'

Felix looked at his village elder and friend. He didn't look right here. His layers of ragged clothing, which seemed to blend into the forest, made him look like a vagabond here. And he moved like he was wanting to break free. Felix just wanted to rest and sleep, but suspected both would be in short supply.

'So what do we do? What are we meant to achieve here? Lord Gutta is coming with his army and the walls are partly down. What can we do that Lord Mofty and his men can't do?'

Donald snorted. 'He's brought Lord Gregory and me here because we're meant to know how to defend the place. He hasn't a clue, he's just hidden behind the walls all his life. Took them for granted. Well, that won't do now. And you,' he looked at Felix, 'you are meant to put our plans into action. Know much about siege warfare?'

Donald laughed again. 'Me neither.' He slapped Felix on the back. 'Let's go up and look at these walls again shall we.'

The view from the walls south was stupendous, looking out over the farmland and cleared land around the city, out over the apparently endless expanse of forest that stretched in every direction to the horizon.

The walls were high, that was for sure, but what was equally certain was that they had fallen in the south west corner. The blocks of stone were colossal. Nobody, it turned out, knew how they had been made or how they had been put in place. It was a knowledge lost to time.

'How are we going to get those blocks back up?' Felix gazed down at blocks the size of small houses which littered the ground outside. Without them in place the enemy would be able to pour through the gap.

Donald sighed. 'To be honest I have no idea. Nor does Lord Mofty. Nor does anyone. But if we don't find a way Lord Gutta's army is going to flood through that gap like a river. I don't see how we can defend the place. The West Gate is damaged too, although not as badly. This whole corner is a mess and I don't know how to fix it.'

He looked out again over the forest. 'And now we don't know where the boys are. Or what they're doing. Or why they left. And I'm not certain Pad is safe in Frith either.' He paused. 'I like those boys. I'm fond of Tom, treat him like a son almost. And I know you like Rick, clumsy oaf that he is.'

Felix smiled and nodded as Donald continued. 'And even that Grant has shown he was worth bringing in to the village.' He looked around. 'I think he said he came from here, the Shambles.' He looked out again at the silent forest.

'And now he's out there somewhere with Tom and maybe Rick.' He shielded his eyes and peered out at the forest as if his gaze could penetrate the canopy. He sighed again.

'Who knows. It may be that they're safer out there than they would be here.'

Chapter 14

'So that's the plan is it?' Pad looked at the others then looked at the forest, as if unsure where he was.

'You think we should sneak up on Gutta's huge army, find out what they're doing – maybe go up and ask them – then trot back to Burgh to let Lord Gregory know? Is that it? Anything else? Maybe we could fight Gutta's horde all by ourselves. Why bother all those people in Burgh?'

Pad threw up his arms and wandered in a circle. Tom looked uncomfortable.

'You told us yourself Pad that all the Watchers have been withdrawn. There's nobody out here to see what's going on but us. We can keep out of trouble, spy on them, then get that knowledge back to Donald and the rest. We don't have to get too close.'

Pad laughed derisively. 'Right.' He looked at each of them in turn. 'I've spent my life in the forest, I'm a forester. What about you lot? You've spent your lives hiding behind those big walls in Burgh. Until a few months ago if you'd been out here like this you'd have had to go home and change your breeches. Your idea of fighting was to say "Ow" before the other person hit you. What use are you?'

Grant stared at Pad until Pad had to look at him. 'Where I come from,' Grant said evenly, 'if I had to fight I had to fight until my opponent wasn't moving. And he usually had some mates. You have no idea about my life.'

He kept staring until Pad broke the stare.

Beth snorted. 'Forgotten me, Pad?' She smiled sweetly at him. 'Hope I didn't hurt you the other day, kicking you to the floor?'

Pad waved his arms. 'Well, Tom and Rick are pretty useless. They should just go home. We can handle it.'

Tom had heard enough. 'You seem to have forgotten I volunteered to come with you to rescue Grant and the others from Jubu. And we succeeded. And Rick killed a warlord on his own. And here you are, you followed me. You all followed me. And now you can follow me if you like or you can go on to Burgh.'

He stood up and walked off. This time there wasn't much delay before he heard footsteps following him. He didn't turn round but he smiled with relief. He was glad he wasn't on his own.

'We've been walking hours. Do you think it's time for something to eat?' Rick did look like he needed a rest.

Tom nodded. 'Let's take a break. Who has any food? I've got water.'

It turned out they all had water. Nobody had any food, apart from Pad and Beth, who had a few nuts and seeds to eat.

Tom shrugged and picked leaves off a nearby hawthorn bush and started eating. It would do for now. He was reminded of Langdon, the man who gave his life protecting them outside Jubu, and who was now buried under his spirit tree, a hawthorn. Tom ate the leaves and gave thanks to Langdon.

Rick wandered off for quite a while but then returned with some greens to eat. 'Here, everyone help yourself. I've got sorrel, dandelion, thyme, bush vetch and lots more. And there are some roots for later, when we have a chance to have a fire – some dandelion and some earthnuts.'

The others ate sparingly, as Pad once again approached Tom. 'What direction are we going in? Why are we heading this way?'

Tom squinted towards the sun. 'Because Lord Gutta has one advantage. I mean, apart from a huge army and an enemy whose walls have fallen down.' He grinned, but Pad only grimaced. 'Lord Gutta has Reese doesn't he? He'll have told him the quickest way to Burgh. Straight up from the south. He won't veer west and go through the Silver Belt like his brothers will he?'

Pad thought about that and nodded. 'True.'

'So we head south east, we find his army soon after it hits our forest and we shadow it from there. That's the plan.' Tom shoved a handful of plants into his mouth so he didn't have to explain more.

He wasn't sure what they'd do when they found Lord Gutta's horde of warriors. And quite a lot of him didn't want to find it at all.

But they did find it. The next day Beth scrambled down from a high beech and the others gathered round.

'There's smoke on the horizon. Looks like they're burning as they're advancing. We're about half a day from them if we keep moving. Tom, your sense of direction is really good. They're right ahead of us if they're not too far ahead of the smoke.'

There was just a hint of a question in that last remark. Tom just smiled and didn't meet her eye. 'Lucky I suppose.'

Rick pulled his axe from his belt and checked it over yet again. 'Right. Then let's press on and see what we see.'

If they'd had older, wiser heads with them perhaps they wouldn't have set off straight away. But they were eager to find what they'd been heading towards for what seemed like ages.

By late afternoon it had clouded over and Tom wondered if more rain was coming. In their excitement they'd given no thought to looking after themselves. Pad thought they'd all be dead before nightfall anyway, or that's what he said. Tom wondered where his cheerful friend had gone to and whether he'd ever return.

Tom pulled his thoughts together. By now they could all faintly smell smoke. A few wisps of ash were floating down. And there was a background noise that was hard to place. The group moved forward more cautiously, keeping to shadows, using tree trunks to mask their progress. How close were they going to be? What were they going to see?

He could feel the tension in him and the others. He stopped and turned to the rest. He pointed to Beth then pointed upwards and raised an eyebrow. She nodded, looked around and disappeared among the trees. The others looked about to see which one she would most likely climb.

Nobody saw Beth climb the twisting sweet chestnut. She went nimbly up to the crown, settled down so she had a good view, and looked out. She froze.

While they waited in cover, Rick sidled forward to Tom.

'You know, Tom, I've been meaning to talk to you about your hair.'

Grant guffawed and clapped a hand over his mouth. Tom stared at his friend. 'My hair? Really?'

'Yes,' said Rick, not put off in the least. 'Your hair. It's too blonde and too long.'

'I see,' said Tom. 'And you think now is a good time to discuss haircuts? I know it mattered in Burgh but I'm not sure now is the time.'

'What do you think,' asked Grant with a smile. 'You think maybe some plaits or something Rick? We could weave some flowers into it.'

Rick looked sulky. 'It's just that we've all got dark hair and you've got really light-coloured hair. As we were creeping along I was thinking how much it showed up against the dark of the tree trunks. That's all.'

Tom nodded slowly. He ran a hand through his flaxen hair. It had grown long, he hadn't thought about it before.

'Rick's right. We need to make ourselves blend into the background more. We need to be invisible. Has anyone got a spare bit of cloth?'

For some reason Grant did. It was a dirty square of dark material that he'd been hoarding in the small bag he carried. Tom used it to cover his hair, tying a knot at the back of his neck so most of his hair was covered. The others grinned, but it worked.

Grant looked at them all. 'You know, I was reading stories of old hunters. They made sure they never washed with soap or anything when they were out hunting because it made a strange smell. The animals would react to it, run away. And they made sure their skin was covered in earth or stain so it didn't stand out.

'Not that that's a problem for me, but it is for you lot.'

Tom nodded. 'True. But that applies to you too Grant. Black or white, any solid skin colour is going to show up against the wrong background. Everyone, get some mud, and wipe it on your faces and hands.'

The others crawled around and were soon muddy. They were briefly enjoying themselves, this was every boy's idea of fun. They had just got back together as a group when they heard a slight rustle. They went still, but it was Beth.

She paused for a moment when she saw how different they looked. They grinned self-consciously at each other. She walked quickly over to where they crouched. As she crouched down she lifted her eyes and looked at Tom. She didn't say a word. As he looked at her face, Tom's smile faded and he felt the hairs on his neck standing up.

Chapter 15

'While you've been playing at boys in the forest, I've been looking at the enemy.'

Despite her brave words Tom could see the shock and fear on her face. Nobody spoke. Beth drew a deep breath and told what she'd seen, as she'd been taught by her brother.

'We might be about half way down the column. It stretches from horizon to horizon in the forest. Men on foot, men on horses. Oxen pulling wagons. Didn't see what was on them, supplies I suppose. It's the biggest army I've ever seen. It goes on for ever.'

Tom moistened his lips. 'Did you see the head of it, who's at the head of it?'

Beth shook her head. 'That's already past, out of sight. And they're burning trees as they pass. They're throwing burning branches into the trees, into the undergrowth, they're trying to burn the whole forest.'

Tom looked to where the constant noise was coming from. 'How close?'

'They're only a few hundred paces ahead.'

Tom looked at the others. 'We need to see for ourselves. Keep low, use the shadows. We need to see, not be seen. We get close enough to see, but no closer. Agreed?'

The others nodded. This didn't seem such fun now. Tom led them forward, keeping low, moving cautiously through the understorey beneath the canopy of trees. The sound grew louder until Tom could make out creaking of wheels, oxen lowing and the constant tramp of thousands of feet and hooves.

He peered through some bracken and there they were. He forced himself to stay there, to stay still. He prayed Rick was being careful. He trusted the others not to give their position away but he worried about his big friend from the city.

He watched for a few moments then gradually eased backwards, keeping his eyes forward. He flicked a glance left and right and saw the others doing the same, backing quietly away.

It was a terrifying sight, so many men, all looking fierce and warlike, so many weapons, so much equipment. It was an army, moving forward for one purpose. To destroy Burgh and then the whole forest.

A sound behind him filtered through over the noises ahead. He turned very slowly. What a fool he'd been getting this close. He hadn't thought. They had a flanking patrol out. It was behind them. They were trapped between the main army and the patrol.

He could hear the men pushing through the undergrowth and in the gloomy, smoky light of the overcast afternoon he could see the odd glint of flame. With his back to the main army, Tom watched the men coming from his left. They'd be in plain sight in a few moments.

Tom looked left, saw Beth, Pad and Grant already sinking into the undergrowth, aware of the threat. Tom started to sink, his eyes scanning for Rick. He saw him. He had stayed back, been sensible, kept clear of the main army in case he did anything stupid. Which meant he was now in the line of the patrol as it pushed through the bracken and brambles around them.

Rick looked back desperately at Tom, but all Tom could do was gesture for him to get down, stay down. Rick disappeared and Tom went to ground, his face pressed into the earth. The noise of the patrol grew louder. Tom inched his head up, looking through the roots at ankle height.

He could see Rick, lying on his front. He'd got into some brambles, but his arms were spread out, caught on the thorns. Tom figured if he was seen they'd have to attack and try to get clear but he didn't rate their chances.

He saw what happened. The leader of the patrol drew parallel with Tom and Rick, with the rest of the patrol spread out behind. They'd be in line with the others, lying hidden just feet away. Tom saw the boot come down on Rick's right hand. There was a quick command and the men stopped. The leader had stopped with his boot crushing Rick's hand. Tom looked on in horror as the man turned, his boot grinding into Rick's fingers.

Tom could hear the men trying to listen, thinking they'd heard something. He couldn't believe Rick was silent. Was he unconscious? There was another quick command and a burning branch was thrown out. Tom saw it coming through his eyebrows, arcing up into the air, and landing with a crackle close to his head.

He tried not to flinch as the burning brand instantly caught the dry grasses. Flames and smoke rose quickly. The men still stood, listening. Tom slowly moved his head to one side, as smoke drifted his way. With his eyes stinging, Tom tried really hard not to cough as the smoke got into his nose and eyes and throat.

He put his mouth to his sleeve and breathed gently through the cloth. He could feel the heat on his face now. Still the men stood, still Rick stayed silent.

Even amid the green ferns and brambles, the flames were finding fuel, and the heat and fire licked higher, spreading slowly to where Tom lay. He could smell the heat of his clothing now. He'd have to move. But if he moved he knew he'd cough. He was trapped.

To his left he heard a noise. His lungs were screaming and his eyes were weeping, but he tried to hold on. There was a commotion in the undergrowth and Tom's heart sank. One of the others had lost their nerve. But instead there was a flutter of wings and the alarm call of a blackbird, receding fast.

Ahead he heard the men exclaim and they trampled on. The heat was burning Tom's face but he waited, going deep inside himself, until he was sure they had gone. Then he moved, crawling right, coughing into his sleeve. Behind him the vast army tramped forward.

He forced himself to crawl forward to where Rick lay. The others crawled out of hiding and they looked at Rick with concern. His face was grey and sweaty, his eyes closed. He had scratches of blood on him from the bramble thorns but everyone was looking at his right hand.

It was crushed, a bleeding mess. Looking around, with the enemy so close, the others heaved Rick up, no easy task. They staggered away from the main column and its protective patrols. They'd hardly even seen the enemy yet they were already injured, forced to retreat. Tom wondered if they should just head straight to Burgh. At least they had some information to give.

It started to rain. As dusk fell, the five youngsters slunk away through the forest, melting into its shadows and gloom.

Chapter 16

Lord Gregory stood four-square on the cold stone tiles in front of Lord Mofty. He noted Lord Mofty was keeping him waiting, deliberately. He was sitting behind a long table, with a few men either side and they seemed engrossed in some papers.

Lord Gregory recognised the city Steward, Steward Browne, next to the city lord. Steward Browne always looked very wealthy and sleek and smug to Lord Gregory, and his presence, deliberately ignoring him, caused Lord Gregory a moment's irritation before he dismissed it. A few other senior people of the city also stood in the chamber, watching Lord Gregory, but he ignored them all.

He was a patient man, he knew the power of patience. Lord Mofty looked up sooner than Lord Gregory had expected.

'Ah, Lord Gregory, good of you to join us.'

The forest lord stood impassive, his face impossible to read with his eyes covered by the huge grey brows and his mouth covered by the grey, full moustache. He didn't bother to point out that Lord Mofty had sent two guards to bring him from the Shambles, where he was overseeing the work on the walls.

Lord Mofty plunged on, smiling, in the face of Lord Gregory's lack of response.

'I am looking for progress on rebuilding the south-west corner. How are the walls looking now?'

Lord Gregory's moustache twitched. 'You could come and see for yourself Lord Mofty. I am surprised that your commander of the guard hasn't been overseeing things. We are just foresters after all.'

Lord Mofty heard the barb. 'My Guard Commander is a busy man. Perhaps you saw him drilling the men in the main square as you came here? We are preparing our defences.'

Again, there was a faint twitch of the moustache. 'I did. I did see them going through their drills. And I'm sure if the enemy were to approach and fight in nice straight lines your toy soldiers would do a good job.'

He paused while there was a rustle of annoyance in the chamber. He glanced about, beneath his brows. Even in the summer there was a small fire burning in the huge grate at one end of the stone room. He wondered if the cold stone was getting into these people's heads.

He spoke up to silence the whispering. 'You have never seen Lord Gutta's army. We have fought and beaten one small part of it. With no support from Burgh. But what is coming is many times the size of that.

'He has scoured both the Open Lands and the Empty Lands for tribesmen and warriors. He has bribed or terrorised the Edge People, brought them all together, for one purpose. To destroy Burgh and then to destroy the forest. That is what is coming.'

He paused. 'And Lord Gutta knows your walls are down. He is coming eager for slaughter and rich pickings.'

He felt the alarm run through the cold chamber, echoing up into the wooden rafters.

Lord Mofty jerked upright from his chair. 'Then I charge you with repairing the walls. We must have them repaired before he gets here.'

Lord Gregory snorted. 'Yet you cannot tell me how they were built or how to repair them.'

Lord Mofty opened his mouth but it stayed open. Lord Gregory heard the door open behind him, but he didn't turn. He heard the pad of bare feet approaching, heard the intake of breath from the others. He didn't need to turn.

It was a shocking breach of etiquette, to approach the city lord while another lord was in the chamber. In theory it couldn't happen because the guards would stop anyone entering. Yet here he was. He padded up beside Lord Gregory. He gave a cursory nod to Lord Mofty.

'Lord.'

He turned and nodded again, deeper. 'My Lord Gregory.' He lowered his voice and spoke quickly and quietly to his lord. Nobody else moved.

The stranger looked an apparition, as much animal as man. His wild hair was like a black mane, streaked with grey, teased out into fantastic shapes from his head. His beard covered half his chest and was pulled into forks with leather bands. He wore a pair of faded breeches and a dark pair of fingerless leather gloves and nothing else. His skin was tanned and weathered and scarred.

And he wore a wide leather belt, from which hung a sword and scabbard that was one of the largest anyone had ever seen. And he was wearing it in the chamber, which again was impossible. But again, here he was.

Lord Gregory simply nodded. The man turned, gave a piercing stare from blue eyes at Lord Mofty, and then walked out of the chamber. Everyone could hear his bare feet slapping on the stone in the silence. The door closed quietly.

Lord Mofty looked shocked and furious. 'Was that Lord Blakelock? That hairy beast was Lord Blakelock? What is he doing here?'

This time Lord Gregory raised his huge head and stared at the other man. 'You could have asked him while he stood before you. You demanded every able-bodied man come here. He has come. But he does not use his title in the forest. He was a lord of the city, and that ended when you banished him.'

Lord Mofty waved his arm. 'He was scheming against me. I was merciful to let him live.'

Lord Gregory slowly shook his head. 'No. He was the best Guard Commander this city has ever seen. He spoke to everyone, knew what was going on, he wasn't plotting against you.

'And when he was in charge, the guard were the best troops this city ever had. Now they don't even dare stop him coming in here. They're weak, and the strongest enemy this city has ever faced is a few days' march away.'

Lord Mofty flung his head back and put his hands on his hips. 'I should have him arrested. I will have him arrested.'

Lord Gregory cocked his head. 'I see. And how many men would you send to arrest him?'

'What? I don't know. A squad of six should be sufficient, surely. I shall see to it.'

Again, Lord Gregory's great head shook ponderously from side to side. 'You need all the men you can muster. You can't afford to lose six men.'

Steward Browne snorted but Lord Mofty didn't. They both knew the truth of the words.

Lord Gregory had had enough. 'If your Guard Commander could attend us tomorrow morning I should be obliged. We will have to stop now it is getting dark. But there is much to do.'

And, he thought, as he walked back through the city, he now had some news for Donald. He was grateful to Blakelock, but he wasn't sure if the news was good or bad.

Chapter 17

The rain fell gently as the five struggled away from the enemy column. The erratic wind pursued them, blowing gusts of smoke and ash over the forest. With the smoke and the fading sunlight above the clouds, anyone would have been hard-pressed to see them moving steadily away.

'We have to stop.' Beth was breathing hard. She lifted Rick's head up in her hands and looked at him. 'He's done.' He was half-supported by two others, but even so Rick was barely able to keep walking. Everyone was panting, sweating, anxious.

'I hear water,' said Pad. 'A bit further.' They pressed on and came to a stream. If was fast-flowing and deep. They looked around. Pad spotted a dry gully that ran down to the stream. He had a quick look and came back, nodding.

'That will do. It's facing away from the enemy, we can hide in there, and we'll need the water.'

They found a comfortable spot in the bottom of the gully, protected by what had obviously been storm debris at some point. There was a rough wall of branches and roots and stones that gave them shelter from the wind. The sides of the gully were above them, so they were hidden. Although they wouldn't see an enemy approaching until they were very close.

The gully opened out onto the stream and they all drank their fill and refilled their flasks. Grant helped get Rick down to the stream and bathed his hand in the cool water. He and Beth looked at the bleeding wound ground into the back of his hand. Beth winced and put her hand on Rick's shoulder.

'You were so brave Rick. How did you manage not to cry out?'

Rick grimaced a smile. 'It hurt so much I couldn't speak. But I knew if I made a sound then he'd find not just me but all of you and then we'd all be dead or taken prisoner. Anyway, I think I must have made a sound. That's why they stopped.'

He winced as Grant tried to gently rub off the blood so he could see underneath.

Pad hunkered down by them. 'That was brave Rick. Gutsy. I'm not sure I could have kept quiet.' He slapped Rick on the back and moved away. Everyone chorused their agreement. Tom, walking down to the stream, grinned. What a little team they were becoming. A stand maybe.

But Grant's voice was serious. He was looking at Rick's big hand. 'We need to get some hot water somehow. There's lots of dirt and muck ground into the wound. If we get all the dirt out then it should heal. Otherwise it may get swollen and go bad. He could lose his hand.'

'Is it safe to stop here?' Beth looked around anxiously. Tom walked up the bank, and steadied himself against a young oak trunk. He was silent for a moment. The others watched him. He came back down.

'I think it's safe. We're far enough away from the enemy, and their patrols are just protecting the flanks of the column, they're not exploring. And there's smoke and fire everywhere. If we build a small fire we should be safe here for tonight. The enemy won't camp for a bit yet.'

The others just accepted his judgement without arguing. Even Pad.

'What about wild animals?' asked Beth. She seemed more thrown than her usual calm and confident self.

It was Pad's turn to answer. 'The noise of the enemy, all that smoke and flame – everything has run away or will stay in its burrow tonight. Which means there will be no game for us to hunt. And Rick's too hurt to go and get some of his famous greens.'

Rick smiled but it was a wan smile. 'I'll be fine in a bit. We won't starve.'

There was a pause as everyone tried to work out what was best as Rick was obviously going nowhere. Tom stood to try to make some suggestions as to what people could do, but Grant beat him to it.

'Does anyone know how we can get hot water? Does anyone have a metal container? We can't heat our water flasks. Anyone?'

The others shook their heads. It had all been such a rush and a muddle. Grant sighed.

'Right then. We try it my way. I read about it in a book. I haven't tried it but it might work. We need to do this for Rick.'

He looked at the stream. 'We'll need some clay. Riverbanks are the place to find it. Beth, will you help me find some clay? It's like grey, a bit blue, all thick and claggy?' She nodded, eager to help Rick.

'Tom, we'll need a fire. Can you get a fire going?' Tom nodded. 'And, Tom, find some stones, big stones. Not wet ones, not from the river. Get a pile together, here at the end of the gully.'

Tom looked mystified but nodded. He had no idea what Grant was planning but at least he had a plan.

Pad saw that Grant had finished for the moment. 'And I'll get a shelter up. For all of us.'

Rick lay back up in the gully and everyone else disappeared on their various missions. Rick frowned as he looked up at the sky. 'Hope someone has thought about some dinner.'

The gentle rain fell on his face, and he tried to laugh, but his eyes seemed wet. He pulled his damaged hand onto his chest and began to tremble.

'What do we do now?' Tom was intrigued. Grant and Beth had come back with armfuls of yucky grey sludge. Grant had dug a hole and they'd lined the hole with what was obviously clay. It had taken quite a while for them to fill their bottles at the stream then pour them into the hole. But it worked. The hole filled up with water and it didn't leak away.

'Now we put those stones into the fire.' Grant started picking up the rocks and tipping them into the red-hot fire. The others joined in and they waited.

'Oh,' said Beth, trying to get her arms and front clean of the sticky clay, 'then we put the hot rocks in the water?'

Grant nodded, but looked anxious. 'Like I say, I read it, but a while ago. I hope I've got it right. If you use the wrong rocks they explode in the fire, or when you put them in the water – I don't remember which.'

The others moved away from the fire.

'Shame we haven't any nice meat to cook on the fire,' mused Tom. He looked around, thinking of all the lessons he'd learned when out in the forest with Pad and Donald. He looked at the stream again. Deep, fast-flowing, sandy bottom in places.

'I'll be back in a bit,' he said and wandered off. The others went to help Pad get the shelter finished while the rocks heated up. Or exploded.

Pad had wedged two long poles a few feet into the mass of debris in the gully. Then he'd covered the gap between the poles with small branches and lengths of wood. After that he'd leant more small branches side by side on the outside of the two poles. This made a sort of tapering shelter from where the poles went into the mound of debris one end, and where they were pushed into the ground the other end.

Now he was covering all the little branches with armfuls of bracken and leafy boughs to make it watertight. And all but invisible. The others joined in and soon they had a snug shelter. Beth then carried on cutting vegetation with her axe to form bedding inside, to keep them off the soil and to help keep them warm. It may have been summer, but the steady light rain was dampening everything and would chill them during the night.

Pad and Grant went back to the fire and, using bits of wood, they rolled the hot rocks out of the fire and into the basin of water. They flinched as the stones hissed, expecting bits of rock to explode in their faces, but the water bubbled briefly instead.

'Keep going,' urged Grant. 'Keep adding rocks. And then we take the old ones out and heat them again. We can get this boiling.'

It took a while, but they managed it. 'It's boiling!' Grant looked thrilled. 'We've boiled water!' Pad grinned, amused at Grant's enthusiasm. Despite himself, he was impressed. He'd learnt something from some city boy.

Beth came to see and clapped her hands. 'Now we can make Rick better.' She paused for a moment, looking at the bubbling water, thinking. She went through her bag and pulled out a thin garment she liked to wear if it got cold. She ripped off one sleeve and dunked it in the water.

'Ow! That's hot.' The others laughed at her surprise.

They looked up into the gloom of early evening as Tom appeared. He had his tunic off and was carrying it carefully. Obviously he had something inside. He put it down gently, wrapping the ends over. Intrigued, Pad went to say something but Grant spoke quickly.

'Right. Now, everyone, we need to get Rick down here.' The boys went to rouse him but found he was all but unconscious. Tom frowned. 'He's in shock I think.' They carried him down so he lay between the pool of hot water and the fire.

Beth hesitated. 'Grant, do you want to do this?' She looked down at the boy as she crouched beside him. 'I don't want to hurt him.'

Grant nodded briskly and took the cloth from the water. Wincing with the heat, he used it to bathe Rick's hand. It looked horrid, but he kept working away, until it was at least clean. There was a lot of skin missing and Grant noticed that one of the fingers was actually dislocated. He looked at Rick.

He gestured to the others to hold him down. They did so, their faces looking fearful, but Rick seemed unaware of what was happening.

Grant took a deep breath and pulled really hard on the middle finger of Rick's hand. He felt it move slightly towards him. He let it go as Rick gasped in agony, some sixth-sense making him still stop himself from crying out. Grant looked again. The finger had popped back into its socket. He breathed out slowly.

He cleaned the rag once again and then tied it round Rick's hand. He knew when it dried it would get a bit tighter, and would better seal the wound. Tomorrow maybe he'd try to find some cobwebs, but for now he was done. Rick stirred and opened his eyes.

'Ouch,' he said quietly. Beth laughed and kissed his head and the others sat back, feeling exhausted. And hungry.

Tom moved back to his tunic and emptied the contents into the hot water. He looked at their faces.

'Mussels. I found mussels on the stream bed. And a few crayfish. It's not a lot but it will do. A few moments and we can eat. Even Rick, if he's still awake.'

Later that night the five lay in their shelter. They were close together in the cosiness of the bracken and moss. Beth had found some small pine branches and they made a fresh smell to go with the comfort. Exhausted and anxious, the five were at least all together still, and they'd eaten and drunk. And now they slept, quietly and deeply.

In the distance the forest smouldered in the rain and the enemy encampment burned with fierce fires in the night. Curled up uncomfortably in a damp, dirty blanket, Reese tried to sleep but kept being startled awake by the sounds of the warriors, snarling and gambling and cursing. Dawn felt like a long way away.

Chapter 18

Soon after dawn Lord Gregory stood with Donald and Felix on the ruined ramparts of the southern wall of the city. The rain had stopped during the night, but there was a morning mist that made the forest look beautiful. And invisible. Donald stared hard, but the mist hid everything. He knew the enemy weren't that near, but they were closing. Not today, but a day soon.

And now he knew who was out there. 'Blakelock is sure?' Lord Gregory just nodded. Of course Blakelock was sure, and Lord Gregory knew it was a sign of nerves in his faithful and trusted elder that he'd even asked.

Below them, men were trying yet again to build a gantry mechanism that could lift one of the huge cut stones that lay on the ground outside the line of the walls. Their shouts drifted up but Donald seemed unaware. He spoke but almost as if to himself.

'So if Pine Leaf saw them heading towards the enemy that would have been yesterday. They might have found them yesterday or more likely today. That's still a couple of days away from here I should think, given how slow his army must be moving. All that equipment, food, men getting tired, trying to get a lift on the wagons. Hmm, a couple of days away at least.'

Felix nodded agreement, but kept quiet beside the two elders.

Donald gazed into the mist as if sheer effort would part the tendrils of vapour. 'And what will they discover? What are those young people hoping to achieve? Damn Lord Mofty, forcing us to pull in all our Watchers. I know you've given your word we won't send any out. We'll keep them all here, doing nothing behind these tumbling walls.'

Lord Gregory grunted and moved away. He wasn't going to get anything further out of Donald for a while so he let him be.

As soon as he'd moved away a girl approached them cautiously. 'Excuse me, sirs, but are you from that place in the forest, Frith?'

Felix turned, his expression unfriendly. 'We are. What of it?' He saw a girl, not yet a woman. With the sort of colouring and dark eyes that meant she might be from out there, from perhaps Jubu or somewhere. There were plenty of rumours of Lord Gutta's spies trying to find out information.

The girl looked frightened but determined. 'I was hoping you might have some news of my friend, sir. I heard he'd been at something called the Silver Belt? And he'd been fighting?'

Felix didn't trust her. He didn't want to talk about the Silver Belt, the defensive position deep in the forest. What if Lord Gutta was planning on sending another attack through there again, to divert from his main attack?

'I don't know what you're talking about.' Felix gave her a hostile look and walked off. The girl put her head down and turned away.

Donald called her back. She came hesitantly now, looking more scared. He could see she didn't know what to make of him and his strange appearance.

'Yes, my lord?'

Donald smiled. 'I'm no lord.' He looked at her, but he didn't look like Felix looked, he looked at her like a Watcher would look.

He saw a girl, very pretty, not far off womanhood, darker skin and very dark eyes, clearly originally not from these northern lands. Some wealth there. A good dress. And nervous, not just because of standing in front of him, but nervous of her location, looking around her. So not from the Shambles. No, from a nicer part of the city. So what had driven her here?

She dropped her gaze as this strange, ragged man stared at her. She sensed authority there and had seen him talking as if as equal to the other lord, the one from the forest. He was probably too grand to know anything about what she wanted to know.

'What is it you want, girl? You're not from this part of the city are you?'

Oh no sir, I'm from Park Side.'

Donald worked out that must mean from somewhere near the park, the Centre Park, which was in the north of the city. 'So what are you doing here?'

She hesitated then raised her eyes again. 'I came to find out about my friend. To see if anyone knows anything. I haven't seen him since he came here to talk to Lord Mofty.' Despite herself she smiled. 'He had this funny crown made of twigs on his head.'

Donald laughed, but he was careful. 'And what is the name of your friend?'

'Tom. Tom Haywood.'

Donald nodded carefully. 'I know of a Tom Haywood.'

'Have you seen him? Do you know where he is? Is he here?' The eager questions tumbled out.

Donald thought about his reply but the girl misunderstood why he hesitated.

'No. He's not here,' Donald said gently.

The girl's big eyes filled with tears and she put her hands to her mouth. She twisted away and started walking quickly back the way she'd come.

Donald sighed and strode after her. He turned her round.

'He's not dead if that's what you're thinking. He's a very tiresome fellow who doesn't do what he's told, but he's not dead. Last heard, he was very much alive and well.'

The girl smiled a radiant smile through her tears. Donald noticed it. Beautiful he thought, and scratched his beard. He turned and walked back to the wall, ignoring the look Felix gave him. The girl followed.

'Thank you for telling me sir. Thank you. But can you tell me where he is if he isn't here?'

Donald hesitated. He remembered what he could of what Tom had said about the people in Burgh. He vaguely had a name of a girl. Could this be the one?

'What is your name girl?'

'Abi. Abi Chattan.'

Donald nodded. Yes, Abi was the name he remembered. He sighed and looked out from the high, broken walls.

'I don't know exactly where he is Abi. He's out there somewhere.' Together they stared out into the rising mist. Abi shuddered. It looked scary and wild out there.

Chapter 19

Tom sat up carefully. He looked along the line of sleeping bodies. Rick, in the middle, was on his back, his injured hand on his chest, mouth open, sounding like stones dragged along the bottom of a stream. Beth was beside him, one of her arms half draped across him. That sight gave Tom a strange feeling.

He cautiously got up and wriggled out into the day. There was thick mist, but it felt warm, like it would clear into a sunny day. He walked down to the stream, pulling bits of bracken out of his hair. He felt tired and worn and his head lolled forward, unobserving.

He pulled off the dirty rag from his hair, knelt by the stream and dunked his head in. He rubbed his hands over his face under the water and pulled his head out, gasping with the refreshing chill, his eyes closed. The side of his head was still red and tender from the burning undergrowth and the water felt good. He took a few mouthfuls.

He opened his eyes with his head still bowed over the running water. He couldn't see anything, as the surface of the water was broken by the water dripping off his face and hair. Peering down as he knelt there, he started to come awake and started to become aware.

Something splashed hard into the water right by his head.

Tom reared round, realising how defenceless he had allowed himself to be.

'Admiring yourself again?' Pad sniffed. 'Can still smell that smoke, guess they'll start again today.' Pad too dunked his head in the stream, then shook the water out of his black hair and ran his hands over his face. 'That feels better. We slept well. Let's see if we can find something to break our fast.'

They rootled about. Tom found some mushrooms but Pad shook his head. 'There's a thing we use for wild food, like a ratio, risk and reward. Mushrooms. Risk – death. Reward – not much energy. Not worth the risk.'

Tom went to thank him but Pad was looking over to where the stream lay a short distance away. Tom heard it then, ducks quacking in alarm. Pad didn't even glance at Tom, he just headed in that direction, his scaramax materialising in his hand.

Tom followed. Ducks, so some meat. But something alarming them – a threat to the ducks, like a fox or an otter, or a threat to them all, like a death worm? He trailed Pad.

Pad was hunkered down at the base of some firs, their dark low branches giving him cover as he looked out. There was long grass along the banks, and there was something in there. Pad picked up a stone, paused, and threw it where there was a slight movement.

A pair of ducks flew past, quacking urgently, making Tom jump. A fox put its head up. Pad threw another stone, hitting the fox on its glossy coat. It put its head down and ran. They could see its movement by the grasses waving.

Pad moved forward, carefully, and parted the grasses. The duck's nest looked a bit of a mess, the dry grasses it was made of trampled and pulled. There was a string of yolk from a broken egg, obviously one the fox was eating when they arrived.

But there were other eggs. Tom moved in and grinned. He counted another nine, still intact, looking large and inviting.

'Wow! Look at these! Let's scoop them up and get back.' He reached out and started collecting the still-warm eggs into his arms. Pad put out a hand.

'The fox may not come back. We might have scared him away.' He looked at the eggs, then at the ducks, circling frantically round. 'Those are the parents. We take five eggs, we leave the rest.'

Tom actually felt a bit ashamed. He was hungry. He took five, and left the other four in the nest. They backed out, Tom clutching the eggs carefully.

'Aw come on,' said Grant. 'We don't have time to do that whole thing with the fire and the hot water again. How are we going to cook the eggs? We haven't got a pan have we.'

Pad looked at Beth. 'You know how?'

She nodded. She looked at her belt. 'I've only got axes. I need someone to use their blade to gently make a hole or take the very top off each of the eggs.'

Given the size of the scaramax blade, virtually the length of arm from elbow to wrist, this was clearly not an easy job, but Rick eagerly stepped forward. He seemed much more himself after a decent sleep and some care on his hand. Everyone looked doubtful, seeing their breakfast smashed to bits.

Ricks' big hands, one of them bandaged tightly, were surprisingly delicate. The others watched in amusement and concern as he gently worked on the eggs with the tip of the blade, his tongue sticking out between his lips.

'When one is done, someone put it in the embers,' said Beth. 'But not in the really bright red bits, it needs to cook not burn. Make sure they go in upright with the hole at the top.'

Fortunately the others had got the fire going in Tom and Pad's absence, and there was a good bank of hot embers, some just reheated from last night. Soon all five eggs were roasting gently. Beth lay down by the fire, watching them, turning them every now and then. Rick joined her, and she let him turn them, teaching him what to look for.

Tom watched them lying side by side, chatting and working together. It gave him a funny feeling in his stomach.

He coughed and spoke up, sounding harsher than he'd intended.

'We have to decide what to do together. We can't spend all day just lying here shoving food in our faces. We either head back to Burgh or we make a plan.'

The others looked up, surprised at his tone. But he was right. Secretly, they all just wanted to stay where they were. It was safe, there was food, and not much chance of being found. The very last thing any of them wanted to do was head back towards that great long fiery, smoking death worm of an enemy column.

Nobody spoke, but instead watched as Beth wrapped her hand in her sleeve and pulled the eggs out. She handed one to each of them and they had the sense to wait for them to cool.

As Pad juggled the hot egg in his hands, Tom broke the silence.

'Pad, what would the Watchers do?' Tom knew Pad had dreams of being one, and his father Donald had been one of the best ones, and maybe that's what they should try to aim at right now.

'The Watchers?' Pad looked taken off guard. 'They'd really watch. They'd find out how many men there were, and if they could they'd find out the enemy plans. Then they'd report back, probably split up so at least one of the pair would make it back with the information.'

'And how would they find out the enemy's plans?'

The question clearly made Pad uneasy. He looked down and spoke as he peeled the shell off the egg. 'They'd get close. Maybe at night. Try to listen in to conversations or briefings. That's what they'd do.'

Tom looked at the others as they tucked into their breakfast. It would give them some energy for a while. He looked at them clearly. Three boys, including him, who'd only recently left the life of the city, and one of them was injured. A girl who'd never fought although she knew the forest well. And Pad, angry Pad, who was an unknown quantity.

The egg tasted delicious, but he felt it sticking in his mouth. He said what he had to say.

'If that's what the Watchers would do, then that's what we should do.'

Chapter 20

Donald looked down from the walls as shouts floated up. The gantry trying to lift a huge block of stone was slowly toppling over. He watched as figures ran desperately in all directions as the tall structure collapsed. He glanced across to where Felix was standing further along the wall.

'That's it. We're done,' he called out. 'We're out of time. We're going to have to get the other plan into action and fast. Get them started now.'

Felix nodded, looking fed up. Around him some of the city men stood, clutching big sheets of diagrams and blueprints. They looked lost and scared. Without the stones in place they felt horribly vulnerable, and it was obvious now those stones weren't going to be restored before the enemy arrived. Felix rolled his eyes.

Donald grunted to himself and walked along the walkway behind the wall, sometimes having to detour down to the streets where chunks of masonry were missing. He walked slowly, missing nothing, and by walking slowly he didn't draw attention to himself.

His steps took him across the ruined south-west corner and up towards the West Gate. By now he was at street level, where the stench from the slaughterhouses was enough to make your eyes water.

But his eyes were staring at the gateway itself. He tried not to stare, just let his eyes wander naturally. He didn't know who could be trusted in this city now. There was no doubt about it, the masonry above the gateway had collapsed. It was only held up by the huge wooden and metal doors locked below the arch.

To his annoyance he saw some of the city men standing there, more men with rolls of paper, and they were all looking anxiously at the stonework. He wandered over.

'Time to stop staring at the gateway gentlemen.'

They turned and saw a raggedy man they didn't recognise. But he had the voice of authority.

'And who are you exactly to tell us what to do?'

'I am overseeing the restoration work. My name is not important. You can ask Lord Mofty if you doubt me. And now I'm telling you to disperse. We know what the situation is here and we don't need to draw attention to it. Go.'

One of the men looked around quickly, as if he'd just understood what he'd been told. He rolled up the sheets of parchment in his hands. 'Time to go gentlemen.'

The others looked put out but followed him away, heading quickly out of the area, sticking together.

Donald looked again. There was no way to quickly repair the gateway. It was a weakness. He was fairly confident they could shore up the other gaps in the walls, but this would take too long to fix. Better if nobody knew about it.

He turned round. The road was fairly wide here where it came through the gateway, but there were houses either side, virtually touching each other. The road continued into the distance, somewhere meeting the Centre Square, and then on to the East Gate. It was too far for Donald to see but he knew the farmers from the area were all driving their animals into the city through there.

Lord Mofty was emptying the nearby land, bringing all the food and livestock into Burgh as a precaution. Donald hoped they didn't have to endure a siege. He rather suspected Lord Gutta had no experience or appetite for a siege, he'd try frontal assaults. But if he knew of a weakness that wasn't obvious? Donald nodded to himself and started walking, deep in thought.

A figure caught his eye. It was that girl again. She was still here. He frowned. Was she watching him, following him? She looked nervous, her dress of a fine material standing out amid the others who lived in this quarter. He wandered along, apparently unaware of what was around him.

Three young men over there. Watching the girl, or watching him? She was aware of them. She was scared. There weren't too many people about and they seemed preoccupied, dashing about as the tension in the city mounted. A smudge of smoke was now obvious on the horizon to the south.

Donald kept watching under his brows, walking slowly away from the gate, intending to get to the end of the row of houses and turn north, back towards Lord Mofty's realm. He sensed the girl approaching to walk beside him.

'Sir, I was hoping you could tell me a bit more about Tom. Tom Haywood.' She smiled but Donald saw that there was little humour in it, mostly nerves. She seemed to pull herself together a bit. 'So you knew my name? That means he's talked about me?'

Donald grinned. 'Well, I think it was Abi. Maybe it was Anne. Yes, I think it was Anne now I come to think of it.'

Abi looked crestfallen and Donald laughed. The three boys had drifted ahead and were now waiting where the line of houses ended. 'No, I'm teasing you Abi, it was your name he mentioned. Many times.'

Abi looked up, her face now genuinely smiling. 'I'm glad. Although,' here she looked down again, 'I'm sure there are lots of pretty girls in the forest.'

'Oh yes, the place is thick with them. Beauties hiding behind every tree. We had to get Tom a special stick to beat them off with. You know, with his fancy city ways and fancy shoes with buckles and things.'

Abi smiled, unsure whether he was teasing or not. But it distracted her and by then they were at the corner.

'Well, if it isn't Abi Chattan. Come to visit us in our neighbourhood. Nice of you to come and pay us a visit.'

The three boys were lounging by a fence on the corner, and Donald and Abi had to walk by them. Abi stopped.

'Matt. Good morrow.'

Matt nodded and looked at his mates. 'I seem to remember meeting you before, when you had your little blonde friend in tow.' He scowled at the memory of their last meeting in the park. 'I didn't like that. I pointed out I was in charge now that Reese has been banished. And I am in charge down here. Until he returns.'

Donald stood, smiling slightly, completely still.

'And nice of you to bring your granddad with you. Come down to see a nice bit of slaughtering have you?' His mates sniggered. They stood either side of Matt. They felt bolder confronting the girl again now she was with an old man who looked like a bit of a vagrant.

Abi looked scared but uninterested. 'Very funny, Matt, you're very funny. We're heading home, so it's nice to see you but we're going.'

Matt shook his head. 'No. No you're not. You promised me a kiss last time. Time to collect.' He stepped forward grinning nastily.

'I did no such thing! I'd rather kiss one of the goats down here for slaughter.' Abi tossed her head.

Matt snorted and looked at his mates again. 'You won't be quite so high and mighty when Lord Gutta gets here will you? He'll be told about people like you. Perhaps he already knows.'

He smirked and sauntered forward. He had a new type of tunic on with pockets attached, and he kept his hands in his pockets to show how in charge he was.

The axe head slashed the front of the right pocket and, a moment later, the left. Matt let out a gasp and brought up his hands, which seemed unscathed.

'Not polite to talk to a girl with your hands in your pockets.' Donald swung the axe idly. He hardly seemed to have moved. Matt stood still, looking at his hands in front of his face. One of his mates snarled and flicked out a knife to gut the interfering old fool.

Without apparently looking Donald backswung the axe so the back of the axehead hit the boy's wrist. The knife went flying and they all heard the crack of bones. The boy whimpered and reeled round, clutching his broken hand. Donald seemed unmoved, still smiling slightly.

Matt and the other young man seemed frozen. Donald stepped forward and the smile was gone. Definitely gone.

'That was interesting what you said. Matt. How would Lord Gutta know about goings-on in Burgh, hmm? And you think Reese is going to come back? How would you know that?'

Matt made a small noise but stayed very still. The axe had disappeared between them and by the way Matt was standing on his toes Abi could guess where it was.

'The thing about axes,' said Donald conversationally, 'is that you really need to get a swing to cause real damage. But if you hook the lower point over something and pull back hard it can cause a surprising amount of damage with hardly any movement. Which is interesting isn't it? Isn't it?'

Matt nodded slowly. Donald continued in a reasonable tone.

'The thing is you're not acting like much of a man. A man helps those weaker than himself. Like girls.' He inclined his head to one side towards Abi. 'Or poor defenceless old men.' He waggled his head to indicate himself.

'You're acting like a boy, who doesn't know how a real man acts. And if you ever want to be a man then I suggest you answer my questions. Now.'

Matt breathed out carefully then breathed in. 'Maybe Reese still has friends in Burgh. I wouldn't know. Maybe some of them think Lord Gutta will win, and then if they'd helped him they'd get rewarded. I wouldn't know.'

Donald looked into the boy's face for what seemed like ages. He stepped back so quickly that Matt made a squealing noise and looked down. The axe had somehow disappeared.

'Go away.' Donald didn't need to say it twice. As the boys disappeared Abi stepped forward again, her eyes wide.

'How did you do that sir? You moved so quickly. Is that how it is in the forest?'

Donald sniffed. 'No, we don't have people like that in the forest. And my name is Donald.'

He started walking, and she tagged along. 'You want to walk with me back to the square?' He asked it kindly and she nodded gratefully.

But Donald didn't speak again, his face unreadable. Abi kept by him, but kept the many questions she had to herself.

Donald was worried now. It seemed likely that there was information getting out of the city, and that could only aid Lord Gutta.

He thought how he and the foresters had taken Reese in. He shook the thought away. It wasn't helpful right now.

Right now, after getting back to talk to the city elders about the new defensive measures, he needed to go to the East Gate. He needed to talk to the guards, not so much about the people coming in, but the people leaving.

As they left the Shambles Donald sensed the fear and panic receding. Like all good hunters, he had more empathy with the prey than anyone who didn't actually kill their own meat. He sensed the distress and the fear from the animals being slaughtered.

He knew, if things went wrong, it wouldn't be only the animals feeling the panic and the pain and smelling the blood in Burgh.

Chapter 21

'So we think about three thousand soldiers.' The others nodded. They'd all done a rough count and come up with a different number, but the snaking column had taken at least two hours to pass them they thought. 'And about fifty wagons bringing up the rear.'

They hunkered down quietly, even though they felt a bit safer. For hours they'd been sat in the trees, watching the column approach, then pass. At least it was now past, bar a few stragglers.

Pad kept his voice to a murmur, and the others leant in, hidden under some bushes. 'We know how many, sort of. We know where they're going. But we don't know their plans.'

Rick shrugged. 'That's obvious. They're just going to attack where the city walls have fallen down. With that many soldiers how can they fail?' He looked at the ground. 'I'm really worried about my parents. And everyone. What happens if this army breaks through the walls?'

Neither Grant nor Tom could meet his eye. It was what they were thinking. They'd seen this swarm of snarling, shouting enemy soldiers, and they could now imagine what would happen if they broke into the city. Tom could see them running down his road, killing and terrifying. What would his parents do? Could Abi get out? And if so where could she possibly go?

Once again he wished he were in Burgh to help. And to have all those tough foresters and soldiers around him.

Pad took a sip from his water flask. 'The best way we can help you city folk is by finding out if Lord Gutta has a plan. Maybe he's going to make a diversion, attack one gate then the other. I don't know. But if we could find that out we would really help.

'If we can get the information back of course.'

They argued about what they could do while Tom settled down, his back against the trunk of the oak he'd been watching from. He didn't speak for a while as the others put forward ideas, clever or crazy.

There was a pause in the quiet but intense talking. He spoke.

'The enemy army is like a huge burning death worm, crawling through the forest. When mortals wish to control a death worm they get a forked stick, a piece of the forest, and pin the head down. We need to be at the head, there we will find out what is planned. We can use the forest to help us pin the head down.'

He'd sounded very serious, almost not himself, but now he looked up and grinned. 'And maybe we can annoy it by grabbing its tail too.'

'Oh that's great. Pad didn't want me and now you don't either. That's not fair. I'll be as quiet as a dormouse.'

'Ssshh. Rick, for Frith's sake, keep your voice down.' Tom waved his arms and looked around.

The day was done. The evenings were long at this time of year, but that was just as well. It had taken them hours to get forward to the head of the enemy column. The army seemed to have just stopped where it was, making no effort to form a perimeter. They were very confident and lazy Tom thought. But they were right, there was no forest force or Burgh army to attack them here.

There were still fires burning, but some of them were now the enemy making camp fires to cook what little food they had. Tom had spotted the odd patrol out but he felt confident they could keep clear of them. He just needed to sort Rick out.

'Look it makes sense. Pad's the best out of all of us for sneaking about and not being seen. And Grant could look a bit like one of them if the light is dim. They stand the best chance of finding out what's in those wagons.

'And Beth is the best at climbing trees. And, well, you're not. Your job is really important though. If we get seen you're going to have to cause confusion. Shout, run about, attack someone if they're on their own, throw some fire about. That way Beth and I can get down from the trees and we can escape. See? You're the biggest and strongest.'

Rick nodded reluctantly. Tom realised his big friend didn't want to be left on his own. They'd already left Pad and Grant at the rear of the column while they made their way alongside it, and now he and Beth were going to disappear into the trees. Leaving Rick all alone surrounded by the enemy.

And a Rick who was still too injured to use his right hand. Good thing, thought Tom, that Rick had been taught to use his axe left handed. He smiled at his friend, put his clenched fist to his chest in a formal gesture, and turned. It was time to climb.

Tom put all his faith in Beth. He wasn't bad at climbing trees, but he knew she was as natural in them as a squirrel. She'd already navigated a route through the branches that would take them near to where they could see the reflection of a big fire. That was Lord Gutta's fire.

Tom tried not to think too much as they climbed higher. He was already struggling to keep up with Beth, who moved with incredible grace and strength. She moved out onto a big branch and Tom caught his breath. She just walked along it, balancing easily as the bough nodded slightly.

Tom followed, trying to mimic the way she moved, like she was fluid, like she was a slender branch. The wood they were on was thinning, and he kept back as it started nodding more. But it wove into branches on the next tree, and Beth was already on its boughs. She moved to the next trunk and stood there waiting.

Tom was breathing uneasily but he managed the transition to the next set of branches. His balance started to go and he flailed out an arm and just caught a higher bunch of leafy twigs. He breathed out, balanced again, and walked forward steadily towards Beth.

He kept his eyes on her, because then he didn't have to look down. The ground was already a long way away. Just ahead he could hear voices. He realised they were soon going to be travelling above enemy soldiers. Beth reached out a hand.

Tom moved steadily forward, took her hand, felt her pulling him to safety. It was a thick branch, like where a strong man's arm reaches his shoulder. They stood immobile. Tom realised he was pressed against her, his breathing ragged.

She stared into his face. Her green eyes seemed to glow slightly in the dark. She wasn't smiling. Tom licked his lips. He felt the need to say something.

'I don't think Rick would like seeing us right now.' He whispered it near her ear, her hair tickling his nose. He tried to smile.

Beth put her head on one side. 'Actually, he'd be making less noise than you are.' Her voice was just the faintest whisper. 'You need to calm your breathing down. And relax. If you go all rigid you'll fall. Sway, like the trees do.'

She swayed gently where she stood to show him. That wasn't helping Tom concentrate at all. But he heard the message in the words. He focused on slowing his breathing, making himself quieter, more still, more like the tree.

Beth watched, nodded, turned and was gone. Tom followed, any thoughts of her replaced by the sound of soldiers beneath them.

The transition into the next tree was harder. There were voices under him all the time now and Tom could catch the odd glimpse of movement far below. He hoped nobody would look up, but he knew in the dark they were just vague dark shapes against the dark trees. He was glad he'd tied his hair again, inside a black rag.

He had to balance on a branch, then stretch right up to a sideways branch of the tree next door. He got his fingers over the branch, kicked up and swung himself onto the branch, lying flat. Below he heard a shout.

He lay still. It went quiet below and he knew soldiers were looking up. Had he made a noise? Had he kicked off some bark?

After a long moment the harsh voices returned, and Tom very slowly crawled along the branch to the relative safety of the trunk. Once again Beth was waiting. Her eyes were wide. 'You kicked off some green leaves. I saw them fall.' Her voice was almost inaudible, but her fear was all too real.

Tom grimaced. She rolled her eyes, turned, and swung round the trunk. She found a thick branch heading further but, instead of walking along it, she lay down so her legs and arms were along the branch, invisible from below.

We must be there, over Lord Gutta's position, thought Tom. He calmed himself again, trying to think himself into the tree. There was a branch near Beth, angled a bit further out. He moved round the trunk, found the branch and lay down as Beth had. His boots scraped on the bark and he saw Beth turn towards him, her eyes huge in her face.

There was shouting and movement below. He heard the unmistakable voice of Reese calling out.

'Ha, look who's come to join us. My old mate from Burgh.'

Chapter 22

The next morning Donald stood by the East Gate with the Guard Commander. He watched the roll of wagons coming in, boys herding flocks of goats and cattle, children herding geese, families bringing belongings, grain, food of all sorts. Everyone knew it could be a siege.

And he watched even closer those going the other way. He was wondering if that brat Matt or one of his mates might try and slip out and find Reese. There were few leaving, mostly farmers heading out to get another load of food or belongings, but it was impossible to check everyone.

'It would have been easier if we had both gates operating.' Studge, the Guard Commander, sounded like he was complaining.

Donald shrugged. 'True. But if we open it it'll probably bring the whole gateway and arch down. You want that?'

Studge pulled a face. 'Be better if we hadn't had that earthdin.'

Donald looked the other way and rolled his eyes. 'Yes, Guard Commander, that is the case.'

'And is it me,' said Studge in his deliberate way, 'or is there more smoke than there was?'

Donald had already seen what was on the horizon. 'Yes, more smoke, definitely. Looks like they're burning more and more of the forest. And they're getting closer.' He paused. 'Which means we have less time. And you still have to get those holes in the walls shored up and get your men down there to help and to get some practice in defending them. Don't you think?'

Burgh's Guard Commander looked at Donald. Donald saw how the folds of skin on Studge's chin were bulging over his chainmail doublet. The man's done his chainmail up too tight, he thought, as he's getting fat and he doesn't want it to show. And he's trying to stare me down. Donald returned the stare.

Studge snorted and looked around, to check his squad was still with him. 'Well, I don't have time to waste talking to the likes of you, I've got responsibilities me. Lads, looks smart, we're off.'

Donald watched him go with his squad of soldiers trailing behind him. That's what is technically in charge of defending the city, he thought. And they used to have Lord Blakelock. He was still staring after Studge when he sensed someone beside him.

Blakelock looked after Studge and his squad as they disappeared towards the Shambles. He said nothing. He turned and met Donald's eye.

'Donald, I've just had a report from one of ours. There are five of our people out there. Tom is one, Pad is another. I'm guessing the other three are Beth, Rick and Grant. They're very close indeed to the enemy column, virtually among it.'

Donald stared at the smoke. There was definitely more this morning, part of it a great big black column that was dissipating as the day wore on. It didn't look like wood smoke. He wondered what it was.

His son, his adopted son, was right there, right now. Donald had faced many dangers with equanimity, but the thought of Pad facing them out there made his stomach churn.

'No message?'

Blakelock shook his great shaggy head. 'No message.'

'Anything else, any more information?'

'No. It wasn't Pine Leaf, she is tired and being rested. It was a younger messenger, Rotten Tail. He found all the smoke frightening I think. But if what he says is true, and I believe him, then they are putting themselves in great danger. What are they doing do you think?'

Donald thought, scratched his beard, wiped his hand absent-mindedly on his ragged cloak.

'I don't know. But I can guess. Pad wants to be a Watcher. So he'll be watching. Maybe they'll find out something useful, I don't know, but it's way too dangerous for them. Imagine what happens to them if they get caught by Lord Gutta.'

The two men fell silent.

Donald went still, watching the wagons and people coming in, and a few leaving.

'So Lord Mofty made a stupid command that we had to pull back all the Watchers didn't he?'

Blakelock nodded slowly.

'And Lord Gregory for some reason agreed and gave his word so now we can't send out anyone who is a Watcher, isn't that right?'

Blakelock nodded again and turned his head to look at Donald. His expression didn't change but his eyes showed his increased attention.

'So anyone who went out from here couldn't be a current Watcher, could they?'

Blakelock nodded again, then shook his head. 'We need you here Donald. That fat fool Studge couldn't defend this city against a flock of elderly goats.'

Donald grinned. 'True. But they've got you. And Felix. And I'm no longer an official Watcher. I retired, remember? I'm just an old man wandering about getting in the way. And trying not to get beaten up by local toughs.'

Blakelock looked at his old friend. He didn't smile but he put his clenched fist to his chest. Donald returned the salute. They nodded to each other, turned and walked away. It was agreed.

Chapter 23

High in the tree Tom closed his eyes. Perhaps he could just pretend this wasn't happening. He could hear horses snorting and stamping, people moving about. But that jarring, sneering laugh cut through.

'What are you doing up there? You look stupid. Get down.'

Tom turned his head, resigned. He caught Beth's eye and made a gesture for her to stay still. She just put her head down into the branch and all but disappeared in the dark among the leaves and branches.

With a sigh Tom sat up and swung a leg either side of the branch. Perhaps if he came down quickly they'd not think to look for anyone else. He just hoped they didn't shoot him full of arrows before he could even climb down. He looked past his foot to the ground far below.

There in the light of the fire he saw the tops of soldiers heads, some with helmets on, some wrapped in cloth or rags. And there was Reese, bare headed, standing with his hands on his skinny hips. He was looking at something Tom couldn't see, further over. Tom frowned. Why was nobody staring up at him?

A horse moved sideways and Tom saw through the leaves the rider had someone in front of him, virtually sitting on the horse's neck. Tom vaguely recognised him. His mind seemed to be working very slowly. He looked down the other side of the branch and stopped breathing.

There was Lord Gutta. He could just make out his bulk by the fire, the flames and shadows slithering over his mail. His big black beard looked in the dark like the opening into a hideous pit, and from it there came his voice, flat and commanding.

'Bring him.'

Soldiers lifted down the boy from the horse, none too gently, and shoved him towards the fire. Tom realised he was still sitting upright on the branch, his feet dangling. If anyone looked up he'd be seen for certain. Slowly, while everyone's attention was on the new arrival, Tom swung himself back until he was lying flat again.

He put his face into the rough bark and felt his heart hammering so hard he could hear it in his breathing, feel it against the tree. He tried to get control of himself. He realised how scared he was at the thought of being found here. What would Lord Gutta do to him? He shut his eyes and tried not to panic. He could feel the pressure building. He had to get out of here. He forced his limbs not to move. An earwig crawled over his hand.

Beth stayed still, listening.

'So, Lord Gutta, this is my mate Matt Barnett. He's here because I set it up. It's because of me he's here. I'm proving useful aren't I?'

'Tell me what you know, Matt Barnett. Tell me now.'

'Lord Gutta. I'm Matt Barnett right enough. Pleased to meet you. Honoured. And Reese said that if we told you stuff then we'd get to help run Burgh after you win. That's right isn't it? We'll be in charge?'

'After I have crushed Burgh I shall raise you higher than anyone else in the city. I give you my word.'

It was taking all Tom's will to keep his limbs from moving. He was sweating, close to breaking. He focused on his heart, feeling it thumping so fast he was amazed nobody else could hear it. Any movement, any noise and they'd be found. He knew now that he'd be hanged if he was lucky.

He focused on his heart again and felt an erratic rhythm, like he had two hearts. He stayed focused, and found his heart slowing, slowing. His breathing slowed. His heart slowed more until it was just a measured, heavy beat that bumped in his chest, deep and old.

He felt at one with the tree, the sweat cooling. He felt tired, and his face pressed deeper into the rough bark.

The sound of Matt's young voice floated up to him as Matt clearly tried to make sure he was going to get something out of this. Tom could hear the fear in the voice, confronted as Matt was by a group of rough warriors, deep in the night forest, with the fearsome warlord staring at him the whole time.

'That would be great Lord Gutta, great. Because I've risked a lot to come here. People are suspicious in Burgh. One old man threatened me with an axe, wanted to know about Reese and stuff. But I didn't tell him anything. Even though he killed one of my mates. We're really suffering to help you. Got to be worth our while.'

'Who was that?' The sharp question came from Reese.

'Connor. Well, he didn't kill him, but he smashed his wrist. He was going to come with me but he had to stay home.'

'And who was the old man?' asked Reese suspiciously.

'I don't know mate. Some raggedy old man with a grey beard. He seemed to think he was in charge of fixing the walls or something. Oh and he had that girl Abi with him, that one that used to hang around with that blonde boy with the stupid hair. Got outlawed with you. Tom someone.'

'Tom Haywood. And that would be Abi, Abi Chattan. And that old bloke sounds like Donald. What was she doing hanging about with him?'

Reese was thinking hard. But the names had floated up to Tom, bringing him back to the present, and the present danger.

A voice down to Tom's left made him raise his head. A new voice.

'How very interesting. We're so glad your friends are having a nice time in Burgh. But we brought you here for information. Give us information.'

Tom glanced down through the branches and leaves. The pale cowl and robes were gliding forward towards Matt. The boy stepped back as the shape advanced steadily on him out of the dark. Soon Matt could feel the heat of the fire at his back, but the flickering shadows still didn't light up the face within the cowl.

Tom watched Zala advance, knowing how much he'd terrify Matt. He looked down on the cowl, wondering what lay beneath it.

'We want to know about the city walls, the preparations, the defence. And I want to know about this raggedy old man. We want ...'

Tom saw the pale apparition pause as the voice trailed away. He saw the cowl turn, to the left, to the right. Tom jerked his head back and lay flat on the branch. Fool, fool, what a fool he was.

How many times had Donald told him that a prey will often feel it is being watched? And hunters were more sensitive to it still. And below him was the arch predator, and he'd stared at him for what seemed like ages.

There was silence, broken by the sound of men shuffling about, and the fire crackling. At least the army hadn't set fire to the forest near their night camp, thought Tom. But mostly he thought about blending in to the branch. He deliberately stopped thinking, focusing again on the dull rhythm of the tree, ponderous and timeless.

After what seemed like all night to Tom, Zala started talking again. But Tom knew that the tracker would be on his guard now, and he needed to be doubly careful and vigilant.

Tom and Beth lay silent and still as Matt, backed up by Reese, stood and told the enemy everything. With Lord Gutta and the fire before him, and the dreadful pale shape of Zala behind him, Matt spilled his guts. He'd pictured this scene in his mind, but this wasn't how it had looked. He realised only his knowledge was keeping him alive. He worried about what would happen when he'd told them everything, but he couldn't stop talking.

Eventually he wound down. There was silence. Lord Gutta lifted his heavy-lidded eyes and stared once more at Matt. He guessed the boy had told him everything, but it was possible he'd forgotten some useful piece of information. The boy was swaying with fatigue and tension. Lord Gutta nodded.

'Take them away. Show them somewhere to rest. Let them eat. We march in the morning.'

He looked up as Zala came round the fire to sit down on a pile of skins. He beckoned over his senior commander, the most senior left and motioned him to join them.

'We have information. Now we make a plan.'

Above them, unseen, undetected, Beth and Tom lay deathly still, using just their ears as the enemy sketched out a plan that would guarantee them success in their assault on Burgh. Because now they knew how to get in.

Chapter 24

Tom began to feel weary and chilly as the night wore on. With the men having stopped talking about their plans, he wanted to get away, get back to Burgh. But neither he nor Beth dared move yet. He looked to see if he could edge backwards, like a caterpillar, but a violent shake of Beth's head in the gloom told him to lie still.

He heard Zala start to wander around, talking about boring issues like patrols and the amount of food the army had. Tom heard how Zala's head was turning here and there, the sudden clarity when he spoke while clearly looking up into the trees. Tom's weariness left him.

'Put more wood on the fire. Let's get some more light on our surroundings.' Zala's command confirmed what Tom feared. Zala was still suspicious. Tom and Beth lay still amid the branches and green leaves and acorns. The colours grew more pronounced as the fire blazed. Soldiers threw on more and more wood until the tiny clearing was bathed in light.

Tom glanced across at Beth. He caught his breath. One of the axes on her belt had slipped slightly down, even though the head was still held secure in her belt. There was the beginning of a gleam from the axe head as the flickering light increased. He wondered if he was betraying the same unnatural metal flicker up in the tree.

'That's better.' Tom could hear that Zala was right below, looking up, scanning the trees, looking at the bushes nearby. He couldn't move, all he could do was wait. The night was still, with no wind to disguise any movement. He knew Zala's sharp pink eyes would spot something at any moment.

Once again, Tom had to fight the urge to just run. But his heightened senses heard something approaching. And he thought there was more light off to his right somewhere. He didn't dare raise or turn his head, just kept it jammed into the bough, his arms straight above his head, his feet together, as invisible as possible.

A horse thundered up, its rider jumping off as soon as it had slid to a stop.

'My lord, Lord Gutta, I have to report an attack at the rear. They sprang out of nowhere.'

Kneeling before his lord, panting with exertion, the soldier waited with his head down, looking at the earth.

'How many?' As ever, Lord Gutta's voice sounded almost light, but there was no possibility of not replying.

'We don't know my lord. Only a handful, but they pressed their attack fast and retreated just as fast when we counter-attacked. We beat them back and they disappeared into the forest.'

'And what of the wagons?'

The man hesitated. 'They set fire to the wagons my lord. But we have saved some, pulled them clear, kept them safe.'

There was a pause then Lord Gutta spoke again and the man shuddered at the tone.

'There were six special wagons were there not. That had to be kept away from the fires we set at all costs. Tell me about those six wagons. Tell me you protected them with your lives.'

The man threw himself on the ground in front of Lord Gutta. 'We managed to save some Lord Gutta. It was chaos in the dark, and they came from all directions, but we have saved some.'

'How many?' Everyone could hear the building rage in the question. Men stepped back.

'One is safe my lord. Perhaps we will be able to save the contents of some of the others. But they burned my lord. They burned so hard we couldn't get near. And we have dozens of the other wagons safe my Lord Gutta.'

Zala stepped forward. 'Did you see who did this? What did they look like?'

The man shook his head. 'They seemed…slight, very nimble. Faster than our men. It was hard to see them.'

Lord Gutta stood up and the man stayed where he was sprawled at his feet.

'A handful of little warriors beat you. What were they – women or children? And now my wagons are gone thanks to your cowardice and incompetence.'

'Please, my lord, we…'

Lord Gutta drew his sword in one smooth movement and plunged it into the back of the man beneath him. The soldier screamed as the blade hacked and tore at him until he was dead.

Nobody moved, everyone kept their eyes down. But Zala had watched every movement, every twist of the blade in the man's body. Now he refocused and thought about what had happened at the rear of the column. They had just been dealt a blow, but as yet he wasn't sure how serious a blow. He stood, looking back at a column of fire he could now see clearly in the night.

Above him, unnoticed, a branch nodded gently and then was still. A slight breeze arose. It gently stirred the leaves, making a susurrating background noise and movement that would stop anyone hearing any other gentle sounds receding into the distance.

Zala's eyes narrowed and he looked upwards again. A hard green acorn let go early from its cup and fell to disappear into Zala's upturned cowl. The men heard him swearing.

Tom twitched and opened his eyes. Something. He kept still. A small rat. Just a small rat. It scuttled over him and away and Tom relaxed. In the past, back in Burgh, he'd have screamed and jumped up. Right now a small furry creature seemed such a friendly thing. He turned his head.

Rick and Beth lay nearby, all of them sheltered by the drooping branches of the fir tree. The others were looking grubby now, hair tousled and entwined with bits of twigs and debris, their skin dirty, their clothes dishevelled. He guessed he looked the same. They were tired too. Tom felt like he'd only had a few hours sleep and it wasn't enough.

He sat up and quietly woke the others. There was just room for them to sit up under the fir, as it had fallen and wedged itself into another tree, forming a hidden triangle beneath its drooping green boughs. A bit of undergrowth and it was a shelter where they could rest.

Rick sighed and rubbed his hand. 'Can we just stay here today? And maybe get some food delivered.'

Beth tried to run her hands through her hair, and rubbed her face. 'We need to get out of here Rick. We need to be back in that city of yours.' She yawned. 'And then I can have a bath and sleep in a bed. I don't care if Lord Gutta is knocking on the gates, I'd sleep right through it.'

'Come on,' said Tom quietly as he looked out from their den, 'we need to find Pad and Grant. Then we can head home.'

They moved off reluctantly, back towards the head of the column, or where it had been. They could hear in the distance the army was moving again, but they were sure they were far enough away to be safe even from wandering patrols. It had been nerve-wracking heading away the previous night, knowing that Zala was on the alert behind them. At least they'd hooked up again with Rick without incident.

'Are you sure we're in the right place?' Beth rarely betrayed nerves and the question got Tom's attention. But the others were taking a long time. Tom wondered if something had happened. What if they'd been caught? Or if they'd been injured in the attack on the wagons? Tom had such faith in Pad that he realised he hadn't even thought of that.

He wasn't sure if Pad was even a friend any more, but Tom had total confidence in Pad's abilities in the forest. Even so, they should have been here ages ago.

'How will we meet up with them exactly?' Rick's question broke the lengthy silence.

Tom grunted. 'You asking questions that loudly should do it.' Rick looked abashed.

Nearby a blackbird made a cry of alarm and they heard it flying away, its call fading. Tom slowly dipped his head down. They were hiding in the space left by an uprooted tree. Above them the roots reared up like a wall, the tree's trunk flat on the ground, and where its root ball had been there was a neat space for the three of them. Now they all got their heads down. What had alarmed the bird?

Tom thought. Then put his head up. He grinned and gave a tiny wave. Moments later Pad and Grant tumbled in to the dip. As they caught their breath Tom wondered out loud.

'So that was you Pad, who made that patrol give up and stop standing on Rick's hand? You can mimic birds?'

Pad grunted agreement. Like Grant he was streaked in dark soot and he had some angry red marks on his hands. Tom sniffed. 'What have you two been doing? What is that smell? You smell really weird.'

'You don't smell so great yourself,' said Pad, turning to look out of their hiding place. He turned back. 'We know what's in those wagons. We have to tell you about it so everyone knows. Then we have to get out of here and back to Burgh. Right now.'

Grant looked shattered but he managed to raise a smile for the others. 'Good to see you lot again. And I bet you found out stuff didn't you?'

Further to the north, nearer Burgh, a dark shape moved through the forest. It was like a shadow moving amid shadows, seemingly never drifting into direct sunlight. Frequently it stopped and became all but invisible, its ragged outline merging perfectly with the forest. Moving forward, the shape drifted silently south, unseen, unobserved by much of the wildlife or even the forest.

In single file the five ran through the forest. They dodged bushes, scrambled over fallen trunks and followed animal trails. Somewhere off to their right was the head of the enemy column, moving slowly forward. By now Tom reckoned they must be ahead of it, but they stayed clear in case of enemy patrols.

The last thing they wanted was to run into the enemy now. Each of them had all the information they'd found out, information they knew would help Burgh's defence when they got back. They ran on, through the dappled shadows of the forest, slowly getting clear of the enemy, clear of the danger. Ahead lay Burgh.

Their fatigue faded as they loped on and on, knowing that every pace brought them nearer safety. Tom, following Pad, saw him hesitate at the front as they came to a small clearing. Unlike him, but a sign of the need he felt for speed, Pad ran straight across the clearing instead of skirting it. The others followed, and were soon swallowed by the forest again.

High above, a ragged shape drifted on the currents. It had been searching for hours but now it wheeled north. Now it had information. It flew in a straight line towards Burgh. Some time later it flew over a darker patch of forest. Looking down, it saw nothing to take its attention. But a shadow amid the shadows moved forward, focused forward. Above, the black shape flew on, unobserving, unobserved.

By now the minor tracks were starting to join up. The trackway towards Burgh just got bigger and bigger from now on. Pad called a halt. They heard a small rivulet, and everyone drank deeply. It was going to be a hot day and already they were damp with perspiration.

Rick was breathing heavily but keeping up, and the others just looked determined to keep going. They all felt the responsibility of the information they held about the enemy's plans and what they carried with them, but partly they just wanted to get clear of the dark threat they still felt behind them.

Pad looked back. 'I don't think we should get onto the main track for Burgh. We should stay on the animal tracks. It'll be safer.'

Grant grimaced. 'And slower. We can make much better speed going straight. I want to be out of here as fast as we can.'

The others mostly nodded. They were clear of the enemy now and didn't see why they'd send a patrol right out the front when Lord Gutta knew everyone was cooped up in Burgh. Pad sucked in his cheeks.

'That sort of makes sense. We go on the main track. We run for one hour. Then we get off the track and walk on animal trails for an hour. Like

that. We should be in Burgh this evening if we can keep this up. Let's
go.'

Pad called a halt about an hour later and those with water bottles
drank deeply and passed them around. They were all sweating now,
breathing heavily. But they felt triumphant at the distance they'd covered
away from the enemy column behind them.

'We should probably head off the main track,' said Pad, glancing
back the way they'd come. The track was clear for as far as they could
see. Around them the forest was opening up.

Tom glanced back. 'I think we should get off the track right now.'
He looked anxious and the others nodded. Pad looked off to their left.
The forest wall grew again perhaps five minutes' jog across more open
ground, while ahead they'd be running for much longer than that to
reach the cover of the trees.

He was going to suggest heading left and heading for cover when
Tom stepped forward. He looked agitated. 'We have to go, right now,
come on.' Without looking back he headed off to the left, heading for
the shelter of the treeline. Once there they could carry on parallel to the
main track. The rest followed, made slightly uneasy by Tom's insistence.

However, they were close to where the trees started to thicken within
minutes and they started to relax. Grant was at the rear and glanced
back.

'Oh no, oh no, it can't be happening again. Horses! Horses!' Tom
looked round. Like Grant and Pad he remembered being run down by
men on horseback before. His stomach jolted and he started to run even
faster.

It took a moment for the men on horseback on the main route to
notice the small running figures in the distance. But soon the five heard
the shouts, the fierce cries and they knew they would be hunted.

It felt to Tom like he was running on the spot, the trees never seemed
to get nearer. He could hear the gasping of the others as they ran flat
out. But the trees were nearer, then they were passing the first ones out
on the open ground. They were in the shade of the trees and Tom felt
they could outwit men on horses now.

They ran on, hearing the chase falter as the horses tried to go round
the thickening trunks. He heard the others breathe out in relief as they
left the pursuers behind. Unlike last time, this time they'd made it.

Pad in front cried out in dismay. Ahead, beyond the immediate trees,
was another clearing. Not a big one, but he could see horsemen starting

to file into it from one side, then the other. They were caught in a net. It was a big net and they couldn't yet be seen, but they knew the net would get tighter and tighter.

Pad turned, his eyes wild. 'What do we do? What do we do?'

Chapter 25

Ahead it was fairly open with the trees on the other side of the clearing not that far away. To the right the forest carried on but they could hear horsemen pushing through the trees, trying to form a line. Tom ran in that direction and hunkered down, the others around him.

He pointed and spoke quietly. 'It looks like there's earthdin damage here. See how the ground is all churned up? There are little gulleys and dips over there. That will be hard ground for the horses to run on. Hard to see us if we stay low. We have to get out before the soldiers come in on foot.'

He looked at the others. 'That's the way out.'

They nodded, looking, assessing where to go.

Tom hesitated and spoke again. 'But we have to split up. We're too big a group to get through there.'

The others looked at him with big eyes, the prospect of being separated from their group adding to the fear they felt. But Pad nodded. 'He's right. One of us has to get back, at least one of us.'

Tom drew in a deep breath. 'Right. Get going ahead, get through. I'm going this way.'

Before anyone could speak or act he ran off to their left. He could feel his heart beating yet faster as he burst out of the treeline and made a dash across the narrow clearing. To his surprise it was some moments before he heard the cries of the hunters and even longer before he heard the hooves.

They were approaching fast, but he was going to make the shelter of the thick treeline. He glanced back, not expecting to have made it. He was the diversion and it seemed to have worked.

He cried out. Two more shapes were following him, and the horsemen were riding them down. He hesitated as Rick ran towards him, his eyes locked on Tom's. He was red in the face and puffing but running as fast as he could. Beth was still catching him though, her figure leaping forward like a panicked deer.

Tom knew he had a responsibility to everyone in Burgh to run on, to get the message back. But he just couldn't turn and leave his friends. They'd followed him. They were his stand, like the tree had said, and Tom stood, hesitating.

A rider caught up with Beth but when he was just a few strides behind she whirled round. There was a flash of metal and the rider reared up in the saddle before falling away. She ran on. A second rider coming from the side headed her off, but again he veered away, badly injured. Tom watched with his mouth open, but he knew she was now out of axes.

Another rider reached down from the saddle to grab Rick, but he turned with a roar and lashed out. The rider shrieked and turned away, his arm smashed to the bone.

The enemy were jostling in faster now. Another rode alongside Beth and reached down to grab her. With a shriek she was lifted off the ground by her hair and dragged alongside the thudding hooves of the horse, her legs frantically kicking to keep her upright. Rick was just reaching Tom when Tom ran forward and threw his remaining axe. Beth fell to the ground as the rider crashed out of the saddle.

Her careering ride had brought her near the others and she sprinted to them. But they were surrounded by riders now, milling closer. Tom edged back until he was against a tree, with Rick and Beth either side. Tom had a scaramax blade, Rick had his bloodied axe and a blade, that was it.

Tom looked around and realised they were trapped. Perhaps this was his last stand.

Spears and swords hemmed them in. They parted as new riders approached.

'Put down your weapons. If we wanted you dead you'd be dead.' The nightmare shape of the pale ghost loomed above them on his great black horse. He held a spear in his hand but showed no signs of using it.

The others exchanged glances. They threw their weapons down. It was over.

Beth looked around. 'Rick, don't speak. Go down on one knee.' Her whispered demand made no sense to Rick but he dropped to one knee as if exhausted. With a bound Beth got a foot on his horizontal thigh and leapt up. Her hands grasped the branch above her head and she started to swing herself up. Let them try and catch her when she got into the tree crown.

Zala acted with surprising speed. He reversed the spear and slammed the haft into Beth's stomach just as she was tensed to flick up onto the branch. With a grunt she fell, landing on her side with a horrible thud. She made a breathless groaning noise as she crawled back towards the others.

A couple of the soldiers looked at her with contempt, but a few looked at her with a grudging admiration. A laugh cut through Beth's groans and struggles.

'Well well, looks like the squirrel can't climb the tree after all.'

Reese pushed his horse through the others to stare down at the three. To Tom's dismay he saw Matt sitting on a horse behind, sitting in front of the rider. Riding horses obviously wasn't that simple, even though Reese seemed to have learned.

'There were five of you I think.' Zala's voice floated out of his long cowl, his face invisible, his hands covered by white gloves. 'Where are the others, and who are you?'

Reese spoke quickly to show he knew stuff. 'The one with the stupid blonde hair is Tom and the stupid fat oaf is Rick. They were part of my little gang when we got kicked out of Burgh. The girl, that's Beth, she's one of the forest people. Pity she can't climb trees very well.'

Matt laughed. The rest of the soldiers looked on grimly.

Zala's cowl stayed pointing at Tom and the others. 'And the others? Who are they and where are they? Tell me now, my patience is ending.'

Tom was wondering what to say to Zala when they heard the sound of cries and horses charging away in the distance. It was the unmistakable sound of a chase. Tom felt like a stone was sitting in his stomach. After all this, for it to end with them all caught or dead. He dropped his head.

'You are spies. Do you want to know how we treat spies?' Zala's horse edged nearer, crowding the three until they were all backed against the tree. Tom saw how Reese pushed closer so he could see exactly what happened.

'We're not spies,' said Tom quietly. 'We were just trying to get away from you and get back home. That's all. As Reese says, we're city boys, me and Rick, lost in the forest, just trying to get home.'

'And what brought you so far from home I wonder.' Zala's voice was thoughtful. 'Perhaps it was to chase this girl?' The men laughed as Beth glared at his robes.

'No,' Zala continued. 'You were spying on us. You will now face Lord Gutta and you will tell him everything you found out. Believe me, you will tell him everything.'

Tom gulped at the thought of standing in front of that monster. Through the jostling horses he could see soldiers dismounted and retrieving weapons. He saw a man stand up with Tom's own axe in his hand, retrieved from the limp shape on the ground. It was bloody, and the soldier looked furious as he glanced over to where the three were held at bay.

None of the three resisted as their wrists were tied in front of them and then a rope was tied to the wrist ropes. The ends of the long ropes were held by three soldiers as they mounted their horses and they all turned back towards the head of the column slowly approaching.

Tom's arms were jerked forward and he stumbled to keep his balance as the horses started to walk. He looked sideways, and saw the other two also being forced forward, their arms pulled out in front of them, bound at the wrists. The soldiers had lost men in the chase and were in no mood to be gentle.

Zala sent a rider over to where the pursuit of the remaining 'spies' had last been heard. As Tom stumbled rapidly forward he glanced over his shoulder, expecting to see Pad and Grant following.

Pad had had to overpower Grant to stop him chasing after the other three as they broke from cover. 'Stop Grant, stop. Can't you see? Tom's made a diversion. For us. We have to go. The others should have stayed here, they're stupid.'

'They're not stupid' panted Grant, lying in the brambles. 'They're my friends and they're sticking together. I should be with them.'

They heard the shouts and the heavy thudding of the horses and they knew the others had been spotted and were being run down. Grant sighed and Pad chose the moment.

'Now is our chance, it won't last long. We have to get word back to Burgh. We're Watchers. Come on.' He leapt forward, running crouched between the trees, trying to use the broken ground to keep him unseen. Grant, with the prospect of being left on his own, followed as quickly as he could.

The pair disappeared into the hollows and little gulleys as the remaining horsemen walked their horses, watching, trying to keep the net intact. There were a lot of them.

Matt noticed his rider had the rope that was dragging Beth along. The rope was looped round the front of the saddle, just behind where Matt uncomfortably sat. He looked round at Beth who was being pulled along behind and she stared stonily at him.

Without saying anything, he began to pull the rope in, shortening it until she was walking almost alongside him, bumping alongside the horse's powerful haunches. She stared ahead.

'You won't be looking so pretty after Lord Gutta's finished with you.' Matt scowled at Beth, annoyed he wasn't getting a reaction. She tossed her hair and looked away.

Reese had been watching. He drifted over on his horse and took the rope holding Tom from another rider. Checking Tom was forced to walk behind him, he moved his horse over towards Matt until Beth was squeezed between the two towering flanks that closed her in.

Matt tried again. 'Lord Gutta's going to torture you. Then he's going to hang you or throw you on the fire. You're on the losing side, just like your two loser friends. Maybe if you're nice to me I can get Lord Gutta to go easy on you.' He leaned down, grinning nastily.

'I'm going to be a big man in Burgh after it falls. You ought to be nice to me. Maybe I could keep you alive in Burgh if you're nice to me. You'd better start now.'

Beth glared up at him. 'I hear you come from where they slaughter animals in Burgh. Maybe you'd have better luck with one of the goats there.'

Tom, watching, grew concerned and ran forward, taking in the slack of the rope so he didn't fall over it. 'Leave her alone,' he shouted, although he could hardly see her between the horses.

Reese edged his horse even closer to Beth until she was scared the horses were going to trample her feet. Their muscular flanks banged into her head and she struggled to stay upright as they strode steadily on.

She wriggled and shouted back. 'Matt thinks I should be nice to him. I told him he'd have more luck with one of those goats in Burgh.' The rider behind Matt, who'd been watching impassively, snorted with laughter.

Tom was impressed with his friend. 'Really? A goat?' He didn't know what to say. 'What about the smell?'

Beth tried to push the horses away with no success. She was getting short of breath in the great jostling cavern. Her hands dropped down out of sight.

'The smell?' she shouted, 'Oh I expect the goat would get used to it.'

Several of the horsemen guffawed and Matt sat back up, fuming. With his foot hanging loose, he kicked it backwards, the heel catching Beth full in the face.

Reese moved his horse away, trying to pretend he wasn't bothered. Matt let the rope go slack again and Beth moved back until she was alongside Tom. She looked stunned, and there was blood and dirt where Matt's foot had caught her nose.

She walked close to Tom, who was furious but helpless. He saw the fire in her eyes as she talked out of the side of her mouth. 'I think I've loosened the strap thing that goes under Reese's horse. I couldn't get to Matt's.'

She was going to say more but Reese looked back and saw them talking like old friends. Stung, he called across to Matt. 'This is getting boring. Let's get these horses going shall we?'

Matt's rider shook his head but Reese started to dig his heels in, forcing the horse to speed up. It had taken Tom a few moments to understand what Beth meant, but he saw he had no time before Reese charged off and starting dragging him behind the horse.

With some slack still in the rope, he ran out sideways, dodging across the rough grasses and stunted bushes. He jumped and came down with his heels dug into the ground, his whole body tensed. He watched the rope go taut. The force of it yanked him off his feet, his arms feeling like they were being wrenched out. Then it went still.

Face down, all he could hear was mocking laughter. He looked up. The saddle had spun round on the horse, dumping Reese face-first into the ground. He got up looking deadly, spitting earth out of his mouth.

'I'm going to kill you for that.' Reese completely lost his temper and ran towards Tom, who couldn't run or defend himself. A dagger appeared in Reese's hand and he snarled as he closed in.

But a pale shape on a black horse was faster still. The horse banged heavily into Reese, sending him flying for the second time. He jumped up, but the voice stilled him.

'Lord Gutta wants these prisoners alive. If you killed one what would happen to you do you think? Would you like me to tell you? We have wasted too much time. Everybody, get on. We must get these prisoners in front of Lord Gutta at once.' He looked at some riders nearby. 'And I want news on the other prisoners. Go see where they are.'

Pad and Grant had been twisting and dodging through the broken ground, making progress. They could still hear the enemy but they thought they were through most of them. They came to a small stand of yew trees on a hillock and Pad was drawn to their dark shadows.

After a moment crouched and panting, the pair headed down the slope but as they stood they were silhouetted and they heard shouts from close behind. They ran down the slope, but the going was rough, with lots of the long yew roots twisting everywhere. Grant caught his foot and fell headlong. Pad glanced round and he too tripped and fell, skidding down the steep slope of earth and roots.

They could hear crashing and trampling above them. They rolled down the slope, landing with a thud on the ground. Ahead stretched open land, with nowhere to run or hide.

Pad twisted round where he lay. There was a sort of overhang of yew roots behind them. Gasping, he called quietly to Grant. 'Roll in there, look, tiny gap.'

With the riders at the top of the slope they both rolled back, pushing under the great roots that writhed down. There was enough space for them to lie on the bare earth and they could look out through the narrow ragged gap between the roots and the ground.

The horses thundered down and they saw the hooves pawing and trampling the ground just outside. They heard the voices, calling in confusion. Then they saw boots on the ground. Grant tried not to breathe as the boots went to and fro. But the gap seemed smaller than Grant remembered and even when he saw the edge of a face outside, he knew they couldn't be seen.

The riders milled around, and then charged off in another direction. There was silence as outside the dust settled. Inside it was very dark, the black of endless time. Grant edged closer to Pad's ear, feeling the roots above him pushing into his shoulder.

He looked out. 'Pad,' whispered Grant, 'is it me or has that gap disappeared?'

Pad considered. 'Perhaps the horses pushed it down when they landed on it.' He paused. 'It does make you think though. How did we get in?'

Grant nodded. 'More to the point Pad, how do we get out?'

Chapter 26

The blow sent Tom flying backwards to land heavily on the ground. He put his tied hands up to his face. Lord Gutta's metal glove had left marks all down one cheek. He looked up, taken aback by the sudden violence. A backhand slap with the armoured glove and Beth spun round to hit the dry earth. Then it was Rick's turn. He leant back in advance and Lord Gutta punched him so hard in the stomach he went down without a sound, unable to breathe.

'Get them up.' Lord Gutta's command led to boots kicking into Tom's back until he got to his feet, shaken. Lord Gutta stood in front of them again, close, his vast bulk intimidating the three youngsters who were much shorter than him.

He was in full war gear, with metal plates over his chainmail and a metal helmet on his head which had a nose-piece which came down between his eyes to the thin straight line of his mouth.

Tom glanced around. They were surrounded by soldiers, who looked on either indifferently or with excitement. Torturing prisoners made a nice change for soldiers who'd been tramping through strange forest for days, short of food and drink.

Drifts of burning forest made a nightmare background, where the troops had tried to set the woods ablaze as they trudged through. But now they were halted with the three prisoners in a line, encircled by the enemy.

Tom tried to breathe normally and tried not to look at Matt and Reese, who were in the front row, grinning. He looked at the other two, who looked shaken already, and they hadn't even been asked anything yet.

'I'm sorry I got you into this,' he said, turning to his friends. 'You shouldn't have followed me, I'm sorry.'

Another blow sent him reeling back into the metal of soldiers behind, who shoved him forward again.

'Shut up, scum. You will speak when I ask you a question. And you will answer. Believe me, you will answer.'

He stood with his hands on his hips, the metal glove held in his big fist. He glared at the three, one by one.

'I have your names. Now I want the names of the others who were with you. Give me their names.'

Tom hesitated, trying to think. His heart soared as he realised this meant the others hadn't been captured. Perhaps they were on their way to Burgh now, with the messages. Again, the metal glove smashed into Tom's face, and again he went down. He was so dazed that it was several moments before he realised soldiers were kicking him from the back. Eventually the pain from the blows forced him to his feet, but he stood with his legs apart to keep his balance.

He looked up and saw Reese staring at him, enjoying every moment. But Reese couldn't help trying to look important – and he knew the more he could tell Lord Gutta the safer he'd be.

'I reckon one of them was Pad. Isn't that so Tom?'

Tom glared at Reese. But he was thinking, and decided it didn't matter now if the others knew who the two were, if they'd escaped. And he needed to give Lord Gutta something before the next blow. He could feel blood dribbling down his throbbing face.

He nodded. 'It was Pad. And Grant.'

Reese and Matt looked at each other and laughed out loud. 'Grant? That little runt? Oh we are scared. I'll deal with him next time I see him.' Matt put his hands on his hips and looked genuinely amused.

The pale ghost drifted forward and the voice spoke quietly, but everyone heard.

'How nice it is to see friends chatting together. And how grateful you should be, you three, to Matt here. We were escorting him back to Burgh, so he could find out yet more, when we happened to come across you. Running away.

'And two of you are still running away. So we need to know what you know, which is probably what they know. What did you hear, sneaking around our camp? Eh, what did you find out?'

Rick had got his breath back. 'What's the point in us telling you stuff? You're going to kill us anyway aren't you?'

The cowl moved down the line until it stood in front of Rick. Tom put his head down. Well done Rick, he thought, if they weren't sure we knew anything, they're sure now.

The voice was quiet and even but its tone chilled them all. 'Because if you tell us then we'll let you die. If you don't tell us, and we have to get the information in more imaginative ways, then you'll be begging to die. And we'll keep you alive long after you've wished for death.

'All your men are hiding in Burgh, behind those tottering walls. There is nobody here to save you. No last-moment reprieve. No rescue. Nothing to hold out for, nothing to hope for. Just Lord Gutta in front of you. And me.

'So tell us. What did you overhear? What did you find out?'

The three looked anxiously at each other. He was right, there was nobody to save them. But if they told the enemy everything, then they'd change their plans and Burgh would be caught by surprise. And the three were going to die anyway. Tom felt responsible, but he couldn't see a way out. He hoped that at least the other two were now nearing Burgh.

'Ah!' Grant lay on his front, his face contorted. 'It's no good, every time I hack at the roots they seem to get even lower. The roof is lower, I know it is.' He let his axe fall on the bare, dry earth.

Pad looked around in the darkness. Above him the roots pressed in, virtually touching his back, pressing down with the immense weight of the old yew trees above. Yews. Pad had heard about yews all his life and now he felt the fear.

You stayed away from yews. You never slept under them, never ate their fruit, never let animals eat their leaves or berries. You left them well alone. And here they were, crushed beneath a stand of ancient yews.

The gap they'd rolled through was now just a thin line of light, leaving them in almost total darkness that seemed darker than night. He could hear Grant's breathing, knew he was getting badly spooked. They didn't need to panic or they'd be lost for ever.

They had to get the messages back to Burgh, they were Watchers, they just had to. But here they were, pinned down in the dark. A thought struck Pad.

'Grant, do you have a flint on you?'

Grant grunted assent. 'Why?'

Pad thought about it and felt even more scared. If this didn't work they were going to be killed even quicker. The darkness closed in, smothering him. It was the ancient dark of the warbrock and the death worm.

'Because we're going to get out. We can't hack our way out, the roots are too strong. But we're going to fight the dark. With fire.'

The beating was terrible. All three were punched and kicked until they were too weak to stand up, even when the soldiers used their boots to drive them onto their feet. If anything Beth seemed to be treated worse than the boys.

Lord Gutta stepped back, breathing hard, with blood on his mailed gauntlet. 'You're lying! You know something! Tell us what you know!' He was screaming now and some of the soldiers backed away. They'd seen him like this before and his rage could turn anywhere.

Zala stepped forward. 'You see, we don't believe you. We think you did hear something and we need to know that for our plans. And we want to know what you discovered about our wagons. After all, you sneaked into our camp, set fire to our wagons, and killed and injured some of our men when we tried to stop you.

'You've been very tiresome and badly behaved children. And we've had enough. So start talking. Tell us the truth.'

Beth was the first to her feet. Her eyes still blazed but her face was already distorted by bruising and there was blood on her lips and the side of her face. She just glared into Zala's hood, breathing hard and trying not to cry or tremble. What she saw in the hood made her numb with terror.

Lord Gutta stepped towards her while the boys tried to get onto their wobbly legs. His rage had only subsided a little.

'You're pathetic. You're all pathetic little tree rats. They send children to do men's work. They send a girl to do a man's work. A girl! You should be at home, girl, fetching water, not coming here to die. Because you are going to die.'

He reached out with a huge fist and grabbed the ripped top of her jerkin. With his fist bunched at her neck he lifted her clear of the ground, while her breath rasped in her aching throat.

Matt licked his lips. He wished he'd had more time to give her a beating, but this was almost as good. Reese was quietly convinced that the boys didn't know anything. They were soft city boys, not like him, and he was sure if they'd known anything they'd have told them by now. But he kept the thought to himself. Why ruin good sport?

Both Rick and Tom staggered to their feet and closed in either side of Beth. They didn't know what they could do, and they couldn't think, they just reacted.

Zala's hood moved from side to side. He reached out a white-gloved hand and put it on his lord's great straining arm. 'I have an idea, my lord.'

Again and again Pad struck the back of his axe with the small flint. Sparks flew, but they were small. He didn't have any room to get a good strike and the little bits of dry tinder he had scraped together on the bare earth weren't even smouldering.

He tried again. A big fat spark landed on the tinder and Grant leant in to try to fold the dry material round it. There was a tiny puff of smoke and then nothing. Above them the roots creaked as if moving and they both felt the death cold of the yews.

Grant gasped. 'There's something on my foot. There's something on my foot.' There wasn't room for him to turn. A root seemed to have slightly twisted round his ankle.

'Hurry Pad, hurry, I think we're making the trees angry.'

Pad struck again and again until the sweat dripped into his eyes. Why wouldn't it burn? The tiny bar of light was almost extinguished now and he couldn't really see what he was doing. Above him he heard the creaks and groans of dark centuries.

A spark, a big one. It landed on the edge of the tinder. Grant wrapped it carefully, blew gently, his face a mask of concentration. He could feel the root around his foot, it felt like it was tightening. Panic was moments away.

The tinder smoked. Grant kept blowing gently, then stronger. The tinder ball burst into flame. Grant put it down and both boys reached out in the dark, gathering and adding tiny dried twigs and bits of bark. The flames caught, lighting the tiny cave they were in. They started coughing with the smoke. Now what?

Tom looked at the flames. He didn't understand. The undergrowth had been burning gently but the soldiers had thrown on so much dead wood and material that there was a fierce blaze. They extended it outwards until soon there was a low wall of fire across the open ground, long and deep.

The men looked like they knew what was coming. A big warrior appeared, stripped to the waist, holding a long thin chain. He was much more muscular than most of the enemy, who were slightly built. He approached Beth and looped and bolted the chain to the rope tied tightly round her wrists. He let it drop and walked off.

Beth looked down, puzzled and scared. This wasn't being done to the others, just her. Rick and Tom were pushed forward, inside an arc of the enemy. Strong hands kept hold of the ends of their ropes so they couldn't move more than a pace. A soldier stepped forward and picked up the chain, looping its coils on his arm. The other side of the flames the muscular soldier appeared again. The chain was thrown to him, over the fire. Tom began to get a very bad feeling.

Zala moved forward.

'It's very simple. Unfortunately we don't have the time or the equipment for some of our more imaginative games. But this will do. You girl will tell us what you know or you will be pulled into the fire. So speak.'

Beth looked in horror at the wall of flames in front of her. She tried to back away but the man the other side took up the slack, his muscles bunching in the reflected light of the fire, which was brighter even than the sunlight. Her arms were out taut in front of her and the man began to slowly pull in the chain.

Her feet dug in and she leaned back, panting, putting all the energy from her battered body into resisting. But it was futile. He was too strong. Slowly he dragged her forward, closer and closer to the flames. She could feel the heat, feel the scorching on the ends of her fingers. She bunched her hands into fists and heaved as hard as she could.

It worked. Amazed, she pulled backwards, gaining a few precious strides. She looked up. The man was laughing at her. He jerked her to a standstill, then once more started dragging her forward. She screamed. Men laughed and jeered. Some of them laid bets.

Zala stood beside her, his tone still matter of fact. 'Tell us now. You don't have long before the flames reach your arms, then your hair, and body. Tell us what you know.'

Rick stood as if rooted to the spot. Tom was so shocked that he couldn't seem to move. He knew he should do something, he knew he should step forward and stop this, but his courage failed.

The boys watched as she was dragged towards the licking flames. She said nothing.

On the other side of the fires the muscular soldier raised an eyebrow. He was impressed. She had courage and she was strong and he liked that. But he still pulled her forward, quicker now as the chain was getting warm. He decided to look the other way when it happened. She couldn't leap the flames, they were too wide. He knew what would happen next.

Pad and Grant were coughing continuously now. The flames rose and licked around the chamber, the smoke billowing everywhere. They both tried to push themselves away from the growing flames, but they had so little room to move. Above and around them the roots groaned and creaked and roared as if they were in a storm.

Pad wondered if the whole root system was about to collapse on top of them. He looked anxiously at the opening but in the glare of the flames he couldn't see any strip of light at all.

The heat and smoke started to take its toll on the boys. Pad, fit though he was, could feel his eyes shutting. He just wanted to go to sleep, then it would be better. Grant was breathing in short gasps but he was watching where they'd rolled in.

A light. Was there light there? Grant was getting confused, but he thought he could see a glow of daylight over the fierce red light of the fire. He hung on by telling himself this wasn't any worse than the smells and smokes of the Shambles on a bad night, or that time when the slaughterhouse had caught fire.

There was light. It was growing. Grant pulled himself over towards the entrance, and managed to disentangle his foot from the grasping root. He was rewarded with a gentle puff of fresh air. Smoke billowed out into the daylight, and Grant managed to cram himself through the gap until he lay gasping in the light.

The air smelt the best he'd ever drawn into his heaving lungs. He lay on his back, astonished at the beauty of the green leaves and the blue sky and how sweet the air tasted.

With a start, he rolled over. Pad hadn't come out. Without a thought, Grant forced his way back in and dragged the still form of Pad outside. Pad's boots had only just cleared the last of the tangling roots when, once again, the whole line of roots crushed downwards. A great wave of smoke blew out into the air and then it was gone.

Pad opened his eyes and looked around. He coughed for a while and sat up. He looked at Grant.

'Well, that worked.'

Chapter 27

Beth's boots slid on the dry grass as she was hauled closer and closer to the fire. Through the flames she could see the soldier pulling steadily on the chain between them. He stood with his legs braced apart, pulling the links steadily towards him. He wasn't looking at her now and she had a dreadful premonition of why that was.

She looked at him again and reached a decision. She leapt forward.

Her feet landed in the smouldering edge of the fire. She put her head back and screamed. And lunged backwards. The chain had gone slack as she leapt forward and the warrior staggered backwards, losing his balance.

Beth pulled with almost superhuman strength as her boots scrabbled clear of the fire. The man was still off balance and ended up staggering forward, pulled towards the flames as Beth jerked the chain back, giving herself many strides of space.

But he found his footing before he was pulled into the flames or let go of the chain. Beth saw the sweat on his chest and the alarm in his eyes as he braced himself again. But he was back in control now, and stepped backwards, pulling her forward yet again. He wouldn't be caught a second time. Beth and he exchanged glances, and he made a sort of gesture of respect. But he had a job to do. He had to burn her to death.

Some of the soldiers started laughing, and shouting insults at the man, amused that he'd been caught out by a girl. It was just a game.

Rick started shouting, knowing the end was near. Tom glanced at his friend, the pair of them shocked and horrified by what was happening to Beth. Tom saw Rick was getting increasingly worked up, his face going red, the veins on his temples standing out.

He looked at Beth and didn't understand. Burgh wasn't her city, they weren't her people, it wasn't her home. Why hadn't she shouted out what she knew, to stop this? He wouldn't have blamed her. He'd have done it long before. But still she fought.

He looked again at Beth, struggling and wriggling in vain. Then he looked at Zala standing to one side, unmoving. And realised Zala wasn't watching Beth, he was watching him. The deep cowl was pointing at him and Tom realised. Zala had found the weak link, and it was him. He could perhaps have gone to the fire himself, but he couldn't send Beth or Rick.

'Stop,' he said quietly. 'Stop. I'll tell you everything I know.'

Zala nodded and made a gesture. The muscular soldier stopped pulling. He let the chain go slack and disappeared from Beth's view behind the flames. She collapsed.

Soldiers crowded forward but Zala gestured for them to get back and they did at once. Only Matt got close, looming over Beth, who was gasping and half-sobbing on the ground, her hands still attached to the chain.

'Pity your boyfriend stopped the fun,' said Matt. He licked his lips. Beth was a mess close up. One boot was smouldering, and her hands were raw from the heat and the rubbing of rope and chain. Her bloodied red face was streaked in soot from the flames and even her hair was stinking from where sparks had burned.

She was beyond speech, all her energy used up. Matt kicked her smouldering boot. 'See what happens when you're not nice to me?'

His gloating turned into a shout as he was shoved roughly aside. The muscular warrior bent down in front of Beth and disentangled the chain from around her wrists. Even at the end it was warm now, clearly a lot hotter along the length of it. He held a leather mug of water to her lips and she drank cautiously, watching him.

'Ah, that's sweet,' said Matt, 'looks like you got another admirer.'

Beth saw the warrior's eyes narrow. He put the end of the chain in her hands, his eyes flicking to the coils nearby. The gleam came back to Beth's eyes.

The man pushed Matt aside again and walked off. Matt crouched down on his knees to study Beth. 'Yes, you're a state now, aren't you? You really stink. And what's that got you? Nothing. You're still going to die. And I'm going to watch. You're stupid.'

Beth half stood, and pulled the thin chain up by the end. It coiled round Matt's shoulders and she quickly draped it round again as he struggled to his feet. His shout turned to a scream as the raging hot metal of the chain wrapped around him, its weight dragging its heavy heat into his clothing and skin.

He spun away, trying to get the coils off, but that meant grabbing it with his hands, and it burned his skin. The soldiers laughed, and Reese laughed, keeping his distance. Eventually Matt dragged the chain off and staggered away, screaming and crying in pain. Nobody went to help him.

'And now,' said Zala, 'if you children have quite finished playing, you Tom Haywood will tell us everything you know, everything you heard. You will tell it in front of Lord Gutta. In front of me. We will know if you are lying. Any attempt at keeping information from us, the first time we throw the girl on the fire, bound in chains. The second time, the other boy. The third time you. No more games. We have delayed enough.'

Tom, Rick and Beth stood and watched the patrols leave. All three still had their hands tied, with the rope ends now held by the one muscular warrior, whom they'd heard was called Qut. Tom was glad of a break in the interrogation, but seeing the mounted men leave made him edgy.

By his calculations Grant and Pad must have been back in Burgh by now. The day was going, and they'd been free for most of the day. Lord Gutta had stopped his questioning after hearing about the other two still out there, and had sent out patrols to find them and kill them, just in case.

A horse with Matt on board in front of a rider walked over. Matt had his hands wrapped in dirty rags but he looked like some of his arrogance was returning. He looked down at the three.

'Well, I guess this is goodbye. I'm going back to Burgh, and I won't be seeing you three again.' He grinned unpleasantly. 'I've got one more job to do in Burgh, one more little look round, then I'm out again and on the winning side. And I've got bodyguards because I'm important now.' He gestured to the rider behind him and the two other riders who waited impatiently.

He sighed and looked at Beth. 'Just think, you could have been with me, on the winning side. Instead you're with these losers. Shame. Still,' here he looked craftily at Tom, 'I guess when I'm in a high position in Burgh there will be some other girl who catches my eye. Like that Abi Chattan. She's pretty enough for me.'

He laughed as Tom glared at him. Tom had a cold dread run through him because he couldn't see how they were going to get out of this alive, and the thought of Abi in the fallen city twisted his guts. But he laughed, even if it was a feeble one.

'Oh you'll be in a high position. Like Leigh. Swinging by the neck from one of Lord Gutta's ropes.'

Matt scowled but the rider turned the horse and they rode away. With numerous patrols now out ahead, Zala returned to his questioning. Lord Gutta sat behind him, watching the three like a death worm watches something small and furry.

Tom's mind was racing. He really wanted Matt to get caught before he could sneak his way back in to the city and find out anything else. And what if Pad and Grant had made it, and the defences were going up unseen? Matt could ruin any chance they had of defending themselves properly.

But right now the problem was what to tell Zala and his lord. He squared his shoulders as Zala continued his remorseless questioning.

'It's true. I was close. I saw Matt arrive. I heard what he said.'

'And what did he say?'

Tom recounted bits of the conversation to show he was being honest.

Beth turned on him. 'Shut up Tom. You think I went through all that just so you could flap your mouth like a dying fish?'

Tom shrugged and Zala and his lord exchanged glances.

'And where were you during this conversation?'

Zala's questions sounded so reasonable. Tom had thought about this. 'I was in the bushes behind the trees. To the west of the fire.'

Zala nodded decisively. 'Yes. Yes, I felt you there.' He sounded smug, convinced now of his own instincts. Convinced that Tom was telling the truth.

'And what else did you hear? After that?'

This was the worst part. Tom had been thinking while watching Beth fighting for her life. She'd given him time.

'I heard you planning. Planning your attack.'

Lord Gutta leant forward, his eyes locked on Tom. He stroked his great black beard with one hand, the heavy bangles on his arm clinking, his fingers toying with the bones woven into the black and grey hairs. 'Go on.'

'You, you are going to attack. On the south western corner. Where it sounds like the wall has fallen down.'

Lord Gutta's eyes stayed boring into Tom. 'What else did you hear, tree rat? What else?'

Tom put his hand up to his throat, his fingers touching the rough piece of oak from his spirit tree. He felt its strength. He breathed in and looked Lord Gutta in the eye.

'That's what we heard. That you're going to attack the south west corner. And you have something special in the wagons that will help you. I didn't understand that bit. That's what I heard. That's what the others know. That's all I know.'

Beth kicked him hard, breaking the eye contact, and Tom fell gratefully to the ground. He stood up again and faced her raging anger. 'Sorry Beth, I couldn't see you burn to death.'

Zala and Lord Gutta exchanged looks. They were convinced. Tom's steady eye contact and the rage of the others at him telling what he knew convinced them. The children hadn't found out about the plan for the western gateway. They didn't need to change plans.

And, anyway, the patrols would probably find the other two and kill them if they were still out there.

Lord Gutta stood. 'We move. Forward now to Burgh. We will be there tomorrow.' He turned and moved heavily away as he spoke over his shoulder.

'Slaughter these three. They have no further use.'

Chapter 28

'I'm going to die of hunger soon,' moaned Grant.

'Keep moving, we'll be there today. Tonight we can eat till we burst. I hope this city of yours really does have lots of food.' Pad was flagging, but the thought of reaching Burgh within a few hours kept him going.

'What do you think has happened to the others?' Grant looked worried. 'Do you think they got away? It sounded like they were being chased. What do you think?'

Pad made a face. 'I don't know. I really don't know. Maybe they scattered and got away. I don't know.'

'What will happen to them if they get caught?' Grant was keeping at the thought.

Pad didn't answer.

The summer days were long, but the shadows were lengthening as the two trotted endlessly on. Their tired feet kicked up little puffs of dust although the air was growing hotter and closer by the moment. Pad noticed the gathering mugginess and knew that rain was near. He looked forward to the feel of it on his skin.

They were definitely closer now to the big stone city. The forest had bigger and bigger gaps in it, some of them filled by farms, all empty now. Pad marvelled at how the city could draw in so much produce and so many goods, with an endless and insatiable need for everything the countryside could grow.

They didn't have the time to stop at any of the farms but kept on the main track now, the end not quite yet in sight.

It started to rain. Big drops fell, just a few at first. Grant saw them hitting the ground, spraying little circles of dust as they hit. The air smelt delicious already and they glanced at each other and smiled as they jogged. Within moments the air was thick with water, pouring down, soaking their thin clothes and their dirty hair.

The noise increased, the din of the downpour hammering into the ground and filling the air. Grant put his head back as he jogged, and let the sweet water fill his mouth and wash down his face. He swallowed and laughed out loud, spinning round as he went, spraying water far and wide.

He spun, grabbed Pad and shouted. 'Behind, behind!'

Pad looked round and almost stopped in shock. The riders were almost on them. He heard it now, the thunder of their hooves over the thunder of the raindrops. Three horses, something odd about one of them. He turned and ran, but there was nowhere to run.

Ahead there were just a few stunted, ragged trees in the landscape. Pad instinctively ran towards them.

'What's the point?' Grant was running beside him. 'They're no cover.'

'They'll break the charge,' snapped Pad. He couldn't believe he'd been caught napping. He glanced back. They were on them, no chance to get behind the trees. He stopped and took his stand, Grant beside him, both of them drawing their weapons.

The drumming of the horse's hooves sounded loud now, filling their ears. The men were silent, charging in, the horses making the only noise as they snorted and grunted with the effort.

Pad knew he was going to die, and the knowledge brought everything into sharper focus. Riders and horses looked grey now in the strange light of the thundering rain. He could see spray flying off the huge horses. He focused on the lead rider and drew back his axe arm. He frowned.

What was he looking at? There was something strange about the lead rider. He tensed his arm. Another moment and he'd throw. He wanted to kill as many as he could before he was cut down.

A spear hurtled over his head from behind. It went with such force that it flew completely flat. And Pad realised what he was looking at. He saw a face rear back with alarm but the spear hit with a massive thud and the grey shape tumbled off the horse.

The other two were close behind and he saw Grant's axe fly. But the rider caught it on his shield and it clanged off. Pad threw carefully and hit the rider as he moved his shield away from his face and body again. That left one coming in hard, and now they just had their blades, which were too short.

The spear, where had the spear come from? It was like Pad was in a dream and everything, including his thoughts, was slowing down. A shape came past him and Pad almost stabbed but just caught himself. Grant looked across in alarm and dismay.

The ragged shape, hair plastered down in the deluge, beard spraying water, threw an axe at the last rider. The rider was skilful and jinked the horse aside, losing momentum but also missing the axe head that whirred past his head.

The shape put its hand somewhere in the back of its robes and then roared. It just stood there, like it had been hit. Pad was too confused by it all. This shape seemed to be on their side but was now somehow unable to do any more. Pad dashed forward, waving his scaramax, unsure what he was doing, but doing it anyway.

The rider leant from the saddle, and Pad saw the long blade start its curve towards him, accelerating as it came. He wasn't sure he could dodge. There was a thud and the blade dropped, digging into the ground. The rider slid into the ground with a horrible grunting noise and slewed to a halt. The horse disappeared into the grey gloom.

Pad turned slowly, his blade up in front of him. His black hair was lank over his face, a face pale with shock and fear. He looked at the apparition nearer the trees. Grant was standing like a tree stump, completely immobile, equally shocked and confused.

The shape threw its head back. 'Goats and gizzards, did you ever see such a shambles?' The shape moved forward, roaring as it came. 'I missed. Can you believe that? I missed. And then I get my axe caught in my clothing. For Frith's sake, maybe it's time you put me to sleep under my spirit tree.'

The ragged man was near Pad by now, looking toward the warrior on the ground. 'And then, then, when I do finally manage to get my ancient old arm to actually throw straight, I hit him in the face not the throat. And you know what that means don't you?'

The man stumped forward toward the fallen warrior. 'That means,' he shouted over his shoulder, 'that my blade will be chipped by his teeth. Took me ages to get a decent edge on it too.'

He bent down and stood back up, shaking his axe in his hand. 'Ha! My luck is in.' He laughed and walked back. 'A warrior without many teeth! The axe is fine.'

Pad let his blade drop as the man approached. He wiped the rain out of his eyes.

'Father. Father,' he said weakly.

Chapter 29

Some of the soldiers lounging round moved forward. A few frowned, but others eagerly drew their swords. The three moved close together as the soldiers moved in.

The air felt heavy, grey, full of tension.

'After all we've been through.' Rick looked close to panic but he was fighting it down. 'This is so unfair. We gave them what they wanted. Mostly.' Beth, her hands tied before her, like the others, leant her head on his side. She glanced at both the boys.

'Well, we did our best,' she said quietly. 'And Pad and Grant are probably already in Burgh. Fixing the defences. They'll win. The forest will win, it will be right again. And thank you both for looking after me.'

A soldier stepped forward and stared at Tom. 'You. You killed my friend this morning. I took your axe from his body. So now I kill you and then your friends.'

He waved his sword in front of Tom's face but then his expression changed. He sheathed the sword and pulled out a long knife with a wavy, rusty blade. 'My friend died fast. But you, you die slow.' He paused and his eyes flicked sideways.

A couple of men sniggered as he moved the knifepoint from Tom. He took a pace sideways and looked at Beth and then Tom. 'But first you see her die slow. Then you die slow.' He jerked his head at Rick. 'Someone, kill the big one.'

Beth was breathing fast, but determined not to show fear. The soldier stepped in front of her, his eyes dead as if he was looking at a piece of meat.

It rained. There was no warning. One moment it was hot and humid, the next it was thundering down. Everyone blinked, caught off guard. But it didn't change the situation.

The men in front of Rick and Beth were shouldered aside. Tom glanced up and recognised him. Qut turned and faced the men in front of him. Beth noticed the muscles in his back and shoulders, gleaming in the rain as it poured down. She saw the muscles tense.

'No!' Qut barked at the warriors almost in his face. 'Mine.'

There was a moment of tension and uncertainty. But nobody cared to challenge him. Warriors turned away with a shrug. The one with the rusty knife looked like he wanted to fight but eventually he just made a face.

'Just make sure they die, or Lord Gutta will slaughter us all.'

Qut nodded. He turned to the three, but his eyes were on Beth.

'Brave. All of you brave. So you die like warriors. I kill you fast, no pain. This I can do for you.'

Beth looked up into the rain, her tears mixing with the heavy drops. She'd felt just for a moment that maybe Qut could save them. But she realised he couldn't. There was nobody to save them now. And a quick death from Qut was actually a great gift, given the alternative. She looked at the man with the rusty blade and shuddered as she imagined what he might do.

She looked at Qut who met her gaze steadily. She nodded. Her voice quavered but she spoke firmly. 'Thank you Qut.'

She heard Tom gulp.

'Her first Qut. Kill her first so she doesn't suffer. Be quick.'

Beth realised Tom didn't want her to see her friends dying, to prolong her own agony. She didn't want to die but she realised it was Tom's final act of selflessness.

She put her head down. She heard the long blade sliding out from the metal scabbard.

'But, father, what, what are you doing here?' Pad looked around, completely thrown. He waved his arms, sending water droplets flying everywhere. 'Seriously, what in the forest's name are you doing here, right here?'

Donald shrugged. 'Oh you know, thought I'd come out and see how things were going out here. Fortunate to bump into you really.' He examined his axe head before it disappeared once again back into his clothing layers somewhere. He wandered off to find the axe that had missed.

Grant sat down heavily, even though the ground was now running with water. Pad gave up. 'Right, right. Well, we've found out lots. We were Watchers, we know what Lord Gutta's plans are. We have to tell you so one of us gets back to tell.'

'Yes yes,' said Donald vaguely. He retrieved his last axe and then stopped, looking at the rider whom he'd killed with the spear. 'Oh.'

Grant and Pad wandered over. 'I thought that's what I saw,' said Pad.

Matt looked small and rather pathetic lying on the ground. The spear had gone right through him and into the rider behind. The heavy rain had washed the blood away, leaving just a soaking grey huddle of clothing and armour on the streaming ground.

Donald put his hand over his eyes. 'I didn't realise. All I could see was the silhouette of the rider.'

'It's Matt.' Grant looked down. 'He's dead.'

'He was a traitor,' said Pad. 'You heard what the others said. He came here to tell Lord Gutta about the defences in Burgh. He's betrayed the whole city. He deserved to die.'

Donald looked at the body again. 'I recognise him now. He and I had a little chat some days ago. I thought he was up to no good. Still, bit of a surprise to see him here. Didn't realise I'd killed him.'

Pad snorted. 'You must have killed loads of men father. It's no big deal. I bet you can't even remember how many you've killed.' Pad looked at Grant to make sure he'd understood that Pad's father was a senior warrior. Grant looked up at Donald, unsure what to think.

Donald wiped his hands over his streaming face. 'You have no idea Pad. Every man I've killed up close, every one of them, they're still alive. They're with me in my dreams, my nightmares. They'll always be with me. I see their faces most nights. I smell their breath.'

With a strength that surprised Pad, Donald grabbed his son and pulled him tight, into his soaking wet robes. With his other hand he pulled Grant in tight and they stood in a close huddle in the grey teeming rain for what seemed like ages. None of them wanted to break the moment.

Donald coughed eventually. 'So, you have some news that might help Burgh. Perhaps we should go and tell Burgh. There will be other patrols out I'm sure, we have to get back to bring word. Yes yes, I know you need to tell me first but I think standing here with four dead bodies and three horses trotting about is probably not the best place is it?

'And that's not all.' The boys heard the tension entering his voice. 'There are only two when five set out. First you have to tell me where the other three are. I need to know they're safe.'

Reluctantly, the boys let go of the old man and followed him towards Burgh. Pad swallowed hard and started talking. They soon disappeared into the teeming gloom of a rainy night. They left behind some huddled shapes on the ground, one of them with a spear shaft still sticking up into the air.

Qut drew back his sword, tensing his muscles for a swing with all his force in it, clean, quick.

A hand gripped his arm. With a growl he looked sideways. He saw a white sleeve and a white glove gripping his arm. He went very still.

Zala stood, looking past Qut's shoulder. Beth raised her eyes. She looked dazed. She drew in a great shuddering breath and held it. Zala was so close that she clearly saw inside the great cowl. Rain dripped off the end of the hood but inside she saw the deathly pale skin, mottled with patches of pure white. She met the gaze of those pink eyes and then looked away, her breath coming out in a long moan.

'Perhaps,' said Zala, 'perhaps we are being a little hasty.' He pushed down Qut's sword arm and the man backed away as quickly as he could. 'I'm sure I heard the big boy say that you'd told us "mostly" what you knew. Not all that you knew. And it got me thinking.'

He swayed a step, looking at the three in turn, so close they could smell his dead, ancient breath. 'I'm wondering what else you might know. What you might know that we might like to know. If, for example, something were to happen to that boy Matt then we still want to know what's happening inside the city.'

Deep in thought he turned, and gave orders to the men. They all rushed off, getting ready to get back on the advance again. He called back Qut. 'You will keep these three alive. They may yet be useful, hostages, spies perhaps.'

He looked at Qut directly and the warrior dropped his gaze. 'And you seem to understand these children. So you will keep them alive. And if anything happens to them…'

He faded away, not needing to finish the threat.

Qut looked at the three. He picked up the ropes restraining their wrists and nodded. He hoped they understood his neck was now on the line.

Chapter 30

Tom tugged at the rope round his wrist. He examined again how the rope went over the bough above his head and was knotted up there, like the others.

'You thinking of trying to get those ropes down Tom?'

Rick shuffled beside his friend. 'You fancy standing on a horse like Qut did to get to them?' Rick grinned, fairly certain Tom wanted to get near a horse about as much as he did.

Beth stood and walked over, trailing her rope beside her. 'If you both give me a leg up I could leap that distance easily. I could get them untied in a moment. If we get a chance, why not?'

Tom looked around and thought. 'You know if we did escape they'd kill Qut don't you?'

Beth's fierce gaze wavered. 'He's the enemy isn't he?'

Tom nodded. 'And maybe he helped us. Maybe he saved our lives.'

Rick grunted. 'Only because he likes Beth.'

Beth tossed her hair. 'Well it's not going to be because he likes you is it?' She smirked but then her bloodied mouth twisted down. 'But I don't want to see him killed, not because of us, because of me.'

'Then we can't escape can we?' said Tom. He looked around. The sight struck him again, as startling as the first time they'd seen it, earlier that day.

He barely recognised his own city. He'd only seen it from the outside a few times. But now, now it looked like a ruin. His eyes ran over the fallen blocks, each the size of a house, that littered the ground outside the city limits.

He knew he wasn't the only one to spot the big baulks of timber that filled the gaps in the walls. They looked crude and nothing like as solid a defence as the rest of the stone blocks. He had no idea why they hadn't pulled the blocks back into place. It used to look indestructible to his eyes but now it looked indefensible.

And between where they were held on the edge of the forest right the way to the city itself there was a great field of men, the enemy, straggling into place after their long struggle through the forest. To Tom they looked like one huge death worm, surging and coiling, preparing to strike.

He heard horse hooves approaching and turned. And sighed.

'Don't worry Tom, not long now.' Reese sat on his horse ahead of a small group of warriors also on horseback and stared down at Tom and the others. 'Look at the place, Lord Mofty has really let the city go to rack and ruin hasn't he?'

He sniggered. 'Leaving it wide open. For us.' He sat up on the horse and stared at Burgh. 'And then we'll see who's banished won't we? Then we'll see what happens when you turn your back on me. Then they'll know how it feels to be turned away from your own home, your own city.'

He glared at Burgh with a hatred Tom had never fully seen before. The others exchanged glances.

'For us?' Tom snorted. 'For them you mean. They don't need you now. What do you think will happen if they win? How long will you last before they string you up? Like Leigh.'

Reese wrenched his glare away from Burgh and his cold gaze fell on Tom.

'They still need me. They always will. I've got contacts, I know how the place works.'

Tom feigned a total lack of interest.

'Oh right. You're not even a man. And once they have control of the place they'll soon know where everything is. Where everything valuable is. And they'll destroy it, and kill the people. Kill your parents. And then they'll destroy the forest and everything in it. They're death Reese, destruction. And you're helping do that to your own people. You're a worm.'

Reese's anger burned brighter. He glanced round at the small band of horsemen with him before edging his horse closer to the three who sat on the ground. 'You think they cared about me when they let me be banished? It's their fault, my parents should have fixed it. I've had to live in a filthy wasteland with a bunch of losers while they've lived the life in my city.'

He shifted the horse sideways to Tom so his side was in full view.

'And not a man eh? Well what's this?'

He looked down and Tom saw an axe in his belt. He knew without any doubt it was his own axe, his man axe that he'd managed to get from the oak tree in the Bone Hills. Slowly Reese reached across the other side of his belt and drew a scaramax blade. Tom recognised it as his own.

Reese walked the horse round until his sword arm faced Tom, the horse nearly treading on his feet. There were roots on the surface under the tree, and the horse trod carefully. After the heavy rain the ground and the roots were greasy damp.

'Who's the big man now then Tom?' Reese glared down, his anger building, about to be unleashed as he realised Tom couldn't fight back effectively, with no weapons and his hands tied together. Reese's fingers moved on the handle of the blade as he worked himself up for a slashing stroke.

'If you're going to wave that little knife around, could you cut my rope please?' Beth wandered up, apparently calm, twitching the rope in her hands.

Reese twisted in the saddle, turning to face her. His face worked as he tried to find a clever answer, thrown off balance by the pretty face staring casually up at him. He turned the blade towards her, so she saw the thickness of the blade and the sharpness of the single cutting edge with that wickedly sharp point on the end. She saw it.

He glanced back at Tom and a sly look crossed his face. He knew how to get to her. He turned again to Tom but there was someone else there. Qut stood with his arms crossed on his chest, which just happened to show the size of the muscles in his upper arms.

He stared up at Reese and Reese saw the message in his eyes. Reese moistened his lips. He had the height, he had the weapon, while Qut stood with his hands empty and his arms crossed. But still Reese hesitated.

'Where is that little friend of yours? Why hasn't he reported?' The voice snapped Reese's head round, and his right arm dropped to his side. 'Matt? I…I don't know my lord. He must have got held up finding out something really useful.' He smiled a sickly smile but Lord Gutta just stared at him from his horse, his eyes half lidded, full of loathing. Reese wondered where he'd sprung from.

The white robes of Zala ghosted forward on his black horse from behind his lord. 'But you are responsible for him are you not boy Reese? How are we to know if our plan is to work? We must have confirmation that they haven't changed their defences inside the walls. Such walls as remain. How do you propose to reassure us? And why are you waving your sword at these valuable prisoners?'

Reese pushed the blade away into its scabbard and gulped. 'I'm sure Matt will be here soon. He's been right every time hasn't he? He's one of my best spies. Anyway, you can see their defences are pathetic, they don't stand a chance. Why don't we attack now? Get that gate down, then the fun can really start.' He grinned this time, a nasty, exultant grin that took in the three on the ground.

Zala and his lord exchanged glances. Reese turned round, grinning, and then yelped. Zala's hood was right beside him.

'You speak too much boy. That tongue of yours wags. Cease it wagging or you will be watching it wag on the ground by your horse's hooves.'

Reese gulped and looked away, unable to meet those eyes.

The hood turned, and fixed on Tom. 'And that means nothing to you does it, about the gate?' Tom felt his eyes drawn up until they looked into that dark cowl, into those pink eyes. His mind whirled, and his hand instinctively went to the wudu around his neck. He felt the rough wood beneath his fingers.

'The gate? Attack the gate if you want, it's the toughest part of the defences, everyone knows that. Nobody's ever broken them down.' He shrugged, as if it was of no interest.

'And yet, I see your fat friend smiling at the thought. Why is that do you think? What is it you know about the gate?'

Tom could have sworn that Zala's eyes, deep in his cowl, had never left his face but he was aware that Rick had smiled slightly. Tom's fingers dug into the wood around his neck until a splinter broke off. He rolled it in his fingers, while his eyes stayed on Zala. Out of the corner of his eye he saw Rick look down, horribly aware he might have compromised everything.

Tom dug the splinter into his finger and gazed back at Zala. 'Because it's funny. The thought of you deciding to attack the gate. Everyone knows you'd be wasting your time.' He forced a smile. He could feel the sweat where his rough smock touched his back.

Zala gazed down while his horse fidgeted its feet right by Tom's. Eventually he sat back up straight. He turned to Lord Gutta and Tom saw the cowl nod slightly. Gutta let out a breath mostly of impatience.

'We have talked enough. It is time to attack. We can't wait for some snivelling boy who is probably too scared to leave his mother's skirts. Summon the war chiefs. We attack Burgh. Today.'

Without taking his eyes off the gathering of warlords, Rick twitched his restraining rope and moved across to sit by Tom and Beth.

'Do you think they're stupid? Why are they letting us hear their plans?' It was Rick's usual attempt at a whisper, and Tom saw Reese turn round. He was at the outer edge of the semicircle in front of Lord Gutta. He looked at the three and they saw the smile twisting his lips. He knew.

Tom looked at his friend's open face, currently frowning as he stared at the gathering of the enemy. He hesitated. 'Perhaps because we're not important enough,' he replied gently. He glanced sideways to Beth and she met his gaze.

They both knew.

Tom listened and watched. He'd wondered if the enemy would simply mount a siege of Burgh but he saw that there was no patience. Gutta and his men were too hungry for the ripe treasure within Burgh to settle down to a long siege. And the crumbling walls showed them they had no reason to wait.

Tom noticed how different it was listening to the enemy leader compared to listening to Lord Gregory. Gutta used the force of his personality and threats to stamp his wishes on his men, even though they were experienced warriors. Tom felt his heart beating faster as he realised the enemy horde was going to attack as soon as it could. He guessed what that meant for him and Rick and Beth, as well as for everyone in Burgh.

He just hoped either Pad or Grant had got back and brought news of Lord Gutta's real plans. Either way, he was sure he and his friends were dead. He thought about that, and looked up at the dripping tree above him. It had been there long before he was born and it would be there long after he was gone. He found the thought comforting in a strange way.

He felt the oak's damp roots under his legs as he sprawled on the ground, roots that anchored the great tree to the earth. He knew in his bones somehow that the great rains had helped quell the burning in the south of the forest. The damage was still there, a smoking wound that would take generations to heal, but he hoped the worst was over.

Unless of course Burgh fell, in which case the whole forest would be put to the flame, and everyone in it.

'But, my lord, could we not just launch a screen, a feign, instead of a full assault on the wall?'

The voice brought Tom back from his thoughts. The tone had been anxious and Tom's ears pricked up.

'Why, Pashu, are you afraid to tackle some crumbling ruin?' Gutta's voice brooked no argument, but Tom was impressed when he heard the man answer.

'I am not afraid my great Lord Gutta, you know I have proven myself in battle. But a full assault will incur heavy casualties, and it is not necessary just to draw the defender's attention away and cover our movement.'

'You question my strategy perhaps? You think you would do better if you led this battle?'

'No, no my lord, my Lord Gutta. We all bow to your superior strategy. My concern is simply not to lose too many men if we don't have to.'

'They are of no concern. We have enough. You will lead the assault in person, you will be the first onto the enemy ramparts.

'Azmi, you will lead the second wave across the rear of the first. How many wagons do we have?'

Tom could only see the backs of the men but he heard the hesitation before a voice said quietly: 'We have the one my lord. It is intact. It is enough.'

'One? One left?' There was a thunderous pause. Tom licked his lips, thinking of the damage Pad and Grant had obviously done. He didn't understand why they needed the wagons but the loss was obviously felt. Tom sat still and he saw the others looking at the ground, keeping quiet and trying to be invisible.

'I want those children tied to the wagon when it's pushed into place. That should stop their archers.'

'My lord, they may yet prove useful as hostages or spies. I suggest we hold them back.'

Tom recognised Zala's quiet voice and for once he was grateful. He didn't know what was in the wagon but he had a feeling he didn't want to find out, certainly not by being tied on top of it.

Gutta growled but seemed to lose interest. 'Azmi, you lead the second wave across behind the first. You use them as cover to move round to the western wall, keep the wagon hidden among your men. Get it to the gate, you know what to do.'

Lord Gutta's voice swelled. 'You all know what to do, every leader here. We haven't travelled through that cursed forest to fail here. We attack, we attack the walls, and we attack the gate. It's weak, we will bring the whole gateway down. Then we are in. It will be like the waters breaking in after the dam gives way in the irrigation ditch. Every warrior is to enter the city. Kill every man, every boy, kill the old. Bring terror, bring chaos, bring death.

'Then it will be ours. We will be lords and masters of the survivors, of the city and everything in it, they will be our playthings, our slaves. We will make them burn the forest to the ground so we never again have to stumble through those damned trees. Everything will be ours. All you have to do is carry out the plan. Anyone who shows weakness, or hesitation, or cowardice will die. I will be watching.'

There was a slight pause. 'And Zala will be watching.'

'Go, go to your places, we attack when the sun is at its highest. Soon, my brothers, soon, we will be inside the walls looking out, masters of everything we survey. Go to battle, go to war, go to ruin and destruction!'

The men roared and surged away to their commands.

Chapter 31

The three stood under the oak trees and watched the attack roll forward. Even though it was going away from him, Tom found he was holding his breath, his heart hammering. A glance to his side showed the others felt the same.

The noise rose to a thunderous roar as the enemy army crashed into the broken walls of Burgh. They focused on the most damaged area, to Tom's front left. There many blocks had fallen, all except the base blocks, and already some of the enemy were being hoisted up by others and climbing crude ladders to get to the wooden baulks of timber beyond.

But higher up on remaining parts of the wall the defenders were pouring down spears, arrows and lumps of stone on the attackers. As men fell back wounded or dead others pushed forward, desperate to get to grips with the men behind the wooden defences and out of that deadly rain.

From where Tom stood the enemy horde seemed so vast he couldn't imagine it could fail. And behind those damaged walls were his family, Abi, all his friends from Burgh and now his forest friends from Frith. He realised just how much he cared for just about everything behind those walls. What would he do if it fell?

He glanced round. Lord Gutta's headquarters was nearby, with soldiers coming and going, and Gutta and Zala standing there, watching like hawks. Behind them Reese sat, still on his horse, like some senior warrior. Tom's heart sank. He felt his time running out and those of his friends beside him, and those ahead of him fighting for their lives, for their way of life.

Rick tried to cheer quietly, which drew several helmeted heads to stare at him. 'They're being knocked back. Look, they're not getting in.'

Tom looked again. There were bodies everywhere and he could hear the screams and yells and clang of metal on metal. The deeper sounds of thuds as blade hit flesh or a heavy object smashed into a skull didn't reach as far as where he stood.

The enemy was stalled. The defenders were fighting like the desperate men they were, and the defences were holding. The timber was bigger and better secured than it looked and the attackers were piling up in bloody heaps. New warriors stumbled over the bodies and ran into swords and spears and the big battle axes they'd come to fear.

They were stopped.

Lord Gutta made a gesture. Beside him a man raised a thin horn and sounded a reedy note that carried surprisingly far. Then Tom saw the wagon. It was covered in dark cloth and it was being pushed across the rear of the main attack. A huge second wave was skirting the back of the first attack, probably invisible from the walls. Tom watched as the second wave pushed round to the left. Round to the western gateway.

Despite himself Tom was impressed. He'd seen enough of fighting to know how hard it was to control groups of men once battle started. Yet these men pushed forward steadily, with the occasional glance back to where their lord's headquarters stood watching them.

Tom saw the looks. If this had been Lord Gregory and Donald here instead of Lord Gutta and Zala, he thought, the men would be reassured their lord was behind them, watching over them, ready to jump in if needed. But Lord Gutta's men looked in fear, like goats beaten on with sticks, afraid of what would happen if they stopped.

Looking again, he saw wounded men stumbling back, only to be stopped and turned around and sent back by warriors in Gutta's headquarters group. Tom saw one man, his forehead covered in blood, trudge back, only to be stopped. He argued, there was a brief struggle and he fell to the ground with a sword in his stomach. Gutta nodded and Zala broke his gaze away, back to the wagon slowly moving round to the left.

'So what's in that wagon? What's so special about it?' Beth moved beside Tom, her green eyes fixed on the dark wagon surrounded by warriors pushing and pulling through the mass of men.

Tom frowned, trying to think. 'Didn't Pad say there was stuff in them that burned really fiercely? Some sort of dark stuff, looked a bit like honey, only black? I don't know what that is exactly. He certainly stank of it, weird smell.'

Beth nodded impatiently. 'Yes that's what he said. And we know they're going to roll it up against the gate. I don't see how that works though.'

'But what if it does?' asked Rick. 'What if Pad didn't get back or they can't see a way to counter it? That gateway is going to completely collapse if they burn the gates. And what have they got behind it now, just a row of carts or something? That's not going to stop an army this big.'

All three watched as the wagon and its men moved round to the edge of their sight. From where they stood they could just look along the western wall, although the angle was too much for them to see the gateway in it. They all knew that the gateway and the arch above the gates was now sitting on the huge wooden and metal doors. The earthdin had crushed it down. If the gates broke then the whole archway would collapse, opening up the city to the enemy.

And, thanks to Reese and Matt, the enemy knew it too.

'Maybe one wagon won't be enough. Pad and Grant burned loads of them.' Tom tried to sound optimistic, but he could see the wagon was nearly by the gate. Most of the defenders' attention was still focused on the assault on the broken wall. The attackers were dying in huge numbers, but they kept the defenders focusing on them, not on the smaller group that had slid round the corner.

Peering hard, Tom saw a group of men lock their shields together, above themselves and above the wagon. With a cheer he could just hear the wagon trundled forward until it clanged against the gate. Missiles fell and men went down but the survivors ran back, leaving the wagon in place.

Lord Gutta hesitated then made another signal. Another sound from the trumpet and Tom saw that men had been kindling fire away from the wall. Fire arrows spun forward and landed on the wagon. Within moments it was alight. Tom saw the flames shoot up with the black smoke. He heard the cries of alarm on the walls, cries that sounded thin and helpless at this distance.

With a great belch of smoke and flame the wagon erupted, flames covering the western wall, the gateway and even the grasses nearby. The enemy troops howled with glee while some attempts were made by the defenders to pour water over the walls. But Tom could see that nobody was actually on the gateway above the gate, it was obviously too dangerous, so the efforts came to nothing.

He found he was tugging on the limit of the rope that bound his hands, desperate to get closer to see what was happening. The others were alongside him.

After what seemed like for ever there was a rumbling, grinding crash. A cloud of dust went up with a great gout of smoke and flame. The attackers cheered and charged forward. All along the wall, round from where the initial attack had petered out, the enemy soldiers surged round to pour through the open gateway.

Tom could still see flames everywhere, but warriors charged through and into Burgh, into his city, his home. Rick looked like he was about to burst into tears while Beth just watched, rigid with horror.

More and more men ran through the wrecked gateway and disappeared from view into the city streets. They could all hear the screaming and shouting as hundreds of enemy, eager to kill, eager to destroy and damage and steal, howled forward.

Lord Gutta, triumphant, let out a long bellow, like a predator roaring over a kill. Zala turned and looked at Reese, then his cowl turned to look at the three. They heard him say to Reese, almost conversationally, 'Now, I think. We no longer need them. You can dispose of them, like you asked. You have earned this.'

Reese turned his horse towards the three, who shrank back together, tethered by their ropes, unarmed. Tom saw the hideous look of glee on Reese's face. Reese slowly drew the axe, Tom's axe, from his belt, his eyes never leaving Tom's face. His horse plodded closer, its hooves sounding loud on root-twisted ground.

Tom swallowed. He'd known this moment would come but he hadn't expected his executioner to be Reese.

'Where's Qut?' Beth's voice sounded so small and afraid to Tom. In the background he could hear his city dying.

'Qut? You're calling for your enemy?' Reese sounded amused. 'Afraid he's not around.' He turned and pointed back to Burgh. 'He was in the first wave at the gate. Very dangerous. Don't know how he got sent there. Can't imagine he'll survive.'

His horse stepped closer, its hooves banging on the hard roots of the oak. It towered over Tom. Tom glanced up and around. He moistened his lips.

'Look, Reese, we're all Burgh boys here. Rick and I, we're only here because you got us banished. This is your fault we're here so stop messing about and untie us.'

Reese's eyes gleamed. 'My fault? My fault that stupid old fool got in the way of my knife? My fault my parents wouldn't lift a finger to save me? No, not my fault. And it's your fault for being stupid and getting caught up in things. And you chose the wrong side. That's your fault. And you're going to pay.'

He hefted the axe and Tom opened his mouth to beg, then closed it again. He looked at the other two.

'Then let Beth go. What's she got to do with this? She's not from Burgh. You can't kill a girl anyway. Look at Beth, are you really going to swing that axe at her face?'

He saw Reese's eyes flicker. 'So let her go Reese, nobody cares about her, she's not a threat, just cut her rope. With your axe, do it now.'

Reese hesitated, his face twisted. He made a strange noise and glanced round to where Lord Gutta and Zala were standing. But they were watching the city, not him. Then Zala's cowl slowly turned, turning until it was facing Reese. They couldn't see his face in the darkness of the long hood but they could all feel his gaze.

Reese spun back round and made what he intended to be a war cry but which came out as a sort of scream. He nudged the horse forward and swung the axe.

'Down!' All three dropped to the ground, their bound hands pulling the ropes tight about the branch above them. Reese's swing whirred by but missed any target. The horse snorted, unsure.

Tom couldn't see how they could win, but he knew that Reese's new fondness for being on horseback could work in their favour. He just didn't have the reach unless he got lucky. Or got down.

The three dodged and rolled, trying to keep out of the way of the horse's hooves and the axe swings. They were glad Reese didn't have a long sword, so for now they had a chance. But for how long?

Reese's breathing became more and more laboured, and he started shouting in frustration and rage, flailing wildly. Then Beth and Rick's ropes became tangled above their heads. Beth was caught almost upright, while Rick dived to the ground. Seeing his moment, Reese turned the horse in the tight space and it moved forward as Reese drew his arm back for a furious axe swing at Beth.

She saw it coming and went still, staring at him with her eyes blazing, trapped. Rick saw. He grunted, rolled upright and ran forward, to throw his body in front of Beth.

Tom seemed to have so much time.

He snapped upright, gathering his rope in his hands, and threw himself forward, towards the rear of the horse.

The rope looped round one of the horse's back legs as it stepped unsteadily forward over the tree roots and earth. Tom jerked back and to one side, not really knowing what he was doing.

The horse, already uneasy in the gloomy space under the branches, twitched, and its back leg hit the other one. As it staggered for balance, the damp roots seemed to slide under its feet. With a fearful scream, the horse fell sideways.

Reese screamed too as horse and rider crashed to the ground. He screamed again as the horse came down on his leg.

Tom, caught up in the tangling rope, started to get to his feet, desperate to get to Reese's weapons. But the horse was flailing on the ground, terrified by the rope restricting its back legs. It lashed out. One hoof twitched and caught Tom in the stomach as he rose.

Grunting, he doubled over. The hoof swung back and hit Tom full in the chest.

He was aware of flying through the air, then he hit the trunk of the oak with his back and head. He heard the impact but didn't seem to feel it much. Somewhere he could hear roaring, and some of it sounded very close. He wondered what it was. He saw, idly, that Rick had picked up the axe and he thought Rick looked very angry. He couldn't work out why. His head lolled forward.

Chapter 32

It was hazy, smoky, difficult to see clearly. He could make out figures, but they seemed to be moving faster than was possible. And the sounds they made, sort of high pitched shrieks and wails. He could see blades clashing at impossible speeds, the sounds they made so tinny it was almost comical.

But the blood looked real, and the dead lay as still as the dead do.

The day seemed to be passing so quickly, the sun visibly moving towards the horizon. The sun was of more importance than the little figures rushing about. The warmth of the sun, the angle of the rays, that was what mattered, and the ground, so full of goodness but so dark and cold deep below the surface.

And now nourished with blood.

But the sun was obscured by dark smoke, great ragged rolls of it blotting out the nourishing rays. His gaze was drawn back to the city, which looked to be in its death throes. His viewpoint shifted, above the streets. He could hear the sounds of battle below but also the cries of children, the wailing of women. He could sense the fear as well as the rage and the anger.

It was not all smoke. There were great clouds of birds circling above, the crows and all their kind, the rooks and magpies and ravens and jays and jackdaws. His vision plunged down into a whirl of wings and sharp eyes and sharper beaks, all circling in a wild vortex. One eye stood out, a great, ageing crow riding the thermals, waiting, watching. She saw.

Pine Leaf seemed to draw him down, spiralling down and down, into the noise that deepened into a thundering, howling roar that filled his world. Then Pine Leaf was gone. And Blakelock was there.

'Now!' Blakelock shouted so loud his lungs hurt. His shout floated over the howling mob of warriors who came sprinting through the burning gateway. They ran exultant, certain they had broken the outer shell of the city. And now they could rip out its innards.

They poured in, more and more, running through the smoke. The misty sun shone on armoured chests and heads, glinted on curved sword and shield. Soon it was a flood of warriors who ran forward headlong, their fierce eyes searching for easy victims to terrify and kill, for treasure to loot, for delicate things to smash.

But at Blakelock's shout defenders appeared. From behind wagons and baulks of timber and at upper windows of the houses and even on the roofs. And all the houses and wagons and big blocks of timber and stone were connected.

Houses lined both sides of the road that led from the collapsed West Gate, and every space between every house was filled with obstacles and defenders. Every house doorway was barred and barricaded, so was every ground-floor window.

Filled with the fierce joy of battle and victory, the enemy swept on, until those at the front tried to slow. The road ahead was blocked by a huge wall of stone and wood. It may have been rough but it was the height of two men and on the top of it were warriors several deep.

Men tried to look for a way round but they realised there was nowhere for them to run. They realised this as the pressure built from the number of men running in behind them. They were in a trap. The more experienced warriors knew it had a name.

The killing ground.

And then the missiles came from men high up, out of reach in windows, on great timber walls, on roofs. Arrows, spears, lumps of stone, throwing axes, they hammered down into the mass of men below.

Those at the front tried to turn but the pressure behind them was too great. They were pushed towards the wall at the end, from where more missiles came. Some accepted their fate.

They were warriors, they couldn't retreat so they attacked. They attacked by clambering desperately up the rough wall of wood and stone, but the defenders were ready with shields and blades and the long battle axes the enemy had come to fear. It became a desperate series of little struggles as the enemy tried to simply overwhelm the wall.

In the middle at the top stood a fearsome figure, his great mass of dark hair and beard making him look like a wild beast. His two-handed sword flashed and flicked, powered by muscles all could see moving beneath his leathery skin.

Beside him, in contrast, stood a man with wild grey hair and beard. He looked like a vagrant, in ragged layers of clothing, but he swung a mighty bearded axe like a seasoned warrior.

The enemy searched for a way out, desperate for an escape. They battered on doorways, sprinted down the beginnings of alleys between the houses, tried to break through ground-floor windows. Everywhere they met solid resistance and more weapons. The defenders fought with the desperation of having their women and children, their lives, their city, right behind them.

Arrows and spears and axes slammed into the enemy until the ground was mounded with bodies. The wounded tried to drag themselves back to the gateway but they were trampled by desperate feet.

Slowly the killing ground started to empty of living men. Lord Gutta's army fell back as the recoil of the men in the trap proved more powerful than the men still pushing eagerly to get in.

Again Blakelock raised his voice to a great shout. 'Now! With me!' His men roared and poured down the end wall. They fell on the retreating backs of the enemy, stabbing, chopping, beating down. Blakelock ran, with no shield, just a pair of breeches, no shoes, his hair standing out from his head like a great mane.

An armoured warrior with sword and shield recognised Blakelock as an important leader and turned to kill. His great downward stroke hit the long, strong blade of Blakelock's sword and, as the enemy tried to turn his arm for a sideways sweep, Blakelock used both his hands on the grip to simply flick it sideways into the warrior's face with surprising force.

The nosepiece on the man's helmet saved it becoming a killing stroke but, as he grunted and stepped back, his face bleeding heavily, the long sword flickered again and this time it found his throat. He fell. Blakelock's face remained impassive, his mouth closed, his eyes wide and focused, his nostrils flaring.

He stepped over the body, flicking the blood from his sword as he looked around. Taking in the big picture, then taking in the small picture of the enemy warrior who had turned in panic, trapped. He saw Blakelock, yelled, and rushed at the ragged old man beside him.

The ragged old man brought his great long-handled axe down with surprising speed and force. The soldier made a horrible noise as he crashed to the ground, his head a broken mess.

The old man grunted and brought the axe back to his shoulder as he moved forward. 'I don't know Blakelock, I'm getting a bit old for all this. I ought to leave it to you younger fellows. I'd rather be...' He stopped talking as he swung the axe horizontally, nearly cutting a warrior in half. 'I'd rather be sipping some birch wine by the river, with the willows hanging over.' He went for another strike but the enemy simply ran.

Blakelock's eyes never left the carnage in front of him, never changed expression, but his grim mouth opened slightly. It could have been a smile. 'Yes Donald, you run along for a nap, we'll tidy up here. Perhaps we could let Lord Mofty's men actually do some work.'

He glanced behind, to where a wedge of men in smart uniforms with gleaming weapons were cautiously following the ragged front rows of defenders. Looking forward, Blakelock saw his men winning, but saw them winning at a cost, with men dying and being wounded as they kept the pressure up.

One of them was Ives, pushing forward with his men, exhausted, gasping, battered. He looked so tired he could barely lift his sword but he kept going, pushing forward. Blakelock could see his whole body was shaking but still the man kept the pressure up on the enemy.

Blakelock nodded slightly. He turned and shouted at the Guard Commander behind him.

'Studge! The enemy is falling back. Take your men forward, give ours a rest. Drive the enemy from your streets, back beyond the gateway.'

Studge hesitated but then nodded. Gripping his shield tight to him, he raised his sword arm and led his men forward. Donald paused and leaned on his axe, not minding the blood that dripped onto his sleeve.

They looked so clean Donald thought, so well equipped. He watched the City Guard move through the sweaty, bloody, wild thin lines of the forest men and charge towards an enemy that was already broken.

He wondered how they could get that gateway resealed but realised it was a hopeless job. He looked around at the killing ground they had created. He grinned into his beard as he remembered how much grief they had had from the house owners as they turned their houses into fortresses. Even with the enemy at the gate they'd grumbled about things getting broken and rough men clambering on their roof.

He tried to slow his breathing as he looked at all the dead, and the dying who would soon be dead. He saw a number of forest men, but a tiny proportion compared to the piles of enemy dead. Even so he grieved. They were good men, dying for a city they didn't even live in, for a way of life they'd forsaken, or been rejected by or had never known.

He saw Blakelock moving forward behind the city guards, and grinned again. May the forest help those fancy guards if they didn't get the enemy cleared out soon. His long yellow teeth disappeared as the smile faded. He scratched his straggly beard. With the imminent threat of his own death retreating, his thoughts instantly turned to the others. He hoped the forest was protecting the three out there.

He had no way of knowing if they were alive or what was happening to them, but he was impressed at the way they'd acted like Watchers. The way they'd found out the enemy plans and got that knowledge back. Without them, Donald knew they'd never have had time to defend the West Gate and the enemy plan would have succeeded.

He wondered what the enemy would do now. And what Lord Gutta would do with the three young people if he had them, if he hadn't killed them already. He sighed, and bowed his head, fatigue sweeping over him as the blood dripped down his axe.

Droplets of blood joined together and ran down the metal blade of the long-handled axe. Donald grounded the long haft and leant on the axe, resting his head on his forearm. He could already see the faces of those he had killed this day. He knew he would see them again when he slept.

The drops of blood ran slowly down to the sharp point at the bottom tip of the great axehead. A drop formed right on the point, hung and hesitated.

It fell.

It dropped onto the ground, onto what would have been the main street coming in from the West Gate. But the stone slabs forming the street had been ripped up, used for barricades and missiles. Like other drops before it, the blood fell onto the wet earth without a sound and sunk into the soil.

All along the street blood dripped and soaked into the ground, as the bodies lay thickly strewn. The red soil was soon noticed by questing roots and the fungus that knitted trees together underground. Even here, in the city, there were trees, largely unnoticed, standing alone or in small groups.

As the high-speed, high-pitched jerky movements of the mortals had swirled rapidly round them, they had stood silent, reacting at their own pace. Now, as the noise and movement slowed a little, they started the quest to draw up the nutrition into their roots, their trunks, their leaves.

The viewpoint darkened, it smelt of mould and damp earth and there was a sense of time without end.

You see now that your decision to stay with us, the forest, has brought a rich harvest for the city. The stone city still stands, and the enemy who would burn us all to the ground is confounded. For now. We are damaged, many trees have died, but for now the forest stands and can recover.

But our enemy's rage is growing. We can feel it even here. And he will strike hard. We can move. A stand of trees can move several horizons, but it takes one or more of your lifetimes to achieve. You can move faster and you or one of your stand of friends must face him. You must.

We will help where we can but we can only do that if you bring him to us, we can not go to him in time. Others will help as well, they will do what they can because all of our fates rest on your courage young mortal. Fail, and there will not be time to bury you under your spirit tree because the whole forest will burn.

And your friend will fall. It is a price that will be paid. But it is a death that will not be in vain. Honour her body after death. If we survive.

The horror of what he was hearing seemed to cause some sort of shift. He pulled back, his vision clearing. He was climbing once again up from the wrecked and reeking street, away from the dead and the living. As he pulled back something caught his eye. He wanted to stop but he couldn't. There, in a window overlooking the street.

An arm, a brown arm, it looked like that of a young boy. As he drew away he saw it throw down a bow while the other hand appeared and rubbed the left wrist hard. He didn't see why it mattered but somehow it did. He couldn't control what was happening. He was drawn up through the great crowded throng of birds still circling. Once again Pine Leaf was there, watching something go, something no mortal eye could see, watching until it was gone.

Tom drew in a great shuddering breath, which drew his head up from his chest. He leaned his head against the rough bark behind him as his mind whirled and swirled like the great cloud of birds.

'I will not tell you a third time. Put down the axe. If you do not I will kill you where you stand.'

The voice was familiar. Tom opened his eyes. The first thing he saw was Rick, standing with warriors around him but he had eyes only for Zala, who was standing still, his hands at his sides.

The veins were showing on Rick's face, which was purple with rage and desperation. Tom knew his friend was losing control of himself, beginning to go berserk, and he'd seen what happened then. He didn't want to see it again.

'You threaten me. You haven't even got a weapon. Stand back all of you.' Rick, his hands still held together by the rope, shook the axe at them. Beside him, Beth was trying to get her foot on Reese's scaramax which lay just out of reach. Reese was clearly trapped under the fallen horse although it was rolling to get up, hurting him more.

Tom was confused. So much time seemed to have passed, yet it can only have been moments since he lost consciousness. He watched in a daze as Zala's hand move slowly into his robe. With his back to Tom, Zala withdrew a small knife in a strange sheath. Moving slowly, Zala carefully let the sheath fall away. He seemed to be handling the blade very carefully. Tom looked at the blade and tried to focus his ragged mind.

'Rick, Rick! Put down the axe, it's fine, put it down. Pad and Grant – they did it.' Even to his own ears, Tom's voice sounded strange and far away but it had the reaction he wanted. His friend almost jumped and the look of madness in his eyes started to drain away.

Zala turned, his white robe swirling slowly round. He gazed down at Tom as if he were a vaguely interesting worm on the ground.

'So you have come back to join us. I wonder if your friend will thank you.' He leant down and picked up the sheath and very carefully put the blade back into it. It disappeared once more into his robes. 'The poison would have been excruciating agony but only for a short while before death released him. Perhaps the deaths of you three will be worse than that. I think Lord Gutta is not pleased with your treachery.'

He turned again as Rick threw down the axe. Everyone moved out the way as the horse scrambled to its feet, shook its head and moved off a few paces. Reese stood up, limping, his thin white face twisted in pain.

And then, with a screaming roar, Lord Gutta was in front of them.

'You lying scum! You betrayed us. They knew our plan. And you and your little friends must have told them! Or was it you, boy Reese, did you and your snivelling friend betray my army? Burgh's going to pay for this. And so are you.'

Lord Gutta's wide eyes were full of such an anger that nobody could meet his gaze. Reese hobbled round so the horse was between him and Lord Gutta. 'Not me my lord, not me. I've done everything you asked. And more. It must have been these three.'

Tom found himself staring at the tree roots but he could feel the red heat of Lord Gutta's rage focusing on him. He was aware the enemy soldiers were hanging back, not enjoying the spectacle because they knew they could be the object of his wrath at any moment.

In the background he could hear the chaotic retreat of Lord Gutta's left wing as it fell back from the gateway. It seemed completely silent by comparison where he stood. Then there was a sound. Lord Gutta drew his great sword.

Tom looked up then and his heart quailed. Lord Gutta stood before the three of them, his sword in his right hand. He looked huge, his great dark beard glistening with bits of bone, precious stones and who knew what. His long hair hung dankly round his shoulders, shot through with grey like his beard. His eyes were burning and freezing cold at the same time. Tom saw the muscles moving in his huge arms.

'Stand them together.' It was a voice that would allow no argument. Arms shoved the three upright and in line, their restraining ropes looping up to the big branch overhead. Tom found he had clasped his hands together although he didn't know why. He glanced sideways.

'Pad and Grant, they succeeded. We did it. Burgh was ready.' He said it quietly so he hoped only Beth and Rick would hear. They both nodded but they were watching the sword.

Lord Gutta's mouth worked as he twitched the sword in his meaty fist. 'Now you're going to see what happens to those who betray me. Now those stinking city rats are going to find out what happens when they defy me. When they send children to sneak around. Now!'

With a snarl he drew back his arm and swung the sword round in an unstoppable arc. There were three thuds.

Chapter 33

Lord Gutta stooped and picked up the ends of the ropes. The three stood frozen to the spot. The sound of the blade as it swung over their heads had sounded like their death song. Yet they lived. Lord Gutta jerked on the ropes until all three had their arms pulled out in front of them. Without a sound he turned and dragged them after him.

He towed them after him as if they were just goats on ropes. All three were shocked, but Tom worked out they were heading in the direction of the West Gate. He didn't think it was so they could be set free.

On the way they passed men falling back from the gateway. Many were injured, some still with arrows sticking out of arms or legs, others holding broken limbs. The limping, battered force stood aside for their lord, who churned through them without a glance.

The soldiers growled when they saw their enemy amongst them. Shocked and defeated, scared of falling back with their lord right there, they took it out on the three children they saw being pulled to their doom.

First it was just insults and jeers, then others started kicking and punching the three. Beth was hit as much as the others, if not more. None of them could defend themselves as they were dragged forward by the ropes round their wrists. A kick to the ribs made Tom gasp and he heard Beth yelp as a spear haft whacked into her back.

Someone kicked Rick's legs out from under him and he fell with a thud. Lord Gutta didn't even turn, he just kept dragging until Rick was upright and staggering again. Men laughed. Nobody dared kill them but the blows and insults rained down until all three were close to tears and they just wanted this nightmare journey to end.

Gradually the blows and jostling and shouting and insults slackened. Tom could smell smoke. He'd had his head down like the others but now he risked a glance. They were nearing the western gateway but from his angle he couldn't see through it, could only see the burned wreckage of the gates, where flames still smouldered.

The air stank of burning and blood. It was the sort of smell that made the hairs go up on your body, an old smell of fear. Behind him he heard horses whinnying and neighing wildly. He looked round. He might have guessed.

Reese was on his horse, just behind the shape of Zala on his black horse. They were the only horses Tom had seen since the army had attacked. He guessed they'd tethered them far from the battle. They wouldn't have been much use attacking walls he supposed.

He was yanked to a halt and staggered into Rick. They were close to the walls now, although not so close that they were within range of a spear. Tom wondered if a good bowman could reach the distance. He reckoned one could.

The three stood, beaten and abused, bleeding and bruised. Tom tried to stand up straight and control his ragged breathing. Right now they were still alive and closer to the city than they had been. Maybe they could run for it if there was enough of a distraction. The city seemed so close.

He could see people on the walls. In the ruined gateway, where some smoke still eddied around, he could see a shield wall. He knew that was Lord Gregory or Donald's doing. He smiled grimly. Lord Gutta's men had come up against that shield wall before. And been beaten by it.

Lord Gutta cast around. The track leading out from the city just had a few bushes either side so that nobody could creep up to the gates unseen. His eye took in the bodies lying everywhere, the burned out gateway with its fallen arch and the shield wall in the gateway. He didn't care about that, it just showed they weren't planning on attacking him. They were going to hide behind what was left of their walls. Let them.

He kept half an eye on the tops of the walls. There were quite a lot of townspeople up there but also some spearmen and archers. He guessed the archers wouldn't try and fire yet and he wanted the townspeople there. Frowning he looked around some more and then grunted with satisfaction.

Off to one side was a small stand of trees, and he could see one of the few trees there had a strong set of side branches spreading out. Perfect. His lips twisted but his rage was still burning harshly. They'd be closer than he wanted to be to any archers on the walls, but he'd also be close enough that he'd be able to hear the cries of the people.

He turned back to his men and issued his orders. Time to spread some suffering.

Chapter 34

'People of Burgh! You have defied me. Your rightful lord, not that snivelling Lord Mofty. Has he protected you? Has he kept your walls safe? He has not. And now I am here, Lord Gutta. I am lord of the stone city of Cinetti. I am lord of all the stone cities and I claim Burgh as my own.

'Do not be afraid. Just tell your soldiers to stand aside and let us in. We will bring order to the chaos you see around you.'

Lord Gutta paced up and down, making sure his sword was sheathed but his big shield was half in front of him. Two of his best men kept pace with him. Partly to make it look good, partly to leap forward with their shields if any archers took a shot.

Both men had noted a woman archer. She was slight, and looked old with silver hair, but they saw how she stayed opposite their lord as he paced to and fro, and they saw the bow with a black arrow in her hand. They'd heard about a woman like this and they watched her closely as she watched them.

The walls were filling with people, listening to his shouts, passing it on. He knew he could spread his poison this way. He wished he could get that traitor Reese back inside but for now that was impossible. All he wanted was to get his men inside, then they'd see how reasonable he could be. He drew in a huge breath.

'People of Burgh. I am being patient but my patience is being tested by your cowardly leaders. What say you, good people? Your leaders sent not men but children against me.'

He gestured behind him where Tom, Beth and Rick could be seen standing under the tree. The ropes around their wrists pulled up tight enough over the branch above them that they had to stand with their arms up straight, almost on tiptoe.

'And not only boys, but a girl. A girl! Against the might of Lord Gutta! You insult me!'

He paced some more, gripping his shield tight to regain control. 'But I am willing to believe it was your leaders who did this, not you, people of Burgh. So clear the entrance and let me in.

'If you do not then I will destroy your city utterly. You saw my fire wagon? You saw what just one can do. Imagine the destruction I can wreak with more of them. I will burn your city to the ground. If you do not clear the gateway and let me in.

'Do you need proof of my ability? If you do not accept defeat now then I will start by executing these spies. Their deaths, the deaths of children, of a girl, will be your fault. You will make me do this. Surrender your city now and you will spare these children a painful death.'

He heard the shouts and the counter-shouts on the walls and he smiled into his beard. Let the fear, the threats, do their work. He moved back. Just that bit more out of bowshot.

Miss Goode sighed and put her arrow back in the quiver, making sure she didn't touch the black point, which seemed to gleam.

'Why not? I had a clear shot.' She smiled her own smile. 'Reminds me of killing his brother.'

Donald scratched his grey beard irritably.

'I think reminding him right now of the deaths of his brothers would be a really bad idea, don't you? What with the cause of one of the deaths standing right behind him.'

Pad stood beside his father and nodded. 'I don't see how those three are going to survive though, do you? Lord Mofty's never going to surrender the city to save three kids, and only two of them are from Burgh.'

Studge leaned on the parapet and looked down at the shield wall in the ruined gateway. 'As head of the City Guard, Lord Mofty has entrusted in me the security of the city. And I'm not letting anyone in, not even if he does string up those three.

'And anyway,' he went on, 'that shield wall of yours looks way too thin to stop another attack. What are you going to do about it?'

Pad snorted. 'Gutta's men won't want to break through will they? They know what's on the other side, they won't want to get into that killing zone again will they? The wall is just to make a show and he knows it.'

Studge drew himself up because no boy talked to him like that, but the others just nodded, and then nodded again as Blakelock loped along the parapet behind the wall.

Townspeople either smiled at him or frowned at him, unsure how they should respond. Still, it looked like three young people were going to be executed with no risk to the people of Burgh, so they turned again to watch what was happening beyond the walls. Whatever happened wasn't down to them was it? It was down to the leaders, the lords and all the nobby people.

'I was saying,' said Studge, 'that there's no way Lord Mofty will allow anyone in or out of this city now. We've won the main battle, thanks to me and my men finally fighting the enemy actually out of the city limits, so that's that.'

He made a gesture of finality and looked straight ahead, which meant he didn't have to meet Blakelock's gaze. But he could still feel it, boring into the side of his head. He fiddled with the sidestraps of his very shiny helmet.

Blakelock nodded and gestured outwards. 'You'll certainly have a fine view of them murdering those three young people Studge.'

Studge stared at the three, who were straining to stand up straight. His face worked. 'Look, we're still in real danger, alright? He's right about those fire wagons, and the city wells won't keep the houses from burning.'

Pad shook his head and looked smug. 'That was the only one they've got left I reckon. Me and Grant, we burned the rest days ago. So you can thank us for that.' Grant, standing nearby, nodded, but he looked fearful for his friends.

Blakelock nodded his shaggy head. 'We have a lot to thank you for Pad. The city would have fallen without your information. You and Grant. And,' here he looked out again, 'those three. We owe them. We can't just stand here and watch them be killed.'

Studge actually laughed. 'So what do you suggest? Go and fight him for them? Or ask him politely to let them go because they're nice boys and girls really?'

'You were right first time,' said Blakelock. 'I fight him for them.'

He started to head down the nearest stone steps but Studge half blocked the way.

'As Guard Commander, I forbid you to leave the city. Lord Mofty was very insistent. You and everyone stays.'

Blakelock turned and stared at him, standing close. He didn't say anything. His gaze swept the small number of guards standing behind Studge. Not one met the stare of the former head of the City Guard. One guard turned away but then called back to the others.

'Old Gutta, he's coming forward again.'

'I have been patient. My patience is at an end. This is your doing, you had the chance to save them. I am a man of my word.'

Lord Gutta stalked back to the three, his words echoing off the walls. The trio stood in a line with a semicircle of soldiers behind them. He smiled nastily at the prisoners. 'Now, who shall I kill first? I know, I'll be kind. The girl goes first.'

He walked back under the branch where her rope, along with the other two, had been tied to another branch, too far away for any of the three to reach. He saw it looped up over the branch then down to her sore wrists. Beyond her he could see the people of the city craning for a better look. He really was beginning to enjoy his day.

He untied the rope and hauled hard with no warning. With a cry, Beth left the ground, all her weight being taken by her wrists. Instantly her arms felt like they were being dragged from their sockets.

Rick, standing next to her, shifted sideways as much as he could. Gasping with the strain, he managed to get his shoulder over enough that she managed to get one foot half onto it.

They balanced precariously, neither able to make a move. Rick's face was puce with the effort, while Beth's face was buried in her arms as they were dragged straight. She was gasping with pain but tried to remain silent.

One of the soldiers went forward to smash Rick out of the way with his spear. Lord Gutta gestured him back. He wanted to see how long they could last. Then he'd gut her. He kept his grip on the rope, his muscles bunched, too busy watching to tie the rope off for now.

Focusing on the struggling pair, he failed to see the shield wall part and a figure come loping across the open ground outside the stone walls. But others saw and the commotion broke Lord Gutta's concentration.

He looked up to see Blakelock very close indeed. In his hand he held a green bough of a tree. He gestured to it. 'I come in peace.' The tone was in complete contrast to the words, and the bough looked like a weapon.

Chapter 35

With a grunt, Lord Gutta let go of the rope and stepped forward, his eyes locking with those of the stranger. Off to one side Beth fell to the ground, landing with a thud. Her legs thrashed on the grassy soil as she struggled to get air into her throat and her shoulders down.

Before she could do much more than gasp, a soldier hauled on the rope, heaving her back upright. She tried to keep on her shaking legs. Her chest heaved with the pain and strain. Her arms and wrists were agony. Rick too was gasping, after his enormous effort at holding Beth up.

Tom, standing on the end, could only watch. Beth veered round, her hair plastered to her head with dust and sweat. Her green eyes were unfocused as her mouth fought for air. She focused at last on Tom and her breathing started to return to something less dangerous.

Tom saw she was done, her courage used up, her strength finished. Those final moments hanging the air as death approached had taken all she had to give. Tom felt terrible. He felt it was his fault, his fault she'd followed him and got into this mess. And he remembered the words.

And your friend will fall. It is a price that will be paid. But it is a death that will not be in vain. Choose her a spirit tree after death. If we survive.

He could barely meet her gaze. He realised he too was done in, with nothing left to fight with. He looked at Rick who was standing straight again, staring ahead, breathing deeply.

'That was amazing Rick, don't know how you did that. You saved Beth. Are you alright?'

Rick turned, his chest heaving, his face mottled. 'Oh you know, not bad. Glad Beth's dropped in to join us again. A bit hungry to be honest.'

Tom smiled and looked away so his friends wouldn't see the tears in his eyes.

Lord Gutta kept staring at the man ahead, expecting him to look away but he realised that was not going to happen. He bullied forward, and took in the wild hair and beard, the lack of clothing apart from some breeches and the folded and tanned old skin. He snorted and turned away.

'I don't deal with madmen and vagrants.'

'But you will deal with me, Lord Gutta.'

Lord Gutta wheeled back. Beside him Zala started to pay close attention. He'd been distracted badly by Beth dangling from the rope but now he looked and now he saw.

Reese too, sitting his horse nearby, had been engrossed in watching Beth as she thrashed in the air, and only now he saw who was among them. He tried to make the horse go backwards but lacked the skill. He sat very quietly.

Lord Gutta looked the man up and down. 'And who are you to address me?'

'My name is Blakelock and I represent the city.'

Lord Gutta sneered. 'I can see that. Mad, dishevelled and coming to beg. Well get your begging done and begone.'

'I challenge you to single combat, man to man.' It was said in such a matter of fact way that Lord Gutta didn't get his meaning for a moment. Then he roared with laughter, rudely. He turned to the large number of men watching, and laughed again.

Taking their cue, some laughed. But some had seen this man fighting in the city. A few unlucky ones had also seen him fighting in front of Frith a while ago. They didn't laugh.

'And why should I fight you, mad old man?'

'Because if you win then the city is yours. We fight for the city. And if you lose, your army will retreat out of the forest. And if you lose the three here will be safe. But kill me and all the city is yours.'

Zala glided forward and said something quietly to his lord. Gutta looked again. This time he saw the huge sword hanging from the thick, worn belt. It had no adornments on the pommel like a rich man's would, but it looked heavily used, like a tool used by a craftsman. He saw the muscle beneath the wrinkled, weathered skin. Then he looked into the man's eyes again.

He laughed again, abruptly. 'I am going to take this city whether I kill you or not.'

'You're going to take this city? I think not. You have no more fire wagons, this we know. Do you want to attack the West Gate again? Be my guest. You can probably force the shield wall back and then you'll be in the killing ground again. We've done the same thing at the East Gate but feel free to try.

'Perhaps you think a siege will work. Well, we have brought in all the farmers and all their crops and animals. We have our own well and stream. You and your many men can try to live off the land here if you wish – although I don't think you will find the forest very hospitable.

'And anything you do will cost you a lot of men, men you can't afford to lose. No, Lord Gutta, your best chance is to fight and kill me. I am Lord Blakelock.'

Lord Gutta glowered at the man. 'I have more than enough men to spend. I can take this city whenever I wish. I have no need to kill you, other than for sport, so begone.'

His men looked at each other. Nobody was foolish enough to say anything, but everyone could feel the restless mood that swept through the men within earshot. Blakelock noticed it and his eyes swept the men, the enemy army. Tom, watching him, saw him nod to someone, almost as an equal. Looking round, he saw it was Qut, who was standing close. His shield arm was in a sling and looked battered and broken. He was clearly in pain but he nodded back. Tom could guess how he'd got a broken arm.

He caught Beth's eye and nodded his head in Qut's direction. She looked and Qut caught her glance. His face was pale with pain but he attempted a small grimace and a nod. She looked like death but actually smiled at him.

She turned and Tom saw her steady herself on her feet, the noose still tight about her raw wrists. Blakelock was focusing back on Lord Gutta but it was obvious he wasn't going to rise to the bait. Blakelock was at a loss although he didn't show it. Despite his words he wasn't sure they could survive another major attack. And there hadn't been time to prepare the East Gate. He had to somehow bring Lord Gutta to combat.

Tom saw Beth take a deep wavering breath. 'If Lord Gutta is too cowardly to fight the great warrior Blakelock then I will fight Lord Gutta.'

Her girlish voice had a quaver in it partly due to fear, partly due to exhaustion and pain. But it had a huge reaction. A lot of men laughed, but some looked at her with admiration. They hated having women in a battle, and feared being killed by one, but this girl had courage.

They admired her, and wanted to see her fight Lord Gutta so she could die like a warrior instead of strung up like a sack of dirt. Qut was shouting something but the other sounds drowned out his voice.

Lord Gutta glanced at her. Blakelock saw that he was tempted to take up her challenge.

'What!' he roared, 'You'd fight a girl but not me? What sort of warrior are you?'

Lord Gutta ignored him, and continued to stare at the girl, who stared back.

Tom was so astonished he couldn't move. Where had that burst of courage come from? His admiration for Beth rose to new heights but he knew he couldn't stand there and let that happen. Or was that what the forest had been saying, was this the good death it had meant?

As he tried to think clearly he was aware that Rick was stirring beside him. Oh no, not Rick, don't say anything please.

Rick shouted out Lord Gutta's name and the great hooded gaze swept from Beth to him. 'You can't fight a girl Lord Gutta. Not even your men would stand for that. So fight me instead. You'll want to fight me.'

No Rick, shut up. I know what you're going to say next and it will be the death of you my friend.

Rick drew a shaky breath. 'You'll want to fight me because it was me who...' The rest of what he was going to say was cut off. Tom's leg had scythed into the back of Rick's knees, making him sag so that the rope dug into his wrists. Rick gasped in pain.

Tom felt like he had no choice, no choice at all. This was his doing. He looked up at the tree above him, not seeing the rope, but seeing the tree. He nodded. As Rick staggered to get his feet under him and some pressure off his wrists, Tom spoke up.

'No, Lord Gutta, you can't fight a girl, and you can't fight my friend, who hasn't passed the manhood ceremony so he's still a boy. But I passed the manhood ceremony so you can fight me.'

The men were amused, watching these three youngsters scrabble to get themselves spitted on their lord's long sword. They were aware he was enjoying it too, so they relaxed and watched the entertainment.

Lord Gutta was almost smiling. 'So I can kill you boy, can I? Perhaps I will.'

Blakelock was furious, but Tom steadied himself and said what he knew he had to say. He knew it was his death sentence.

'You'll fight me, Lord Gutta, because it was me who fought your brother. Remember one brother was killed by a woman? Well the other one, Enver I think his name was, he attacked me. I remember the feeling as my blade tore into him. I remember the noise he made. Squealing like a girl. His death was my doing. I enjoyed it.'

Rick and Beth stared at him as if he was mad but Lord Gutta stared at him with a great flaming rage. He drew his sword and stepped forward, his eyes boring into Tom. Tom tried to step back but he was caught like an animal in a trap.

'No!' Blakelock roared and drew his great sword, but at once dozens of men levelled spears and swords at him. Lord Gutta kept going, bringing his sword back.

A white-gloved hand gripped his arm surprisingly forcefully. Snarling, he whirled round.

'My lord, if you kill him now you achieve nothing but his death. But if you kill him in single combat then you will achieve what we want, what you want, you will win the city.'

'You cannot fight the boy.' Blakelock's furious shout was ignored. Lord Gutta stared into the white cowl.

He turned and strode a few paces towards the city so everyone on the walls would hear as well as his own men.

'I, Lord Gutta, have been challenged to single combat by one of your citizens. He is a man, or so he claims. I accept. The prize when I win is that I will take the city. You will surrender the city to me with no further bloodshed.'

'Or,' he muttered quietly to Zala, 'no more bloodshed until I get through the gates.'

On the walls there was shouting and movement. Many more people were coming to watch. But others were rushing away, going back to their homes to get their families and treasures, ready to flee out of the East Gate and take their chances. Because the boy had no chance.

Chapter 36

'I should kill him now.'

'No!' Donald put a restraining hand on Miss Goode's shoulder until she lowered her bow. She kept the arrow tip away from the others. 'You fire an arrow into him, it's the same as firing arrows into the rest of them. They'd be dead in moments, all of them, including Blakelock.'

'I can't believe this.' Grant put his head in his hands, his normally shiny black skin looking grey with the fear and concern he felt for his friends. 'There must be something we can do.'

Pad shrugged. 'There's nothing. We'll just have to see what happens. As a Watcher, I'm going to watch. See how Lord Gutta fights. Get as much information about him as possible.'

Donald gave him a look that wasn't entirely full of fatherly love. His sour expression wasn't helped by the view along the city wall. More and more people had come to gawp, as if they hadn't grasped what was at stake. He saw people smiling and laughing. It made him long for the peace of the forest.

He caught sight of one face full of horror and despair. He recognised Abi in the distance, but she was only looking at the scene beyond the walls. He looked away.

'You know,' he said to anyone listening, 'we have no idea what is going to happen. And if there was one man I'd want with Tom right now it would be Blakelock.' But he didn't look very cheered by the thought.

Blakelock sheathed his sword. Most of the men around him did too. Some didn't. He glared at them then marched over to Tom. They followed. Tom didn't look good to him.

Tom was hungry, thirsty and tired since he hadn't slept properly for days and he liked his sleep. He was also battered and bruised from the beating he'd received on the way to the western gate.

Qut leaned past Blakelock with a grunt, and his dagger sliced through the rope around Tom's wrists. Blakelock saw the raw skin all around the wrists and winced. He took in the desperate look in the youngster's eyes. He wondered what he could say to make that look go away.

Qut turned to his leader. 'My lord, what about weapons?'

Lord Gutta looked irritated. 'My sword and shield of course.'

'And the boy?'

'Whatever he can handle. Why doesn't he try and use the vagrant's sword?'

That got a laugh. Tom shook his head. 'I want my axe and scaramax.'

Lord Gutta shrugged. 'Find him an axe and a blade then.'

'No.' Tom knew he could demand this. 'My axe, my scaramax.'

Lord Gutta waved a hand. Tom turned to Blakelock. 'Reese has them.'

'Reese? Ah yes, I'd forgotten about him.' Blakelock turned and spotted Reese on his horse, which still wouldn't go backwards. He was soon glaring up at him. Reese tried to return the challenge in those blue eyes but failed, not helped by Qut and other warriors also joining Blakelock.

'Tom wants his weapons. Give them to me. And you and I will meet again Reese.'

He held out his hand. Out of options, Reese drew the scaramax and dropped it on the ground. He pulled the axe out and hesitated as Blakelock stood there with his hand out. Reese flipped the axe towards him so he'd have to jump out of the way.

Blakelock's hand moved and it held the axe. He stood for a moment staring up. Reese licked his lips then bit them. Qut leant down with a grunt and picked up the blade, handing it to Blakelock.

'This is a good axe Tom. I feel Mister Weyland's skill in this.' Blakelock swung the axe then handed it to Tom, who nodded. 'It's my manhood axe. I earned this axe the hard way.' His lips twisted. 'Only I'm not sure how long I'm going to be a man for.'

His attempt at humour failed. Blakelock actually kneeled in front of him, putting the axe and blade either side of Tom's belt. He looked up at the troubled face.

'Lord Gutta is huge. His sword is long so he has a very long reach. If he catches you with that sword just once you'll be dead. And remember his shield, that too is a weapon as well as a defence against your weapons. There's no point in giving you a shield – one hit from his sword and you'd have a broken shield arm.

'He's wearing that chainmail tunic and you won't be able to penetrate that. He has armour in his boots and gloves and he'll probably wear a helmet. He's almost impervious to your blows.'

Tom laughed nervously. 'Thank you Blakelock, you're making me feel great.'

Blakelock smiled. 'Now look at it another way. He's huge, which means he's slow. You're faster, much faster. And he's fat, he's not in great condition, which means he'll tire quickly. Keep moving, keep out of his way and don't ever try to block that sword swing. Wait until he tires then try something. Don't throw your axe early because he'll use his shield and then you're down to just a short blade. And he's very angry, and that will lead him to be too eager, and he underestimates you. He'll make mistakes. Make the most of them.

'There are two places you can be. Outside his reach or inside his guard. Get caught in the middle and it's all over. You can do this Tom, you've fought before with great skill and courage. You helped kill one of his brothers remember, you can do it again.'

Blakelock stood up. He took off his fingerless leather gloves. Tom looked at the grubby, stained gloves. 'Are those for me? They'll be too big.'

They were too big but they were also sticky. Blakelock nodded as Tom noticed. 'Sticky with the blood of my enemies. Their deaths will help you.'

Tom tried a few swings with his weapons and was heartened at how much safer they felt in his grip. And it felt like a bit of the great warrior's grim courage was in his hands now. He grinned his thanks.

He looked up as Blakelock put his fist to his chest, then moved it towards Tom. The wild warrior nodded and moved away. The enemy soldiers had formed a semicircle so that they were behind him, with the city folk watching from the front. They had a great view he thought.

He glanced round to see where Rick and Beth were and saw them guarded by Reese and Zala among others. At least the ropes had been taken from their wrists. He tried to smile at them. Lord Gutta charged.

Chapter 37

Lord Gutta came fast, his long sword whirling round for a forehand strike that would cut Tom in half. Tom froze. His enemy looked terrifying huge and powerful and the speed of his attack caught Tom totally off guard. He wasn't ready.

At the last moment he ducked instinctively and he heard the blade swish just above his blonde hair. He heard himself cry out with shock. Still crouched, Tom's mind started to work, but it seemed so slowly.

He threw himself backwards. The backswing. He worked out just in time it would be coming. The blade scythed past right in front of Tom's eyes as he fell backwards.

Sprawled on his back, he saw Lord Gutta spin his sword up for a great downward strike. Here it came, the blade glinting briefly against the late sun. Tom rolled sideways, using his legs for leverage. He heard the blade thud horribly into the ground right by his back. He kept rolling.

He knew he was moments from death and the fear helped him roll to his feet and keep going. Again the sideswing missed, but it didn't miss his back by much. Tom turned. Lord Gutta was completely silent. Intent. It was more unnerving than him shouting. His eyes told Tom he wanted him dead. No games, no bluffs, he wanted him cut into pieces quickly. He charged again.

Tom ran. He heard laughter but he didn't care. There was nowhere to run to. The curve of soldiers weren't going to let him through. They grinned at him as he got close. He hated them for that. He turned as Lord Gutta charged in. Tom backed away and held up his scaramax. His enemy saw the defence and whirled a great backhand swing, coming in from Tom's right side, away from the small blade.

Lord Gutta adjusted the blow as his enemy kept backing away. He lunged forward another pace and then the boy simply ducked, dragging his weapons down with him. Lord Gutta's mortal blow swung in, and at the last moment he realised he was going to hit his own men.

With a hoarse cry, one soldier took the brunt of the blow, but there was enough force for it to injure two more. In the chaos Tom rolled forward and launched a backswing of his own with the axe, aiming for Lord Gutta's right leg.

The blade just caught the hem of the great chainmail but it still had enough force to make the man stagger and half fall into more of his own men. Tom leapt up, breathing hard. Lord Gutta was still tangled up with his men, some of whom were injured and screaming. Lord Gutta turned his head and stared at Tom, murder in his face.

The warlord was off balance and hurt, but the sheer deadly, hate-filled menace of the man made Tom hesitate. He should attack, he knew, but it was too terrifying. He hesitated again and then Lord Gutta was upright, shield across his body, sword ready to strike.

Tom noticed his enemy was breathing hard now, and he could see sweat running down from under the metal helmet. Some of Blakelock's advice came back to him. But what could he do, even if his enemy was tiring? He felt too weak and small against the vast, armoured bulk in front of him.

He ran, again. He didn't see what else he could do. And for how long could he evade those great swings? From the walls there were shouts and screams of encouragement, but he didn't hear them, same as he didn't hear the rough shouts of Lord Gutta's men.

He could hear his own breathing, ragged and wild, as he ran and ducked and dodged. He could see that Lord Gutta was becoming increasingly furious and frustrated, his swings wilder and more violent. But Tom couldn't land a blow on him.

Tom watched his enemy as his mind whirred. What else had Blakelock said? He couldn't remember. I'm faster, keep moving, what else? Tom racked his brains as he dodged another swing and then leapt nimbly aside as the sword swing turned into a dangerous spitting thrust.

He backed away as Lord Gutta drew in a great heaving breath and readjusted his sword and shield. What else? Speed, movement. The words reminded him of what the forest had said. At least, Tom thought it was the forest although in his mind the words always came from his great oak, his spirit tree by Frith.

Tom groped a sore hand up to his throat. Gripping his scaramax tight, he felt the rough piece of wood that had somehow survived on its cord round his neck. Then he remembered.

We will help where we can but we can only do that if you bring him to us, we can not go to him in time.

Tom risked a glance round. They'd been fighting on the ground that was kept deliberately clear outside the city walls. But at the end of the curve of enemy warriors hemming him in were the trees. He heard Lord Gutta's feet thudding on the earth. He ran.

It was like a nightmare, where you run but you run so slowly. He was sure Lord Gutta was catching him, but he didn't dare look round as he ran across the rough ground. He had almost reached the oak he'd been strung up under. His feet slipped on the roots, which spread out even further than the crown of the tree. He turned, breathing hard.

The wild swinging downstroke was already on its way. With a gasp Tom threw himself to one side. The sword thudded into a root and Lord Gutta snarled in annoyance as he had to tug hard to release it. Tom was already on his feet and saw the moment.

He darted forward, fearful of being so close. He came in on Lord Gutta's right side, away from the shield. But he was too late. Lord Gutta's great muscular arm had hauled the sword free. Crouching, Lord Gutta backswung the sword up as Tom ran in, his scaramax strike turning from a stab at Lord Gutta's neck to a desperate attempt at a parry.

The huge sword hit Tom's stocky blade and smashed it out of Tom's numbed hand. Tom winced in pain as he started to bring his axe up. He tried to keep an eye on the sword arm as he knew it would come swinging back again.

So he didn't see the shield. The heavy wood and metal hit Tom with huge force as Lord Gutta swung it across his body and into the hated boy.

Tom reeled backwards, too stunned to think. He cracked into the trunk of the oak and he felt the light turning to dark. His head turned upwards and he saw the branches above him, the leaves not moving. He knew he had to bring his axe up, but it was too heavy.

A long way away he heard a great roar as the enemy watched their lord deliver the killing blow.

Tom sagged against the trunk, his head lolling back, neck exposed, legs shaking. Lord Gutta's leg ached from the axe blow, but it was no worse than that. He stepped in and swung his sword at Tom's extended neck.

Tom's head slid sideways and the sooty scar he'd received when he fell into the hollowed-out heart of his spirit tree scraped against the bark. His feet scrabbled for balance on the roots that seemed to twist beneath his boots. His feet flew out from under him and he fell with a jolt onto his backside.

He heard a great thud as the sword stroke slammed into the oak's trunk just above his head, severing some of his blonde hair. Somewhere he heard a hollow, deep groan. The jolt seemed to clear Tom's mind. He heard Lord Gutta roar in frustration and rage. Tom saw him aim a kick, but he was already moving.

Still slumped at the foot of the tree, he swung a backhanded strike with the axe as Lord Gutta's great boot came for his head. The axe head smashed into the armoured leather boot and stopped the leg in its swing. Tom heard the yelp of pain but he was moving now, rolling forward and swinging another backhanded blow with the axe.

Lord Gutta, his face screwed up, had his hand on the sword hilt and was trying to pull it from the tree. The armour in his boot had stopped his leg from breaking, but he was in considerable pain. He saw the axe head arcing in. Guessing Tom was aiming for his hands, he made a snap decision and let go of the sword, stumbling back a pace.

But Tom was aiming for the sword itself. He'd hefted the axe round so the thick back of the axe head slammed into the sword blade, driving it deeper into the trunk. Then he was rolling forward, rolling twice and then he was up and turned.

Lord Gutta had limped forward and was pulling hard on the sword. Tom really looked at his enemy. Lord Gutta was bent slightly, his right side to Tom as he used his force to pull out the blade. He was focused down on the sword. He was armoured everywhere but Tom saw the muscles straining in his right arm.

The warlord's vanity had left the arms clear of the protective chainmail or armour. Without further thought, Tom drew back the axe and threw. As soon as it left his hand he knew it was good.

The heavy axehead slammed into the straining bicep with a hideous thwack. Lord Gutta reared up. He didn't make a sound but his mouth was a circle of agony and shock. The blade had crushed right through to the bone. He seemed to just turn slightly on the spot, his right arm by his side, blood coursing down. He tried to let go of his shield to draw his left hand up to the wound.

But his eyes refocused on Tom, who saw the vengeance clear in them. Tom looked around for his blade but couldn't see it on the churned up ground. He looked forward. There was only one weapon left.

He ran straight towards Lord Gutta. The warlord swung his only weapon, his heavy shield, aiming to smash the boy to the ground where he could crush him to pulp. But Tom just skidded into a roll and was under the shield as it whumped over his rolling body. Panting, he took another pace and got his hands on the sword grip.

The rough hilt was still warm. Tom pulled with all his might. The blade came out of the oak like it had been released. Almost off-balance, Tom kept the momentum going, swinging the heavy blade round and up in a huge arc with all his remaining strength.

There was a hollow thud as Lord Gutta's head hit one of the roots. A moment later the rest of his body thundered into the ground. There was silence.

Tom stood, his laboured breathing loud to him. He kept the sword tight in his hands. He couldn't yet believe Lord Gutta wasn't going to rise with a roar and charge at him. Tom could still see that last look on his enemy's face as the blade smacked into his neck. Tom looked away at the memory, the sword tip drooping to the ground. He didn't know what to do.

Nor did the remnants of Lord Gutta's army. Lord Gutta was dead. It had been their lord who had driven them on, forcing them to do his will. His reign of terror had brought together different clans and tribes and driven them into a dark and scary forest to attack a city most didn't know was even there.

And now he was dead, very obviously dead. They wavered, looking to each other, looking for leadership. But Zala, the power behind the throne, stood there unmoving, the cowl facing his fallen lord.

It was Blakelock who broke the silence. He drew his heavy sword and held it aloft in both hands. He turned not towards the enemy but towards the city. He gave a great cry, one that started deep and guttural and ended high and piercing. It wasn't a sound a mortal would make and it scared the men.

Blakelock swung his sword and turned to face the enemy army ranged against him.

'Flee!' The roar reached men standing far away. 'Flee for your lives! Your lord is dead. It is done. Flee the forest, flee to your homes, flee! Because vengeance is here.'

Behind him the dark cloud that had been swirling over the city took shape and came swooping over the walls, the wings a great whirring that all men heard. Harsh caws and cries from the crows and their kind filled the ears of the men. The enemy turned, thinking only of saving themselves now.

Chapter 38

'No! Stop you scum. We still outnumber them. We can beat them. Kill the people in our grasp then we take vengeance on the city. The city must fall!' Reese was the only one mounted on a horse and he rode forward, screaming at the men. He drew his sword and aimed it at the city. 'Vengeance! Vengeance! Death to Burgh!'

But he wasn't Lord Gutta. He wasn't one of them. A few hesitated and looked to Zala, but he stood unmoving.

The scold of jays, the mischief of jackdaws, the conspiracy of ravens – and the murder of crows tore into the men.

One face seemed to draw most of the crows. Reese shrieked and waved his sword wildly at the attacking cloud but soon dropped the weapon and tried to protect his eyes and his face from the avenging birds. His horse, terrified by the onslaught, turned and bolted. Reese somehow clung on as the horse careered through the men.

It was too much for the beaten army. They turned and started to run. Not one wasn't thinking how far away the horses were, or how far it was through the dank forest before they would see far horizons again. Flapping their arms above their heads to keep the unnerving birds away, they became not an army but a ragged crowd of desperate men.

As the army broke up Tom just stood, not seeing, not hearing, seeing only the drops of blood that dripped off the blade and fell into the soil. He felt nothing.

Rick and Beth could hardly believe it. Relief made them laugh and hug each other awkwardly. They were oblivious of the men still near, the armed enemy. But nobody paid them any attention. Rick looked to where Reese was, but he was already out of sight. He picked up a sword and waved it exultantly in both hands. 'Victory! Victory!'

He threatened a few stragglers but they ran. And then Zala reacted. There was one horse still there near the trees and he moved towards it. His cowl turned left and he saw Rick jumping with excitement, with Beth off to his left, crouched now in reaction to what had happened. Tom stood not far, oblivious.

Without breaking his stride, his hand flew to his robes and emerged with a sheathed knife. He dropped the sheath.

The shield wall in the gateway erupted outwards. Lord Gregory led his men in a wedge straight towards Blakelock and the others. They killed anyone who got in their way.

Behind them the City Guard emerged on their horses. They looked like they were on parade. They turned as they did in exercises and then charged into the flank of the retreating enemy. It wasn't a fight, it was a massacre. Every member of the guard made sure he returned from the fray with a bloody sword. It wasn't difficult.

Rick was still jumping and shouting and waving his sword. Zala, shifting fast, saw a target. He was moving and he had to throw it with the handle in his hand not the blade. But it was a big target.

Rick had his back to Zala, watching the retreating army, but Beth, slumping down, saw the white of the robes and saw the throw. Without thinking, she leapt forward, driving up from her crouch behind Rick. She threw her arms out to push him but something slammed into her shoulder.

It knocked her down behind Rick, who was still fixated on the fleeing enemy, shouting and jumping with joy. The blade really hurt. She went to get up, knowing she'd been hit but knowing it hadn't gone that far into her. But she couldn't seem to move. She tried to call out but her voice wouldn't work. She felt a terrible chill. Desperate, she tried to get Rick's attention. She lay back, the knife sticking out of her shoulder. Rick was laughing.

Something about Zala's movements finally caught Tom's attention. He saw him jump on the horse and start to move away. Tom looked for his axe but he had only the great sword in his hands. He didn't want to get his axe. He watched Zala go, unable to stop him. The fleeing rider soon overtook the men and was gone. Virtually everyone who was living had fled.

Tom looked round at Rick, dancing and capering with glee. He frowned. He dropped the sword. He ran. Rick saw him running and saw the expression on his face. He stopped shouting and dancing and took a step back, unnerved. He fell over something.

'Beth!' Rick looked in horror at why he had tripped.

'Beth!' Tom knelt beside her. He looked up as the late sun cast shadows over him. It was the forest men, looking fierce and cautious. Lord Gregory looked down at Tom.

'Mister Haywood, you have saved the city. More importantly, you have saved the forest. Come now, come with us. I have to say Tom, you're the hero and I salute you.'

Tom looked down again. 'Careful!' Rick had pulled the short blade from Beth's shoulder. 'Put the blade down, it's poisoned.'

Rick dropped it with a look of alarm and his face crumpled.

'Zala! It must have been Zala. Why would he want to kill Beth? Why did he choose her? I wish I'd killed him.'

Casting around, Tom found an enemy helmet. A bit of the enemy was still inside but Tom just grimaced and dropped the knife carefully into it.

He looked up into the alarmed face of Lord Gregory. 'It's Beth, she's been hit with a poisoned blade. I'm sorry, but I think she's going to die.' Lord Gregory looked troubled at the threat to one of his own. He turned to his men.

'Pick her up, carry her to the city. We need to find someone who might know how to treat her.'

Rick shook his head. 'Nobody touch her. I'll carry her. Only me.' He lifted her with a grunt onto his shoulder and set off as quickly as he could for the city, protected by some of the foresters, who never let their guard down.

Tom followed, protected by more men and Lord Gregory himself. He watched Beth's head and arms lolling lifelessly down Rick's straining back. Ahead, coming out of the ruined gateway, he could see familiar faces, Pad, Grant, Donald and others, although not the one he most wanted to see. They were smiling but he looked away.

It was his victory, his big moment, but it tasted like dirt and ash in his mouth. He knew there was only one person who stood even a chance of saving Beth. Although he was scared of her, and for good reason, Tom knew he had to find Miss Goode. And, remembering what the forest had said, he knew it would all be in vain.

Chapter 39

The stonemasons waved as he walked down West Street. Tom waved back self-consciously. Everyone treating him like a hero was already wearing off. He saw how they were first working to repair the West Gate, to make the city secure. Then they'd have to start the long job of rebuilding the houses along West Street that had been turned into fortresses. He'd already heard people complaining that it wasn't being done fast enough, and had it really been necessary in the first place.

He sighed and wandered out through what was still a ruined gateway. It felt good to be out from all that heavy stone. He wondered how he'd stood it all those years, all that weight above you as you slept, the thick walls shutting you off from the trees and the air outside. Now he found it oppressive and longed to sleep in a room that swayed gently and lived and breathed.

His wandering steps took him towards the small stand of trees to one side of the main track out of Burgh. With summer wearing on, the land and the trees were looking more worn now, more faded, less full of life.

He came to the oak that he remembered so well. He hesitated. He looked down to one side. There. The head had landed there. And there. The body had landed there.

Donald had warned him after what was already being called the Battle of Burgh that it would happen but Tom hadn't really believed him. But in the few nights since the battle he'd seen Lord Gutta's face in his nightmares every night. It looked like the bruises would fade before the nightmares.

Most of the debris and bodies had been hauled away but the grass was flattened and gouged, and there were stains sinking into the ground all over. The air smelt of metal and there were a lot of flies. And birds.

Tom was staring at the trunk of the oak but he registered that there seemed to be a lot of birds around, many of them cawing aggressively. He knelt by the trunk and ran his hand over the long cut in the tree's trunk. It had penetrated the bark into the inner layers and Tom knew this posed a risk for the tree as it would take ages for it to grow a protective layer over the wound.

He knew there was nothing he could do, but he ran his hands back and forth over the cut like it would help. He leant his head against the trunk, his scar touching the rough bark. His other hand came up to touch the rough piece of wood at his neck. He came up off his knee, turning fast and the axe was in his hand.

'Oh, sorry.' He laughed. 'You gave me a fright.'

Abi nodded and let out her breath. 'Sorry. Good thing you didn't give me a fright.' She laughed but kept her hand at her throat. She looked at his hand.

'Is that the axe…the axe you used. To fight him?'

Tom hefted it in his hand and slid it back in his belt. He nodded. In between everything else over the last few days he'd cleaned and cleaned the axe. It was his manhood axe, a battle axe and now it was a blood axe, an axe that had tasted an enemy's blood, and it was all the more valuable to the owner because of it. But Tom still didn't like having it in his hand right now.

Abi swayed slightly, looking clean and elegant and lovely in a long white dress that perfectly offset her darker skin and dark eyes. Tom wasn't looking, he was seeing something she couldn't see. Something she didn't want to see.

'So,' she said teasingly, 'you're talking to the tree?'

Again he nodded, not meeting her eye. How changed he was, how sad he seemed. Although he did manage a small smile. Abi noticed how his blonde hair was so long now it fell over his face and largely hid that strange scar on his temple.

'I've just been to see Beth.' Ah, that got his attention.

'Beth? How is she? I haven't been since yesterday.' Tom pushed his hair back from his face. That didn't make sense to him. How come she was still alive? The forest told him she'd be dead. Every day she got better his hopes rose higher.

Abi smiled slightly. 'She seems well. Rick was with her. He's still so furious that Zala tried to kill her rather than anyone else – like him. Or you.'

Tom nodded. 'Does Beth have any idea why?'

Abi shook her head. 'She says not. She says it was just luck. But she smiles when she says it.'

Tom wondered what that last sentence meant but he could never fathom girls.

'Rick says that he and Beth both decided to follow you rather than stay with Pad and Grant. She must have had a lot of faith in you.'

Tom smiled. 'I don't know why.'

'And you must have spent a lot of time together out there in the forest.'

Tom thought he heard another question there but he didn't know what it was. He hesitated.

'Yes, of course. Every day, every night, obviously.'

So that wasn't the right answer or it was to a different question. He felt he was under attack but couldn't see it coming. He'd have been much happier if she'd drawn an axe and attacked him. He thought fast.

'The three of us. And Rick's been with her all the time since he brought her in. He's spending all his time with her.'

He sensed that was a better answer. Relieved, he carried on. 'You know Miss Goode, she's really scary. But as soon as she saw Beth she found a room for us to lay her in. She knows a lot about poisons. Then I showed her the knife.'

He laughed. 'Well, I showed her the knife in the enemy helmet. There was still a bit of the bloke's head in there as well. She took a look and said "Are you expecting me to make him better?"'

Abi laughed and held out her hands. Tom took hers and winced as her fingers hit the chafed skin round his wrists. He shifted position and she winced too. Puzzled, Tom looked down. The smile left his face and he just stared.

'It was you!' He looked up, his expression hard to read. 'You fired that bow.' It came out like an accusation.

Abi drew away. 'What are you talking about? How do you know?' She looked confused, so did Tom. He gazed at her with his mouth open.

'You were actually there. In West Street. You fired a bow. You could have been killed. What were you doing?' Tom put his hands to his head.

Abi looked rebellious. 'All the forest people, they were working so hard to defend the city. And the guard were stomping about the place looking all tough but not doing much. And all the neighbours, everyone, they didn't lift a finger, like they expected someone else to protect them. I knew if the enemy broke in we'd all be dead. So I wanted to help.

'And that nice man showed me how to use a bow. A bit.'

'What nice man?'

'An old man, got a big grey beard and seemed to be really important. Donald. He knew you.'

'Donald? Ha, I'll be having words with him.'

'Why?'

'Well, because…because you could have been killed.'

'If they'd broken in I would have been killed. So I helped. Or do I have to ask you before I do anything? Oh no, I couldn't could I, because you were running around the forest with Beth.'

Tom took her unresisting hands again. He looked at her and she hoped for some reassurance. She saw him form a question.

'So did you hit anyone?'

She looked away and eventually nodded. 'It's silly. It's like I hadn't really thought. I learned how to fire it – I've got a lot stronger – and then I fired an arrow at this man running and shouting horrible things. It wasn't a huge bow, I can't draw those. But I hit him.'

She tried to pull away but Tom kept hold of her hands. 'When he was on the ground I saw he wasn't much older than me. He died. It took ages for him to die, lying there, with men running past him, and nobody helping. He was screaming. Then he was sobbing. And then he died.'

She looked down with tears in her eyes. Tom managed to bite back the question about whether she'd hit any more. He looked at her wrist and smiled.

'And you didn't have a leather cuff on your left wrist did you?'

She shook her head. 'I forgot. The bowstring hit it.'

'Really stings doesn't it?'

This time she laughed. 'It really hurt!'

Tom dropped her hands and they both rubbed their wrists and smiled. Abi was about to ask how he knew. Tom began to reconsider everything he'd thought about Abi. Pondering, he turned to head back to the city but a magpie flew almost into his face, making a guttural, aggressive noise.

Looking away from Abi, it struck Tom once again how many birds there seemed to be here, it was like that great cloud that had attacked from the city was mostly still here. Puzzled, he looked around more carefully.

Then he knew.

Choose her a spirit tree after death.

'Oh no. Abi, wait here.' Tom ran.

He approached the gaggle of birds on the ground carefully. Some swirled up at his approach but he kept his face up as they circled him, swooping dangerously close. Then a huge crow slid past his face. He heard the cawing and the birds dropped away.

Tom turned his head and made sure the bird saw him clearly. He guessed it was Rustle, who was one of the most important crows after Pine Leaf. He looked ahead and saw a bundle of things on the ground.

The birds let him walk up and kneel down. It was a crow. It was mostly covered in things. Tom moved a metal pin, a bit of broken leather strap, a pretty stone and some twigs and grass stalks out of the way. But he knew who he'd find.

Pine Leaf looked so fragile in death. One of Reese's wild swings had caught her as she tried to stop him gathering the troops or getting away. Tom stroked her feathers and thought of all the miles she'd flown, watching over him and Frith. A small scream made him whirl round.

'Stand still, stand still. I'm on my way.'

He ran to Abi, who was at the centre of a storm of birds. She was bent down with her hands over her face. He stood beside her, his face raised, and put an arm round her. 'She's with me! She's with me!'

With the beaks and claws still whirling close, Tom leant in to Abi. 'Put your face up, put your face up, they have to see you, to remember you.'

Completely thrown, but trusting this confident Tom, Abi stood up and gazed fearfully at the sky. The birds, led by the big crow, whirled away but they didn't go far.

'They'll remember you now. You'll be safe, they'll protect you.'

Abi nodded. It wasn't being the morning she'd imagined. But she liked Tom's protective arm round her. 'So you talk to the trees and you talk to the birds?'

'I do. And now I have to bury one, I have to find a spirit tree for a friend.' They walked over to the sad huddle on the ground. 'This is Pine Leaf, queen of the crows, killed by Reese while protecting the city and the forest. Blakelock's favourite. He's going to be gutted, I wish I didn't have to tell him.'

Tom walked back to the damaged oak. The forest had offered her a spirit tree, and this would be the one. Taking out his axe and blade, he dug a small grave, being careful not to damage any roots. He went back and carefully picked up the light bundle of black and grey feathers from all the debris around her and carried her gently to her grave.

Abi approached, her hands full of all the things the birds had laid over the body. On the top she'd carefully put a pair of stained fingerless leather gloves that Tom hadn't seen.

He had been here. He knew.

Tom laid the gloves either side of the body, as if cradling and protecting Pine Leaf in her final resting place. Then he quickly filled the earth back in and made a small grave mound. On top he laid all the trinkets and bright things the birds had brought to honour their dead queen. He knew he would return with a gift of his own. A silver buckle from his old shoe.

He stood and looked down, Abi beside him. Eventually she took his hand and drew him away towards the city.

They hadn't walked far before the branch above the grave was full of crows. Others were already on the ground, hopping about, rearranging the mess that Tom had made of all their funeral gifts. Mortals, honestly, they had no sense of pattern.

Tom and Abi wandered towards the ruined gateway in silence. Tom looked at the damaged walls and thought how much needed to be done. Inside were friends, family, a whole way of life.

Donald, Felix and the others had already left, heading back to Frith to ensure it was safe from any retreating shards of Lord Gutta's army.

Abi drew a deep breath and swung Tom's hand. 'So Tom, are you going home?'

Tom looked at the hulking tons of stone in front. Then he turned and looked away at the forest, stretching quietly into the measureless distance. He nodded, almost sadly.

'Soon. Soon I'll be going home.'

Did you enjoy this book?

I really hope you did – and I hope you can do one thing for me.

Would you leave a review on Amazon? It can be as short as you like. It would mean a lot to me as I'm self-publishing and don't have the resources of a big publisher.

Thank you very much in advance.

Would you like to stay in touch?

I'm writing a post once a month and it's full of amazing facts about trees and life in the forest with the boys.

It will also mean you're first to hear about the next book in the Treelogy series – and there will be more than three of them!

If you'd like to get this monthly action post then please just send me your email address. I won't send you anything else, and that's a promise. Just click the links below.

Email:
Author@treelogy.world

Facebook:
https://www.facebook.com/Treelogy.world

Twitter:
@TreelogyWorld

Glossary

Here are some of the terms you'll find in this book and the rest of the Treelogy series. If you get confused – check here!

Arul
It's a traditional food, but you might not like it! It was eaten by Genghis Khan's Mongol horde and that tells you all you need to know about it. To make aaruul (to give it its proper name) you boil goats' milk – having first milked the goats. When it's cooled and curdled you strain it and the lumpy curds are then placed on some wooden boards. Another wooden board goes on top, then stones, to compress it all down. When it's become hard lumps of cake you put it all on the roof in trays to dry further. It's quite bitter, but nutritious and will keep you going and, because it sets so dry and hard, it will keep for ages. You can add dried fruit or herbs if you feel decadent. Yum!

Bearded axe
Vikings often used bearded axes. This is an axe where the cutting blade was extended downwards, well past the part where the metal head fixed to the wooden handle. You ended up with a long blade to chop with. It made a fearsome weapon when fitted to a long shaft perhaps the height of a man.

Double-headed axe
Some people preferred their battle axe to be double headed. You could swing to and fro with it, usually with a single-handed shaft. It was heavier but very effective. The forest fighters don't use it because they use axes that they can use for other tasks, like chopping wood.

Earthdin
This is a Middle English term (that would be from 1066 to about the 15th Century). It is another word for earthquake – I like the idea of combining 'earth' and 'din'. It gives a better idea of the sheer noise of an earthquake. The Treelogy books are set in a time when the land was still settling quite a lot so they were more common.

And they remind us that we live on a planet spinning through dark
space, burned and lit by the sun, with us standing on continents that
float on a core of rock so hot it is molten, where the continents move,
bang into each other, ride up on one another and sometimes cause
colossal damage to our way of life. Life is precarious.

Scaramax
Anglo Saxons called this a 'seax' or, like the Vikings, a
'scramasax' while gamers sometimes call it a 'scaramax'.
Whatever the name, it was a type of dagger. In this
case it means one with a long, heavy blade coming
to a point, and with just one side being sharp, the
other blunt to add weight to the thrust. With a short
handle it was a brutal weapon in close combat and
a very useful tool for everyday use.

Telt
Armies and outdoors types have used shelters
made from a single piece of material for centuries. The German army
in the Second World War used a Zeltbahn, a single piece of shaped
waterproof, camouflaged material with eyelet holes round the edge.
You could make a cosy shelter for a soldier with just a few sticks, or you
could join them together for a bigger shelter.
     The telt our foresters use (the word is Old German, just as 'Zelt'
is current German) is made from a woven cloth. One side has been
treated with a mixture of beeswax and oil to make a waterproof layer.
With some holes round the edges and a few sticks, our men have a
snug waterproof shelter they can put up in moments.

Warbrock
History is full of strange creatures that are no longer around, but
perhaps the warbrock is more like a honey badger. Check them out
in videos – they're incredibly smart, indestructible creatures that just
won't be stopped from doing what they want. The name 'warbrock' tells
you though that this is a very aggressive version of the much-loved
badger family.

Watchers
The Watchers are the elite reconnaissance teams, operating in pairs
of men. They go out far into the forest and then remain still, watching,
waiting, observing. They're based perhaps on the 'Lurps', the American
LRRP teams that used to operate in Vietnam. They used to be the
toughest of the tough and would head out on their own into the jungle at

night and then go still, even if snakes slid over their feet or bugs crawled over and bit them in the muggy heat.

Wudu
Every person in the forest has a spirit tree, one that is revealed to them over time. That tree is where they go to restore their energy, to be one with nature. And it's where they will be buried when they die, under the great branches of their spirit tree. Their energy will then help the tree and the forest continue to grow and, who knows, perhaps that person continues to live as part of the tree.

The wudu is a small piece of that tree that the person carries on a cord around their neck. It connects them to their tree wherever they are, and just touching it can bring calm and courage. We could all do with a wudu round our necks.

36902728R00117

Printed in Poland
by Amazon Fulfillment
Poland Sp. z o.o., Wrocław